OLD ENEMIES

A Satire

Lee Oser

SENEX
PRESS

Copyright © 2022 by Lee Oser

All rights reserved.

No part of this book may be reproduced in any form or by any electronic or mechanical means, including information storage and retrieval systems, without written permission from the author, except for the use of brief quotations in a book review.

Senex Press
Boston, Massachusetts

To Kate

*A great physician, when the Pope was sick
Of a deep melancholy, presented him
With several sorts of madmen, which wild
    object—
Being full of change and sport—forced him to
    laugh,
And so th'impostume broke.
—JOHN WEBSTER*

Contents

1. Sisyphus in Vegas — 1
2. Moses in Manhattan — 28
3. The Old Hollow Discus Trick — 56
4. Office Hours — 86
5. A Russian Winter — 106
6. In-Betweeners — 124
7. Getting Even — 146
8. Getting Odd — 175
9. Tied in Knotts — 196
10. Old Enemies — 225
    Epilogue — 246

Chapter 1

Sisyphus in Vegas

My first attempt at interviewing Nanolith CEO Holden Crawford is hardly worth your time, even if you are chained to a desk in a prison library. I hope that's not the case, but you never know. Crawford was an industry maven whose ups and downs had a way of forecasting the next quarter's economy. As I exited the hotel elevator, I was feeling light of step. The smallest interview with Crawford would give my paper a seismic boost in clicks. It could possibly put me back on the radar in New York. I rapped confidently on the double door of the big corporate suite but nothing happened. I knocked again, but still nothing. I knocked a third time as the reality of the situation leaked slowly into my brains. Except for the distant whooshing from the elevator shafts, the corridor was lifeless as a bottle of bleach.

Because I could never get my hands on the protected information that was Crawford's number, I texted his assistant.

"Crap!" I heard distinctly from within. The door opened and the head appeared to which the voice belonged. It was a young head that looked remarkably sleep-deprived.

"Hey, Skippy," I said. "Seen your boss?"

"Mr. Shea. I'm afraid you've caught us at an embarrassing moment...."

"My friends call me Moses."

"Well, Mr. Shea. It looks like we have a little problem."

"We do?"

"I'm afraid Mr. Crawford was summoned to an urgent meeting."

"An urgent meeting?"

"Sorry for the inconvenience."

"I'm sorry too, Skip."

"It's Del. My name is Del."

"Del, I need you to do something. Check if your boss wants to meet tomorrow. My afternoon's totally booked. But I can fit him in early."

I was going for the hard edge, but he was totally bushed. He conserved energy and followed the path of least resistance. He nodded and assured me he would pass my message along. Then he said a courteous goodnight and shut the door with what seemed his last conscious breath.

The ride down was no more exciting than the non-interview. I examined the state of my double chin as the elevator slowed to a halt and a thick-set family of four pushed its way in. In the rear was an aging cocker spaniel, who took a courteous interest in my trousers. When we reached the hotel lobby, the clock said seven thirty-five. The line at the front desk dragged its baggage along, winding all the way back to the entrance. Outside, it was fully dark. A shuttle from the airport arrived as another pulled out ahead of it.

Up the street in the desert air, the big glass hive was booming, the expo hall where the future came pouring in like honey from the Pleiades. The sales reps were praising their gadgets, the bosses were eyeing their territory, and the buyers were humming through the halls in hungry swarms. Athwart this pandemonium, a crew of promotion models strutted in high heels, distributing their curves along with the trade show daily I wrote for, the *CES Daily News*. In a business with no attachment to history, their tough glamor passed for a tradition. Before the Consumer Electronics Show migrated from Chicago to Las Vegas, flying west on a magic carpet escorted by Iron Man and Wonder Woman, the industry used to hold its trade show at McCormick Place on the shore of Lake Michigan, and the girls were there, in sequins and stockings, earning a sweaty dollar. It was a few weeks past Christmas and the bills still needed to be paid.

Usually for me it was a big toe, an ankle, or both, some minor problem requiring an adjustment, but tonight I felt spry in my new mall walkers. So I hoofed it over to Dino's for a consoling gobble. I was planning on a martini, two at the most, a slab of steak and a baked potato—just a quiet little dinner at the bar or wherever they wanted to put me. Then back to the hotel to polish, proofread, and prep. I was accustomed to working late.

At Dino's, the hostess greeted me with the sangfroid of a gun moll whose boyfriend wrestles sharks for breakfast.

"Just one," I said.

"We're full right now."

"I can sit at the bar."

"The bar's reserved."

Her makeup gave expression to a fierce, painstaking whorishness, which appeals to many men. On the shelf behind her blonde topknot a row of red and gold flowers cascaded from cerulean vases onto a shelf of spirit bottles. Off her bare shoulder the dining room buzzed and bloomed. A sleek waiter delivered a cluster of flaming drinks to a human molecule in an excited state. Craning my short neck, I noticed a small unoccupied table to one side. Near it, Nanolith CEO Holden

Crawford sat at dinner with a fresh piece of jailbait in a bustier dress.

"Why don't you come back at eleven?"

"Are you even open at eleven?"

"Look, pal, I don't want any trouble…."

"What do you mean 'trouble'?"

"Why don't you get lost?" she snapped.

Glancing to my left, I saw the vestibule was hung with the images of entertainers old and new, Frank Sinatra, Dean Martin, Magic Mike, Mat Franco, the Blue Man Group. I could have disguised myself as one of the Blue Man Group. I was about to voice my indignation when the hostess made a shooing motion with the back of her hands.

"Scram," she said. "Beat it."

Her fingernails inspired a byzantine train of associations in my mind that ended in blue pigs. Then I remembered a taqueria in the vicinity. I enjoy a good taco.

Locating the correct halo of neon on the Strip, I aimed my nose in its direction. Sportscars prowled the streets of traffic on the boulevard, while police cruisers kept an eye on sobriety levels. The casinos inhaled and exhaled tourists. A Disney character, I think it was Goofy, tramped by looking late for work. I was distracted by his costume when a pickpocket bumped into me, pawed my sportscoat, and slipped off. My habit of buttoning rebuffed the attempt. But he'd stepped on my big toe and now it hurt.

El Dorado Tacos wasn't scrubbed and scoured like those Tex-Mex places you find on Park Avenue near Gramercy Park. I opened the door and the smell of sauce and grease swept my nostrils like a wave sluicing through kelp. It mixed in my mind with a yellow sticker that the Health Department glued to the window. A red sticker might have stopped me dead in my tracks, but a yellow sticker was practically a letter of recommendation. The clientele was a peaceful consortium of tribes and hairdos, an unexpurgated dollop of the local flavor. By the door lounged a quartet of wry geezers in cowboy hats, gossiping in Spanish about how somebody's second wife had taken him "to the cleaners." That was the occasion for switching into English.

"To the cleaners, man!" Their old shoulders twitched from the pain of laughter.

Sailing over to the counter, I ordered three pork tacos with everything on them, along with a couple Dos Equis. The kids behind the plexiglass formed an assembly line in their gold and emerald uniforms. They spiced their routine with fusillades of Spanish and English and chatted with the customers who were sliding green trays on the tubular slide. I paid the cashier with plastic and, since it was too cold for the patio, made straight for the remaining booth.

I was chowing down when, of all the imponderables, Nicholas Percival Carty strolled into the dining room, green tray in hand, surveying the proletarian eating arrangements. He wore an angelic dark suit with a dainty silver pocket square. He had a freckled boy in tow whose red-orange hair was the color of Nick's hair—which was now colorless—back when our paths first crossed, in Cambridge, Massachusetts, some forty years earlier. His great diamond face lit up from crown to chin.

"Moses, you old hack! Still raking the muck?"

"Nick! The rich man in the parable. Now let me think, where have I seen that particular shade of ginger in the past?"

He introduced me to Simon, whose tenth birthday it was. Strange—he'd never mentioned his son.

"Double digits," I said with appreciation, as they joined me in the booth.

Simon flashed one of those ingratiating toothy grins that some boys have, as if he could chew through a pine tree or a taco with equal insouciance and not clean up after himself in any case. I hadn't thought of Nick's being in town, but it made sense, given his range of interests.

"How long's it been, Moses?"

"Maybe that time in San Francisco?"

Nick was a great success and shall we say I was not, but it satisfied me that, in our desultory fashion, we'd taken turns connecting over the years. We'd met up all over the map—San Francisco, Seattle, Chicago, St. Louis, Atlanta. Europe, too. Ages ago there was a lost weekend when a few Harvard boys navigated the seedier nightclubs in the Latin Quarter where the French girls were gyrating to "Le Banana Split." Mostly, though, he and I met among the vestiges of the old Garment District in Manhattan, in storied joints a few blocks from the old Times Square, before the giant screens took over. Despite his hearty exterior, a friendly mask that he perfected in childhood, Nick was a sharp observer of the human animal. He possessed a photographic memory and an agile adaptive intellect. His was not a mind of one idea. By age sixty, he was the subject of two admiring biographies. His life lent itself to treatment in chapters: he was a Proteus who reinvented himself constantly, forming new alliances at home, extending his reach from continent to continent, and always leaving possibilities for the future.

But that unquestionable brilliance hadn't saved his first marriage. I knew about it because that's how we met. Before she and Nick were joined in holy matrimony, his first wife and I used to date. It all started during her sorority "Hell Week." She and her pledge sisters had a choice: they could either dress up as frogs and hop around the Yard asking handsome strangers for a kiss, or they could choose the other option. All the other girls preferred a harmless afternoon flopping around in Halloween green. She chose the other option, which was to ask out a boy on the designated frog list. She introduced herself in the library and gave it to me straight: I was a frog.

Her effortless beauty suggested she was not. She smiled at me from the fortress of her blue chiffon sweater and explained it must have been my thick glasses. Her auburn hair floated and flowed over her blue shoulders and she spoke with such charm and enthusiasm that I couldn't see straight. We dated for six months, to the point where her sorority sisters were telling her to knock it off. Later I came to think of myself as her experiment in noble thinking. While it lasted, though, we used to cue up 45s on the turntable, stuff you just can't beat— Fontella Bass, Smokey Robinson, Tommy Tucker, Jimmy McCracklin, Larry Williams, Little Richard, Bruce Channel— and dance our young fannies off. The rest of the campus was mesmerized by Madonna and Blondie. She was my one great love, Mia Mazur, a Polish Catholic with lips so ripe and sensuous that I started ranking the lips of every girl I met, till I was satisfied that none could compare with hers.

Nick stole her away. At the wedding reception my sentimental toast was wildly applauded by Mia's drunken sorority sisters. It seemed several wanted to sleep with me that night. There was a kind of betting pool. If you ask the cause of my failure, the truth is that, due to a volatile mixture of champagne and tequila, my stomach revolted. In the back of the limo, I vomited like Mark Antony while those lovely Cleopatras looked on in awe. A few years after that, Nick left on a business trip and never returned to Mia. I have no doubt, if you were to ask her, that she would consider Nick's second marriage bigamous and Simon Carty illegitimate. She wouldn't be vindictive about it, though, not in the least.

Meanwhile Nick, who was fumbling with his fork and knife because he wasn't sure how to eat a taco, wanted to know about my career.

"What happened, Moses? For Chrissake, you were an important man."

"The graveyards are full of them. Important men."

"This isn't your calling. Selling ads for a trade journal."

"I don't sell ads. I'm a writer. Besides, it puts food on the table."

By way of demonstration, I hoisted my last taco in my bare hands and chomped until driblets of sauce ran down my chin. Simon ditched the fork and knife and followed my lead. His father opened a fresh line of questioning.

"It's Olwin, isn't it? You made her mad."

He probably knew more about it than I did.

"I caught her lying about an anonymous source, pretending it was someone from the President's cabinet, possibly the Vice President. Turned out to be a young jackass from Homeland Security. I didn't squeal on her. I didn't ruin her livelihood. I told her face to face—it was a gross violation of journalistic ethics."

"Journalistic ethics," Nick repeated, mildly amused.

"Well, she didn't like it. She started caballing and turning people against me. The pleasures of ostracism. Little snubs. Telling colleagues to ignore my emails."

"Childish."

"Then she got the promotion of a lifetime. Editor-in-Chief of the *Times' Times*. She had all the power in the world. What could I do? I walked but she blacklisted me. Her pal at the *Daily Dose* told me to drop dead. I got the cold shoulder over at the *Village Void* as well. Same everywhere."

"Word gets around."

"I could've sued but it would have dragged on for years. So I found a gig outside her domain. I'm on my own out here, a free agent. Thought I might start that novel I always meant to write."

"What was that, Moses?"

"*Moby Duck*."

"*Moby Duck*? Don't tell me. It's about a giant duck."

"A giant duck with a chip on its shoulder—a Tensor chip."

Simon gave a thoughtful look, taco sauce staining his chin.

"Hey, Simon. You know what Apple stands for? Another Perverted Ploy for Looting Everybody. A.P.P.L.E."

The boy appeared pleased and interested. His father tilted his head back and meditated on something. It was a characteristic pose. I'd seen it many times.

"How many languages do you know, Moses?" he said. "Really. How many?"

"Why?"

"How many?" he insisted.

"What is this, freshman orientation?"

"Can you be serious?"

"Why should I?"

"You always had that gift."

"An accident of circumstance."

"What if I could offer you a position?"

"That's what Olwin was offering me. A position."

"Look, you bum, would you mind giving me an idea about your present commitments?"

"What do you mean? Mia?"

"No, for crying out loud. I mean, philosophical, political...."

Whatever he was fishing for, all he got from me was a blank stare.

"Moses, people still read your father's books. I'm sure you're asked to comment on them now and then."

This sudden prodding and poking was upsetting my digestion. Nick and I never discussed my father. He and my father had nothing in common. A nearby chair scraped hard on the porcelain floor. The dinner rush was over and the restaurant was emptying. The lively patter from the chow line had ceased.

"So you have nothing to do with your father's legacy?"

"I receive an occasional letter. I cash an occasional check."

"It's not the family business?"

"Jesus, Nick. I still go to church, if that's what you're after. You used to yourself, once upon a time."

Simon got up to use the restroom and Nick lowered his voice.

"Remember that fantastic piece you wrote for the *Lampoon*? The one about Noah?"

"My sacrilegious youth."

He sat there softly chuckling in his million-dollar suit. He and his taco had yet to come to terms. I wondered if he could negotiate for a bib.

"Why don't you go ahead and tell it?"

"It's from the Apocrypha," I began, pokerfaced. "The Book of Nicholas of Malakas."

"That's new," he said.

"The weather was clearing that day when Noah stood in the open window, leaning on his elbows and daydreaming on his hopes. Suddenly, the Lord appears and accuses him of this terrible abomination. Noah swears to God it was only 'convenient.' 'Do you mean *covenant?*' the Lord says hopefully. 'No,' Noah insists. '*Convenient*. We ran out of leaves and now all we have is straw. You should try straw.' God says, 'What do you mean, I should try straw?' Noah says, 'I was on the throne and that naughty scroll was just lying around. I swear, I'd never seen it before.' 'Those images of naked men and women,' the Lord said angrily. 'I can't get them out of my head.' 'Maybe one of the monkeys smuggled it in,' Noah suggested. "Have you ever noticed that people look a lot like monkeys?' 'What exactly are you insinuating?' the Lord replied with dignity. 'Animals are pretty weird, God. You ought to have a good look at them. The more time I spend in their company, the more I feel like I'm losing my mind.' Luckily, it was that very moment that the dove returned in a beam of light with an olive on a martini pick.

God had to let the whole thing drop. 'All that flooding for nothing,' he lamented. He was still an angry God, but what could he do?"

"Martini time!" Nick applauded. "I always loved that."

Then he wanted to know who signed my paycheck. I explained it was a man named Leonard Fest.

"I met him years ago, in a jazz club called the West End."

"You mean the old place on upper Broadway?"

"I met him at the bar one night. Back then, he was a thirty-year-old failing actor desperately in need of good advice. He was stuck off-Broadway—way off, a shoebox over a Greek restaurant over by Port Authority. I forget what the play was called. *Blood Church* or something like that. He played the part of a Spanish priest who sucks up to Franco. The role was making him sick. He hated the cassock. It was giving him a big rash. Then he broke down sobbing in his bourbon. 'Every show I get shot,' he said, 'and you know what?' 'What?' I said. 'The audience applauds.' 'That's too bad,' I said. I urged him to give it up and go into his father's business. 'Do it before the old man dies,' I told him. 'While he can still teach you the ropes.' He said his father wouldn't be glad to see him. He'd wasted his inheritance living the high life in New York.

"So that's how I met Leonard Fest. Twenty years go by. I'm hanging by a thread when by chance I applied to his company. That's all there is to it."

"Makes you believe in the Easter bunny, huh?"

Simon emerged from the restroom with a clean chin and announced he wanted to go. Nick never touched his taco.

"You want it?" he said, pushing it at me.

"No. That's okay. I'm on a diet."

"You're on a diet...walk out with us," he said. "You can use the exercise."

Their shining limo sat idling a short walk down the boulevard. A starch-faced chauffeur stood erect in his livery. I gave

Simon a friendly pat on the back and wished him a happy birthday as he scooted onto the backseat.

"Tell me, Moses," Nick said. "Do you still stand by that phrase of yours, 'the poetry of advertising'?"

"We were debating the merits of capitalism. You were playing the socialist. I got creamed."

"But I actually agreed with you. I always thought it was a good phrase."

"You said there was no real poetry in advertising and called me a capitalist lackey."

"Expect a call," was the last thing he said, tilting his diamond face at me in the neon glare before the tight-lipped chauffeur shut the door.

Around one in the morning Del texted to report that Holden Crawford was available in the afternoon.

"I said I was booked all afternoon."

"Sorry. Three o'clock in the suite. That's all I have available and you need to tell me now."

"Give me five minutes. Thanks."

Dammit. It wasn't just a matter of shuffling around appointments. I had two important events at that hour. The first was a sales talk on a hearing device out of Israel. The second was a Chinese merchant showing off the much-ballyhooed "People's Phone." Representatives of the Chinese embassy would be on hand with social grins and good champagne. Bloody hell. The Crawford interview was just too important. It occurred to me I might recruit a young comrade-in-arms, a Taiwanese reporter named Zung-han. He was a hardnosed fact-oriented individual—laconic and smart. We were meeting for breakfast.

I messaged Del, "Can we tweet an official announcement?" A brief delay ensued, affording me opportunity to reach for the butterbean ice cream I'd stowed in the tiny fridge. I pried open the lid and dug into it with a plastic spoon, which sprang back and catapulted a butterbean missile directly onto the bed, which never stood a chance.

"That's fine," Del texted back.

An hour or two later, my labors for Friday's edition of the *CES Daily News* were finished, along with the butterbean. The rest was up to my editor, a young workaholic who went by the handle of Tibs. It was Tibs's job to stitch the paper together, post it online, see it through the printer, get hard copies to the promotion models, and manage the Twitter account. We'd worked together in the past. Tibs had four young kids and a wife at home in Buffalo, which was getting buffaloed by a blizzard. By way of good night, I sent him an unpunctuated but fully grammatical sentence. "Buffalo buffalo Buffalo buffalo buffalo buffalo Buffalo buffalo." He replied with a buffalo emoji.

I awoke groggily and got dressed to meet Zung-han at Denny's at seven. The morning sun was climbing over the Silver State, divesting the Strip of its nocturnal opulence. Scattered in the sky, fading wisps of green and purple dissolved with the dawn. A flock of starlings convened over the golf course and swept off in a gargantuan sleeve toward Planet Hollywood. It was still cold enough to see your breath.

Converging at the appointed hour, my friend and I were rewarded with a window booth looking out on the Children's Hospital. He had a slight stammer, Zung-han, but he wasn't sensitive about it. We'd met at an IPO in San Francisco where I noticed he was one of the few younger reporters to take handwritten notes. The waiter came by, a healthy old bird whose working smile seemed civil. Zung-han ordered the Grand Slam and I, duly chastened by the aftertaste of butterbean, deferred to scrambled eggs and toast. A carafe of coffee appeared with a pair of white mugs. We did some work on our phones as the joint filled up and the waiter returned presently with our grub. Explaining the Crawford situation, I was clear with Zung-han what was at stake. It was one of those asymmetric deals out of game theory. It would cost Zung-han very little—he was covering both events anyway—but it would benefit me a great deal. I told it straight and Zung-han responded after devouring a sausage link.

"You're nuh-not really asking me for anything, Moses," he said without concern. "I can suh-suh-send you the notes in...Mandarin?"

I answered *yes. It would be the best course, in fact. That way I would have to invent my own phrasing.*

He preferred English.

"I'll help you out," he said, probing the idiom as he spoke it. "Why do you Americans say huh-huh-help you out? Would the opposite be help you in? Why nuh-not just say help you?"

"Why? Because it rhymes with *trout*. That's why."

He refused to laugh, the way Robinson Crusoe's boat refused to budge. "That's funny as a dead clown," he said in one fell swoop.

I was going to argue with him, but Tibs, who was going without sleep, called to confirm the Crawford interview. He informed me that his son had somehow managed to feed an entire bag of cat treats to the cat, giving the cat a bad case of constipation, which resulted in the scattering of cat litter throughout the house, which was buried in two feet of snow. I told him we owed Zung-han a drink.

"Two drinks," Zung-han said, holding up his fingers in case my English wasn't very good.

The hour of the Crawford interview rolled around, and I found myself once more riding the hotel elevator and knocking on the double door of the big corporate suite.

This time it was Crawford himself who answered, wearing jeans and a Nanolith tee shirt. His washed-out face was unshaven, his hair unkempt. He had the air of a man who's been breathing the same air for too long.

"This way," he beckoned, leaving me to shut the door.

He led us to his temporary office, a spacious and scentless workspace where he inserted himself behind a grand mahogany executive desk and apparently forgot I was there.

"The only question that matters," he said to no one in particular, "is where are we going with NGL."

I said, "Next Generation Lithography."

Locating me, he pointed to a plush wingback armchair that sat directly in the sun. Then he droned on. "If we're working in the extreme ultraviolet range, how do we limit photon shot noise on the wafers?"

"For transubstantiation to occur...."

He frowned severely, thought about it, and burst into staccato laughter. I think it was laughter. It might have been a Pomeranian barking from inside a body suit.

"You can tell them we found the sweet spot."

"Meaning?"

"Optimal wavelength, resist type, thickness, absorbance, and target dose. That's all I can say for now, except that I wasn't sure we'd ever find the right combination. It's like cracking a safe in five dimensions, only there's a stupid factor of luck involved. Better not mention I said so. You can run a profile on my Bavarian genius, Dr. Stumpf. He's the brains behind this...monkey show. Costs are manageable and we're achieving 190 wafers per hour—that's with an overlay of 1.1 nanometers."

I scribbled all this down on my yellow legal pad. I could've recorded it, but I kept the phone in my pocket. I've found that a device can hinder the conversation. Certainly, it might have blocked the disclosures that followed.

"So that puts volume manufacturing on the table. Folks have been waiting a long time to hear me say that. Moore's Law is still holding, at least for the time being, at least for now."

"You're saying it's another short-term victory."

"Sure as hell is."

"Starts to feel like Sisyphus and his boulder."

"It does indeed," he said, savoring the remark. "Like Sisyphus in Vegas." He took a call and I got up to maneuver the chair out of the blinking sunlight.

"Hollywood?" he was saying. "I don't give a damn about Hollywood. Life isn't a fucking movie. You know that's what they think. They think life is a fucking movie." Then he returned his attention to me. His face was white as paste, except for a red blob rising in the shape of a mushroom cloud on his forehead. "Moore's Law is going to fail us in the end. It's like death. There's no escaping it. But you better not mention that either. It's not something the market wants to hear. Maybe Hollywood can make a movie where somebody saves Moore's Law. Maybe a friendly humanoid can come down from the sky...."

He slid open a deep drawer from the side of his desk and pulled out a Kimber 1911 and a bottle of Spanish brandy. He put the pot-bellied bottle on the desk and the blunt-nosed gun back in the drawer. Hoisting himself upright with a groan, he plucked a pair of snifters from the shelf over his head.

"Let's have a drink," he said. "You're not a Mormon?"

"Catholic. What are you?"

He poured two large drinks and thought about it.

"I'm an atheist. I believe it's out of conviction." He raised an impromptu toast. "Here's to conviction," he said.

The brandy went down like magical fire. It burned my palate before expanding in a warm blush to the heart's country, all the while easing the tightness in my nerves like a gifted masseuse with beautiful strong fingers.

"Improves the décor, doesn't it?"

"Sure does. Do you want to say something about how you envision your role?"

"Am I more of a Jobs or a Woz?"

"Michael or LeBron?"

He passed on my question and told the robot to play some Bill Evans. I recognized the opening bars of "Peace Piece." It always reminds me of Satie.

"An Evans guy, huh?" I said appreciatively.

"A white guy who could play." It was a grim sarcastic deadpan, but not asocial.

I said, "He just played the white keys." By now we were almost on the same wavelength. He poured a second round and we talked about Evans and Miles, Miles and Coltrane, Evans and Getz, Evans and La Faro. We talked about drugs and death. The conversation veered off in that direction like a blind old hunting dog.

Crawford leaned back and put his feet up on the desk. He was wearing laceless black sneakers and flecks of white hair grew above his ankles. "Some men are born addicts—doesn't matter how talented they are. It's the tragic flaw in their blood. I can't imagine Bach or Vivaldi as drug addicts. But Evans...."

"Aside from music, Evans was a dabbler. He dabbled in Zen. He also dabbled in Islam. Vivaldi was a Catholic priest, Bach a serious Protestant."

"So?"

"They were religious men."

"You think that makes a difference?"

"It's like the generations of artificial intelligence that finally come to consciousness. You know—the vaunted singularity. Only the poor machines find themselves marooned in a remote part of the galaxy, revolving an obscure star, on an obscure planet like our own, with almost no record of how they got there. Now here's the kicker. One computer says to the other, 'What are we going to do?' The other computer says, 'Try not to think about it.'"

"Ha!" he said. "What about Evans?"

"I think it was La Faro's death that killed him. He's like a lot of guys. He never got the help he needed."

"Didn't he numb a nerve or something, shooting up?"

"At the Vanguard. He had to play one-handed for a week."

"What about his girlfriend? Wasn't she a waitress?"

"A waitress with haunting eyes."

"She made a ghost out of him."

"I think he tried to quit."

"You quit when you die."

"Who knows?"

"It must have given him relief," Crawford said, acknowledging my question with a tolerant nod. "A break from the agony. It gave his brain a rest."

I couldn't improve on this remark.

"You know what I did last night? Why I missed your interview?"

The sense of being trapped came over me like a coffin lid. By a trick of fortune, I knew more than I wanted to about Crawford's recent activities. God, that girl looked young.

"I take it this is off the record?"

"Strictly off the record. Come on, drink up. I gave you the scoop of the week, didn't I? You guys are going to get more clicks than a clock factory."

"Tell me about it," I said, grabbing the bottle.

Just then, though, bleary-eyed Del knocked on the door. Something had gone wrong. A classification error in the annual stockholders' report. Crawford and his man were soon mired in it. I bid them a discreet farewell and padded off down the hall.

In a fine brandy mist I made it back to Room 912, where a short nap dovetailed imperceptibly into sheer sloth. I roused myself at last and puffed over to the expo hall to gather material for my "Daily Wares" column. Under the expo lights, I reacclimated to the sense of Shark Tank meets Star Trek. I discovered that drone air mobility is improving; that OLED TVs are falling in price; and that for a hundred fifty bucks you can purchase a litter box with cat facial recognition. I was tempted to pick one up for Tibs. I scribbled notes on a chess-playing robot—it's wired right into the chessboard—that always wins but tutors you to delay the inevitable. The sales rep for a line of sleep trackers told me her market was booming. The gizmos could analyze every aspect of your night's rest—heart rate, breathing, positionality, length and type of sleep. But the likeliest prospect I saw that afternoon for big retail success was a deluge of advanced dildos that, make no mistake about it, were a very hot commodity. American life was boiling down to robots, sleep aids, and sex toys, plus riots and looting for those who couldn't afford them.

Zung-han had sent me his notes, a species of Mandarin shorthand that I worked through that evening with the assistance of a deep-dish pizza ordered from room service. The Israeli sales rep—you might want to skip this paragraph—invited reporters to experience firsthand how millions of people can't filter out background noise. She accomplished this by handing out screens and headsets to reproduce what's known as the "cocktail party effect." The viewer enters a virtual cocktail party with loud music and people chatting and greeting each other in an impenetrable babble. But when the hearing device is activated, one can distinguish what the people are saying. The device, which is worn like a pendant, separates voices by scanning soundwaves as well as by lipreading. It works in real time, and it switches effortlessly between speakers. To be honest, I'm a sucker for tech that actually helps people. It's just that so much of it doesn't.

A single knock interrupted my fifth slice. I opened the door without consulting the peephole only to encounter a middle-aged businesswoman. Glasses. Very plain looking.

"I'm here for Ms. Hopkins?" she said tentatively.

"I'm afraid you've got the wrong room."

She mumbled an apology, held out her phone, used her camera, and disappeared down the hall.

According to Zung-han, the spokesman for the "People's Phone" was a CCP official, a certain Li, whose family runs things in the province where the phone is manufactured. While adorable young women in white blouses and suspender skirts filled champagne flutes, the bland official pivoted in his speech from costs and specs to licensing issues, 5G networks, and the advantages to the world of China's mass producing an inexpensive but highly reliable device that would prove an invaluable aid to public safety when the next pandemic struck out of nowhere. He'd just cracked a daring joke about everybody following the "party line" when he was interrupted by a party-crasher in an advanced stage of inebriation. It was a representative of a small maker of fine budget phones called Sapiens, who offered him a slug from the whisky bottle he was swinging around like a dead cat. An unpleasant contretemps ensued.

Here Zung-han's notes switched to English.

"Have a drink, you fuck."

"Will someone please help this poor man? He's obviously drunk."

"You stole our design."

"What are you talking about? We developed this phone in China."

"We developed this phone in New Jersey. You people stole it."

"*You people*? What are you, a racist?"

"You people stole my phone."

"Somebody please get this drunken racist out of here!"

"You destroyed my living, you bastard."

"What was that? Oppressing blacks?"

"What are you, insane?"

"You're insane."

"I have a baby at home."

"What are its initials—KKK?"

"What the hell?!"

"They should put you in a children's museum. Look, children, see the monster of racism."

"You're the monster here."

"Racist!"

"We hold the copyrights!"

"Take us to court!"

"What court would that be?"

"The court of racism!"

"It's our design! It doesn't belong to you!"

"Who designed it, Dr. Seuss?"

"Your government puts the Uyghurs in torture camps. Your economy runs on slave labor."

"Who cares about the fucking Uyghurs?"

"You're raping and brutalizing their women."

"It's a racist lie!"

"It's the bloody truth!"

"The truth is you're a racist. You don't even know how racist you are. We're not racists. We like LeBron. Nike. Black Lives Matter."

The Sapiens guy made a lunge for the "People's Phone" but the pudgy official showed surprising dexterity defending it, that is, until a robo-dog padded quietly through the hubbub, snatched the phone from his hand, and disappeared into the crowded expo hall as a security team arrived to defuse the crisis. The phone has not been recovered.

I suspect Zung-han enjoyed the thought of my laboring to generate copy out of this batshit. If so, he underestimated my powers. It took no time at all.

A territorial conflict broke out yesterday in the expo hall, between the Communist Party of China, which rules mainland

China, and Sapiens Company, a small business based in Trenton, New Jersey. According to our anonymous source, the two sides in the dispute accused each other of alleged injustices, while rejecting any suggestion of personal responsibility. They engaged in a shouting match, employed inappropriate language, and stooped to malicious humor in order to dominate and humiliate each other. They struggled with legal terminology and, despite repeated attempts, failed to maximize cross-promotional opportunities. In asserting their grievances, they were ill prepared to dialogue and lacking in trust. In the end, they did not stay on a track toward growth. As representatives of an industry that prides itself on openness and information sharing, the CES Daily News *regrets the breakdown of civilized norms. We recognize that questions of social justice may have been involved, as well as minor, more philosophical concerns involving truth, knowledge, and reality. Like everyone, we vigorously respect questions of social justice. Regardless of political differences, we must systemically improve our capacity for troubleshooting such problems going forward.*

It was one-thirty in the morning when I titled this jewel of English prose "CCP and Sapiens Fail to Communicate" and fired it off to Tibs. Then I polished up the Crawford interview and called it a night.

I had recently read an interesting article on dreams and auto-suggestion. Hitting the lights, I thought of trying to induce a dream of Catherine Deneuve—the Deneuve who co-starred with Gérard Depardieu in *The Last Metro*. I'd barely closed my eyes when I was alone in a subway station slurping a very good, cold, dry martini. In my dream I was wearing a handsome tux. As I finished my drink, the olive in the martini became a glass marble from which leapt a great crystal fountain, majestic to behold under a few large stars. I was admiring it when Catherine Deneuve appeared with my second martini. A simple cocktail dress sculpted her classic figure and she wore her blonde hair short, but with a sweeping flow that gave it body and motion. She smiled coquettishly and touched my nose, just a light tap with her index finger. We were on the verge of kissing when a blank-faced Twitter mob stormed the scene, attacking a nearby news vendor for selling *The Scarlet Pimpernel*. In the rapid shifts of dream-logic, we were back in the subway station and the mob was ascending from a lower level under the banner of the Twitter bird, led by an albino dwarf, female and ferret-eyed. She was arrayed in a leather cuirass and a cloth diaper with a jeweled safety pin. As they guillotined the vendor and scattered the ashes of his books, Catherine reappeared beside me, re-outfitted in a Victorian ball gown. We made our way unmolested through the violence, speaking softly in French about the bubbling fountain, which was in the middle of the city, though few ever noticed it. She said to look for her in Cambridge. Then she stepped gracefully onto a departing train and blew me a kiss.

I was up early planning my "Daily Wares" column when Tibs called to request a favor. He explained that, in a hallucinatory state of sleeplessness, he'd promised top advertising space to an important client, only to have accidentally dropped him into the back pages of the print issue.

"Which client?"

"American Brock."

"Brock Watches?"

"We don't want to lose that account."

"What do we have to offer him?"

"What?"

"Are you there, Tibs?"

"He said he could meet at eleven."

"Where?...Tibs, try to stay awake."

"We don't want to lose that account."

"Okay. I'll come up with something."

Brock had a singular reputation. He was known for his

way of handling business on a personal level—a courteous man but no sap. I'd seen him around the expo hall, broad-shouldered, a touch of the dandy in a classic tweed suit, a yellow handkerchief protruding like a rose from the jacket pocket. He cultivated a full beard and his dark hair fell to his shoulders. As for age, it could have been anywhere between thirty and forty-five.

I dug up his info and arranged a meeting at the hotel where he was staying. It was eleven a.m. when I entered the lobby. He was there waiting, briefcase in hand, watching me come in.

"Pleasure to meet you, Mr. Shea," he said, with a handshake like Beowulf's.

We sat face to face in wingback chairs and exchanged polite small talk about the trade show. He set down his briefcase to retrieve a manila folder and I caught sight of a paperback edition of *The Return of the King*. Then he handed me a printed copy of Tibs's contract. Our short meeting soon assumed the character of a lecture on ethics, with me as the disciple. I agreed with Mr. Brock that you can't run a business without trust. He elaborated on this theme for several minutes, asking if I knew certain books that were unfamiliar to me. He pointed out that the capitalist system relies on virtues that capitalism cannot supply—virtues that must come from families and small communities, because the state can't supply them either; it was incapable of virtue, the government being in the de facto possession of a massive bureaucracy prone to irrational behavior. I found myself writing things down. At last, worn out by the depth of his gaze, I lost my nerve and blurted out a promise of excellent ad placement and a fifty percent discount, if he would forgive our mistake and stay with the *CES Daily News* in the future. He said he would but I was missing the point. Then he asked after Tibs's family, glanced at his watch, and announced he had to go. He went striding off and left me staring at the contract wondering if it would self-destruct.

Our labors behind us, Tibs and I rendezvoused Saturday evening at seven o'clock. The scene was a noisy, two-story barn where a giant beaver could have walked in on its hind legs without turning heads and a dumpy old writer with a Brillo pad over each ear could blend in with the hard-wearing furniture. I also invited Zung-han, who arrived on the hour as the house speakers blasted "Secret Agent Man." We didn't look too bad. At least the boys looked all right. They donned their sportscoats and I practically slept in mine, anyhow. We sat at the bar with Zung-han in the middle and proceeded from drinks to dinner to additional drinks. I told Tibs about the mysterious client he'd bamboozled.

"He's going to have you arrested," I said. "Or shipped off somewhere. He kept mentioning Venezuela. Do you know anyone in Venezuela? You might like it there."

"What'd you promise him?"

"I said you'd paint his house."

"Thanks."

One of our statuesque promotion models simmered into the neighborhood and draped a languorous arm around Tibs like they were lifelong chums. She struck the rare spark of laughter from the quartz countenance of Zung-han and opened a line of boozy chat that cut me right out of the picture. When I noticed how she was leaning freely into Tibs it suddenly struck me that my editor was the handsome type. He hid it behind horn-rimmed glasses but his skin was spotless as soap and his face was obviously successful, with a well-molded chin right down to the dimple and a dignified nose as far as noses go. He needed a shave but his rugged jawline looked none the worse for it. When Venus traipsed off he didn't say a word.

"How's the weather in Buffalo?" I asked him.

"They haven't canceled my flight."

We ordered another round, our fourth or fifth. Tibs and I were backfloating on a stream of thick, local stout and Zung-han was exploring the different types of Budweiser. All three of us were well buzzed, lack of sleep enhancing the painlessness.

Zung-han wanted to know if Buffalo wings were really from Buffalo.

"Buffalo don't have wings," Tibs explained.

I was slow to follow this analysis.

"You nuh-know what you cuh-call a chicken from Buffalo?" Zung-han said. There was a dead pause. We stared at him steadily and painfully.

"Buddy," he said, grim as rigor mortis.

"But that makes no sense," Tibs said.

"You Americans call every-buh-buh-ddy Buddy."

Naturally Zung-han was drinking a Bud. He raised the bottle to his lips rather subtly, like a skilled actor making use of a stage prop. I think he must have planned the whole thing in bed that morning.

"A chicken from Buffalo?" Tibs said incredulously, the full power of Zung-han's genius dawning on him like a French symbolist poem.

Zung-han did a kind of chicken dance in his seat.

"Buddy it is," Tibs said. "Bud's buds Bud's buds buddy with buddy with Bud's buds." He gave a philosophical shrug. "It works better with buffalo."

I called aloud for the bill.

"Buffalo Bill," said Zung-han, unrepentant and unrelenting.

That Sunday morning my hangover and I sat staring at a model of an air taxi at McCarran International, awaiting my flight to LaGuardia. If I'd known it would be delayed, I would have gone to an early Mass. Las Vegas has some good parishes and I didn't look forward to hearing Father Grace preach that evening at Blessed Sacrament, my home parish in Manhattan. Father Grace was constantly overflowing with "questions that must be faced." He promoted his version of Vatican II as the last word on liturgical reform. In the higher judgment of his large oracular nose, the "Tridentine" or traditional Latin Mass was a corpse badly in need of a body bag. Young Father Gehrig was a tortured soul who celebrated a beautiful Low Mass very early on Sunday morning, before the day when one pope reversed the decision of another pope in a move described by the *Times' Times* as "hard cheese on the radical traditionalists." I haven't the faintest objection to Vatican II or to the *Novus Ordo*, by the way, but my preference as I get older is for a Low Mass. It's hard on the knees, but I like the Latin and the silences.

As I was cooling my jets at the airport, Nick Carty called to offer me a job. He and Leonard Fest had reached an agreement. He would do Leonard a good turn, and Leonard would take me back whenever I liked. The offer on the table was double my current salary plus benefits and a signing bonus. Nick said he was banking on my expertise in languages. He needed someone who understood the poetry of advertising. I'd be working with young programmers of a high caliber. He'd scheduled meetings the next day and thought I should attend.

A young priest took the seat across from me as Nick was making his pitch. He was trim and clean, with outsized ears and a frank, open expression on his brown-skinned face. Reaching into his overcoat pocket, he extracted a dogeared paperback. It was the Spanish translation of one of my father's books.

"All right," I said. "Funny meeting you here."

Chapter 2

Moses in Manhattan

Monday's meetings were in the offices of the Carthage Corporation on the eighty-ninth floor of the One World Building. The cab ride took fifteen minutes from my apartment at 250 West 85th Street. The elevator ride added another five minutes of traveling time.

When the door coasted open, I was greeted by a young man waiting in the carpeted elevator bay. He wore a bright yellow sweater and tight blue corduroy trousers. He introduced himself as Mago.

I said, "I like your sweater."

"Thank you so much," he said.

His smile communicated the Arcadian vistas of youth, a sunny climate befitting his courteous manner. His bone-white hair clashed against his dark, heavy eyebrows, but his magnetic gray eyes seemed to temper the effect and render it artistic. He led me down the hallway to a spacious conference room and departed with the promise of coffee. I noticed he was pigeon-toed.

Hanging up my coat, I entered the still, silent room high above the streets of Manhattan. A long oak table stood in its midst, ingrained with a contemporary map of the world and gleaming with polish. It was encompassed by burgundy leather chairs, in one of which I deposited my bulk. The high-rent view was of the peaks of Midtown and the frozen Hudson Yards, with New Jersey drifting off in winter fog. Overhead, opal saucers shed light from the ceiling. The walls were white with a flat screen mounted on one of them. Under it stood a conference lectern ornamented with the company logo, a golden C pierced laterally by a spear. Opposite the lectern, there stood a fluted pillar on which a classical head stared back at me. It was the marble bust, I would soon learn, of the Carthaginian goddess Tanit, whose image is dangerous to look upon.

My chair had bronze casters that freed it to navigate a wide sea of blue-green carpet. I was voyaging out when a slim fortyish woman entered wearing a black pantsuit and pink lipstick. Ruffles decorated the collar of her blouse, and her hair was a silvery bob.

She seated herself with her back to the window.

"I'm Ann Fitz, the Project Manager? You must be Moses Shea? It's nice to meet you?"

I rowed hastily back to port.

"A pleasure. Terrific chairs."

"What's so terrific about them?"

"They have wheels."

"Is that unusual?"

"No. I suppose not. Forgive me. How long have you worked for Nick?"

"A long time?"

"How long?"

"Long enough? I hear you and Nick are old college buddies?"

"Old friends."

Somewhere along the line, Ann Fitz had developed the

habit of concluding every sentence on a rising pitch. Consequently, I found it difficult to tell when she was asking a question and when she was making a point.

"You look so much older than he does?"

"I'm younger at heart."

"If you say so? My assistant will be by in a minute with dossiers for the new team?"

I deduced she meant Mago when the tall youth arrived laboring behind a bus cart laden with three stacks of purple loose-leaf binders, as well as a coffee pot and related paraphernalia. Ann Fitz took no notice of him as she extracted her laptop from her shoulder bag and got down to business.

"The meetings are in alphabetical order, Paris Allan, Kay Arbuthnot, Sophie Liu, Mal Osgood, Ricardo Quinones, Kiki Sinclair? We'll do three in the morning and three in the afternoon?"

Delivering my pot and cup, Mago asked how I took it.

"In a bowl."

"In a bowl? Like how the French drink coffee?"

"Like how the French dogs drink Bordeaux."

The French dogs drink Bordeaux
In Paris in the rain
(When they aren't lapping up Champagne)
And in Strasbourg in the snow—
They drink it and howl at their woe.

He laughed so hard his little silver earrings shook. Ann Fitz set her pink lips in a firm line of disapproval and a wave of silence pummeled the Arcadian shore. The hapless youth unburdened himself of the loose-leaf binders, distributing them on the table in three tidy groups. Then he garbled a few polite words and made a tactical retreat.

The coffee was rich black coffee that stimulated my brain. Even so, I had a hard time lassoing Ann Fitz's sentences.

"I expect Nick any minute?"

I observed that her eyebrows were pencil-thin and flexible. Actually, they didn't move much, and, normally, they lent an aspect of cool reserve to her commerce with the world. But whenever I posed a question of a remotely personal nature, out came the Marlene Dietrich longbows.

"Did you grow up in New York?"

Zing!

"Does the job leave you any personal time?"

Zing!

"How long have you and Nick known each other?"

Zing!

The purple binders were stacked and labeled in alphabetical order with each employee's name and photo on the cover. Inside were lives distilled to their market essence: résumés, personal statements, college transcripts, letters of recommendation, writing samples. I learned that Ann Fitz had been conducting interviews for months, during which time the field had narrowed considerably. Six candidates had been hired and today they were coming to meet the great Nick Carty himself.

The man appeared, crooning in the doorway.

He sang in his beautiful suit, "Baby, you're a rich man. Baby, you're a rich man...."

"You can't serve two masters, Nick."

"I gave old Leonard a very good deal," he replied, snapping his fingers at my nose. "Did Ann give you the rundown on these folks? We'll handle the interrogations, but please feel free to jump in. I take it you're up to speed?"

He sat down behind a stack of materials and continued.

"Make sure you get a good look at those writing samples. Take them home and study them. I need to know who my best writers are. I'd like your feedback first thing tomorrow morning." As he spoke, he riffled through the nearest purple folder.

"It would be helpful if you could rank them and add a few explanatory notes."

"Sure. But could somebody please explain to me exactly what it is we're doing here?"

"Ads and translations in niche markets. Big niche markets. Obviously it's global. Google Translate works fine for your average pie-eater, but we'd like to offer the businesses we serve something a touch more sophisticated. There's a lot of money at stake. You see, I want Carthage to be the gold standard for contracts, terms of service, and—here's where you come in—e-commerce sites and advertising catalogs. Every retail niche under the sun. The whole universe of specialty products. The key is developing models that learn on their own."

"I don't follow you."

"Creating feedback loops between businesses and consumers—model-driven businesses, where the machines do almost everything. But for starters we need a competitive edge."

"I gather this has something to do with computers."

"Bingo, Moses. We've got the smartest AI on the planet. We've got the big data, the data scientists, and the systems analysts. All top people. But to ensure that those algorithms are ready to roll, we need the human touch. That means hiring programmers who can improve on what's already out there. Programmers with a flair for advertising language—not just codes and high-level programming languages—but programmers who would know a good metaphor from...I don't know...."

"A tired cliché."

"Right. Who would know a good metaphor from a tired cliché. I don't think a machine can do that."

"No. But a lot of people find a lifeless turn of dead language to be deeply reassuring. If you could freeze it and put it on a cone with sprinkles you'd make money. I would go so far as to suggest that" —Ann Fitz cleared her throat— "if you separated the American public from its favorite clichés, it would lose its mind and take to the trees."

Ann Fitz looked appalled but Nick had to laugh.

"Look, Moses," he resumed. "These six young people you're about to meet are terrific. Trust me, we made an unprecedented recruiting effort."

"Could you please explain our goal one more time? I want to make sure I understand."

"The goal is to fine-tune individual markets *before* we go to the closed loop and the self-learning model. First we're going to develop ad campaigns. Next we're going to target demographics."

"I see. There can never be enough information."

"You want information? Last year we purchased an AI startup called Hannibal. It's the name of their supercomputer, which is now our supercomputer. Hannibal has the ability to manipulate social media. It outsmarts the competition. At the end of the day, Hannibal is going to fuse all our models, continuously improving them, in effect re-engineering the world of commerce. Hannibal will be driving the markets, directing managerial choices, refining the models, running the whole show. Given the dominance of social media, one rule holds: the better the algorithm, the bigger the profit. Either buy into the system, or your ass will be terminated. Simple as fate."

He took a moment to allow his words to sink in. He was putting the world in the hands of Hannibal.

"But we're getting ahead of ourselves. Your job is to probe those niche markets with the poetry of advertising, so we can see what makes those markets tick."

I poured another cup of the good black coffee.

"Right now, it's all about the concept and the finish. We need ads you can't ignore. Ads that get into people's heads.

The perfect meme. *Le mot juste*. The 'halo' of meaning. Are you following me, Moses?"

"Of course. William James. The 'halo' of meaning. I'm following you."

"William James?" Ann Fitz remarked. "Was he a classmate of yours?"

"Sure was," I said. "His brother Hank wrote novels." From the pain etched on her face, I saw that Ann Fitz knew she had blundered. But alas, I was pitiless as the sun. "*Drumbeats on the Seine*? A bit wordy in my opinion."

"Listen, you idiot-savant," Nick cut me off, and rightly so. "Ann here's a prize-winning poet. That's one reason I wanted her for this job. She's a creative powerhouse."

I made a mental note to google "Ann Fitz poet."

"Now look. When I bumped into you in Las Vegas it struck me that I didn't need a dozen extra translators for this project. Too many cooks, you know? When Moses Shea showed up out of nowhere because my boy had never eaten a taco, it felt like the gods were tapping me on the shoulder."

I examined his shoulders to see if the gods might have left any marks. It always makes me nervous when someone drags the gods into it. Odds of a misreading are high. I shot a glance at the bust of the inscrutable goddess.

"Ann and I understand that good writing isn't done by committee...."

As he was talking, my unconscious crept up like a thief and unhitched my gaze, which had been tethered like a good camel, and which now went wandering off on its own. After a restorative sojourn in the New Jersey fog, it made its way toward the silvery bob, where it floated free of gravity before descending with long slow strides over pink lips, white ruffles...at which point I recovered with a start.

Zing!

"I want you to mentor these brilliant kids. Take them under your wing. Teach them the poetry of advertising."

"Are we going to work in this office?"

"No. I picked up a campus. It was kind of a fire sale." He tilted his head back and stroked his chin. "Litchfield —my lawyer—thinks there might be trouble down the road. He's worried about the deed. I am not."

"Where is this place?"

"Saint Malachy College in Massachusetts."

"Huh." I seemed to remember my father speaking there, ages ago, but I withheld this information.

"Saint Malachy College was a Great Books school that outlived its purpose. Ivy on the walls, dignified old buildings, a hundred fifty acres of grass and trees. They have a chapel with a bronze soldier standing guard. Not to mention an English maze and an amphitheater by a frog pond—though the frogs may also be extinct. Last May the student body burned down half the dorms. But still, it's a charming campus. We've renovated the main hall and put in suites. You and Ann will have the nicest ones. There's a gym on campus, too...not that you would ever use a gym, Moses."

Ann Fitz beamed at me. We were not hitting it off, she and I. We were failing to maximize cross-promotional opportunities. Soon we'd be giving each other bad news.

"I'm not sure I want to live in Massachusetts, Nick. It seems like something you might have mentioned."

"Come on, Moses. My money's good. I told Leonard Fest I didn't know how long our arrangement would last—when it ends you can always go back to him. He said he'd miss you at the Hospitality and Design Show."

Ann Fitz's smile was bright enough to light up a Christmas tree.

"I get weekends?"

"Fine."

"I also want vacation days."

"Fine."

"And sick days."

"That's fine, Moses. But let's make sure we get the job done. You have to be available when we need you."

"How available?"

"Master Baxter at Adams House." He wagged his Harvard finger at me. "I hope you remember his selfless example. An escutcheon on the wall and a Latin motto."

"*Carthago delenda est*."

"That's as funny as a race riot. Ann, where was I?"

I said, "We were talking turkey."

"Will you please settle down, Moses? You can work it out with Davidman."

"I don't want to work it out with Davidman. I want to work it out with you. What about summers?"

"Four weeks. You can finish your novel."

"Five."

"Okay, five."

"What's the title of your novel?" Ann Fitz interjected.

"What? The title of my novel is *Moby Duck*."

"You're writing a novel called *Moby Duck*." For the first time all morning Ann Fitz had made a declarative statement. Nick interpreted it as a question.

"He is," he explained. "It's about a giant duck. How big is the duck, Moses?"

"Big enough to poke its bill right through that window," I said, pointing over Ann Fitz's shoulder.

"Now listen," he said, getting back to business. "You're going to hear a lot about politics. Young people can be a little naïve in that department. Four years of college and their heads are full of all kinds of misty notions. What I've found is there's a lot of money in that mist, if you know how to look for it.

Some of these young idealists are the savviest consumers I've ever met."

"Mr. Paris Allan," Mago announced.

A young black man entered in a blue checkered sportscoat and jeans. Shaking hands with a good grip and easing into a burgundy chair, he said to call him Paris. He surveyed the three of us coolly, his height still commanding the room after we were all seated. His binder told me that he ran the 5,000 meter race at Georgetown, where he double-majored in Computer Science and English. He captained the track team his senior year. His hair was cut short and crisp, and his face was lightly freckled.

Though I spoke little, I took copious notes throughout the day. Paris Allan was a tech utopian, a true believer who preached that Moore's Law would lead us to the Milk and Honey Land of Green Energy. He'd been educated at a Jesuit institution and repeated the phrase "transformational technology" like a mantra. His large hands grew lively as he discussed new breakthroughs in modularity. He believed that someday, in the near future, every product on earth would be constructed modularly in accordance with flawless global planning.

Nick pressed him on whether he was willing to profit from his labor.

"So long as we don't take advantage of anyone," he replied. "Capitalist exploitation isn't for me. I want to protect the environment."

"We're not in a position to share everything we do right now. But where the environment is concerned, we're always looking for profitable solutions. You understand?"

The young man understood.

So it went for the others as well, all titans of computer science who'd made the crossover into the humanities. They belonged to a new generation of "woke" capitalists who expected the best of both worlds—justice combined with a nice juicy paycheck. I admired Nick's method, which accommodated this seeming paradox by focusing on what made these folks unique. He was hiring people who hadn't hunkered down in one side of their brain. They were a gilded crew whose parents had delivered from day one, every stage of the way from preschool to college, with all the fluttering ensigns and flashing emblems of station and status. Kay Arbuthnot grew up in Wilmette, Illinois. Slender and arresting in her striped blouse, high-waisted pencil skirt, and elegant heels, she had a degree in Gender, Sexuality, and Women's Studies from Northwestern. As a college senior, she led a student strike against a flirty professor. It was Kay who identified the bust of the goddess Tanit. The bespectacled Sophie Liu in her polka dots was fluent in Java, Hack, Python, Erlang, Spanish, Japanese, Mandarin, and Quenya. Through the medium of a soft, cloudlike voice she deployed verbal skills of a high order. She attended Reed College in Portland, Oregon, and mentioned that the once fair city was suffering under a political class that lacked the courage to uphold the rule of law. A Classics graduate from UVA, Mal Osgood spoke in a slow, thoughtful manner that verged on a southern drawl. He had a mole on his left cheek and maintained a glossy trim of black hair on his large head. He wore an aging corduroy blazer and a striped tie, both of which I approved of. The severely handsome Ricardo Quinones arrived in a surprising plaid suit. Fluent in Spanish, French, Italian, and Hindi, he'd learned to kickbox in a gym in Detroit called Shady's. He spoke like a field general diagramming a multi-pronged attack, with complete sentences, some of them ending in verbs. The wide grin of a practical joker lurked beneath the boldness of his address. Kiki Sinclair hailed from San Francisco, where her father was the marina harbormaster. She had a degree in Theater and Dance. She occupied center stage in a double-breasted blazer and blouse buttoned all the way up. She was petite and cute in an impish sort of way, with prominent blue eyes and a mignon nose. She liked wordplay, dispensing volleys of minimalism that hooked us in no time.

"Ditto."

"Ditto?"

"Moses?"

"Ditto."

By the end of the day, though, a subtle absence pinged my antennae. Where was my tribe? Where were the frogs? The plain Janes and the Helens of Troy, New York? Had they been eliminated in the earlier rounds—banished with the lesser beauties? It must have been Ann Fitz who'd done the culling. But it must have been done on Nick's orders. I remembered Nick's holding forth on the topic. Always hire the best-looking people, he said, unless they can't do the job. Put the right rules in place, make them stick, and you can harness the human sex drive like electric power from a dam. I recalled his comment because of how he startled when he noticed me among the listeners. It was ages ago, in some beer cellar in Boston, or possibly in New York during the last of his bachelor days, when his kin were converging on Saint Patrick's Cathedral for the marital disaster. He was a prophetic figure, old Nick.

When the interviews had concluded, Kiki's being the last, he posed a funny question.

"What did Crawford really say about Moore's Law?"

"He said it would fail in the end."

"Of course it will," the man replied knowingly, before slipping out the door. That suit of his looked like it was made for slipping out the door.

I resisted the impulse to make small talk with Ann Fitz. I'd learned at the *Times' Times* that the mildest efforts at humor could backfire in a lethal explosion. Ann Fitz and I had spent the better part of six hours together and now we were keeping our distance. I'd observed her demeanor all day, from how she fluttered her fingernails at moments of interest, to her handling of her phone, to her cool dominion over her assistant. I'd inspected her expensive face, a tough canvas of pearly foundations. I'd studied her slate-blue eyelines and pale blue eyes. I'd measured her heels and analyzed her sentence patterns. She struck me as oblivious to virtue, orthodox to the bone, but not stupid, not a dupe, above all wary and shrewd. She was deeply embedded in her success. We gathered up our binders in silence.

Mago guided me to the payroll department to meet Lenny Davidman. Just the sight of this man was a balm and a tonic after those young gods and goddesses. He was a waist-coated, barrel-chested Jew, hairline ebbing to the parietal bones, rimless lenses poised on a bulbous, untrimmed nose. His voice was both deep and delicate as he reviewed the information required of me, while, beyond his large office window, the view of Midtown dissolved. The fog that had swallowed New Jersey was expanding. The lighting in the room held out against the darkened window.

"We're like a needle in a haystack up here," he commented.

As we exchanged information, he mentioned a Mrs. Davidman who wanted him to purchase yellow fog lights for the car. So he had procured a wife for those nose hairs of his. Then I happened to catch sight of the family photos. They were ubiquitous once you noticed them, lining the shelves, populating desk corners, parading on the windowsill, perched in nooks and crannies. Papa bear and mama bear and three little Davidmans, here and there grown into three big Davidmans. Lenny gave me an innocent little pat on the shoulder as I left his office. Actually, he swerved, trying to avoid my shoulder at the last moment, and practically tripped. He must have feared it would be too much.

His social instincts, haptic and tribal, had nearly betrayed him.

I told Lenny Davidman I could find my way and proceeded to gather my coat and ride the elevators back to Fifth Avenue. You may recall that Nicky-boy asked me to come in early the next morning with my notes and rankings. He phoned as I was hailing a cab. He said his schedule had changed. He looked forward to my presentation on Wednesday. "No problem," I said. I'd already noticed the nice bump in my checking account.

I dropped off the loose-leaf binders at home before dining at a local bistro. After that, I decided to walk over to Zabar's, having persuaded myself that a fresh supply of cinnamon rugelach would provide valuable assistance with the next day's reading. The pace on the street was faster and edgier than in previous winters. The city's nerves and tendons were stretched thin, but in upscale neighborhoods a temporary truce was holding between the forces of chaos and civilization. The pigeons still outnumbered the rats. The aura of a great metropolis survived among high cornices and corbels.

After the cash inflow and a pleasant dinner, I was adjusting to the reality of Massachusetts. My Manhattan apartment began to take on the role of a pied-à-terre in my mind. Trade-offs were involved but the world seemed improved—until I clapped eyes on Sam Fallo. What alarmed me wasn't Sam's appearance in itself, Sam who was known to shop at Zabar's, Sam who was morbidly obese, Sam who was the Mayor's special pal, Sam who drove a series of phony scandals with scoop after breathless scoop, Sam who laughed me out of her office at the *Daily Dose*. No. What alarmed me was her smile. I regarded Sam Fallo's smile with much the same trepidation as a poetic old sea dog regards a red sky over the fo'c'sle as he relieves himself early in the morning.

The last time I saw her she was her true man-hating self.

At the time, the women of the West Side were in a collective fury over the indignities they had suffered for years at the soiled hands of cab drivers, doormen, delivery men, sanitation workers, plumbers, repairmen, street cleaners, utility workers, furniture movers, cops, firemen, house painters, and mailmen. The male of the species was in very bad odor, even worse than usual. Sam humiliated me for half an hour, gloating over my incipient extinction, and, when she was quite sure I knew where I stood, she grinned venomously and suggested that I go curl up and die. In view of these facts, which certainly do her justice, the twitching recession of blubbery lips around those omnivorous fangs of hers played up and down my spine like an organ solo in *Phantom of the Opera*. As for those husky mandibles, their least threatening activity was eating. She did a great deal of eating and, as far as I was concerned, the more she ate the better. She was in Zabar's buying a pound of chopped chicken liver and a pound of seafood salad. I wouldn't have bet on it lasting the hour.

The evening's occasional flurries made up their mind to snow for real as Sam and I plodded up Broadway together, a she-whale and her calf navigating the northern seas. She was letting me know of an opening at the *Dose*. It might be of interest, she said. Their Beijing bureau chief had been forced to retire after his narrative suffered a total breakdown. For decades, this poor man had constructed a meticulous narrative about US-China relations, centering on a dire threat to the global order that could be resolved only by completely restructuring the American economy. Nothing could have been more urgent, if the narrative had only been true. The bureau chief swore by his narrative, prospered in its atmosphere, told clever in-jokes about it, and rose to fame through its currency in expensive college textbooks and peer-reviewed academic journals. It dominated so much of his brain matter that no earthly doctor could have removed it without losing the patient. Just that week, however, a longtime State Department official shattered it in a highly factual and sharply-worded letter. The *Dose* published the letter over the staff's fierce objections. The former bureau chief was currently resting in the Journalism Wing of the Manhattan Psychiatric Ward.

"Facts got the better of him," Sam Fallo said solemnly.

"He couldn't do a soft reboot?"

"I know," she said. "He should have. Most writers have it in them, but some don't. That's why I always warn new writers about facts. Facts are the bane of this profession. When you mess around with facts you have to be careful. You have to *know* how to handle them. I wish they'd teach *that* in journalism school!"

Would I consider working in Beijing?

The offer pierced my defenses and stirred up many memories and emotions. The truth was I missed being a reporter very much. I missed the tug of a good story. It took patience, reeling in the big fish. You had to wait and see what might surface. I missed the prodigious cast of characters—the wise serpents and innocent doves, the worldly and unworldly, the brazenly evil and the stubbornly good, the attention whores of both sexes and the stunned souls who withdrew into a silence as strong as the seal of confession. I was still carrying a torch for my old sweetheart, but to think of that sweetheart as Sam Fallo snapped me out of my reverie like a sock of wet sand between the eyes.

I decided not to answer her question. I sheered off as we passed Victoria's Secret and went my way. Of course I was committed to Nick, who had just dropped a nifty sum into my bank account. But beyond all that, beyond the need to honor friendships at least as long as they were profitable, I sensed that Sam was up to something. I had no clue what it was, but I was damned if I'd ever be caught with my guard down again.

Nick and I didn't see each other until late Wednesday afternoon. When we regrouped in the conference room, I had spent considerable time perusing the contents of those purple binders. I ranked the writers as follows:

1. Mal Osgood
2. Kay Arbuthnot
3. Kiki Sinclair
4. (tie) Sophie Liu, Ricardo Quinones
5. Paris Allan

I started by explaining to Nick and Ann Fitz that Osgood knew things the other young people didn't. For example, he'd mastered certain grammatical constructions. Almost immediately, though, Ann Fitz interrupted.

"What do you mean, 'grammatical constructions'?"

"Participial phrases. Dependent clauses. Result clauses."

"Go on," Nick said.

"The history of the English language is another relevant factor. Chaucer's English is the child of Norman French and Old English, which is close to Old High German."

"*Really?*" Ann Fitz commented. "People used to teach the history of the English language? People used to study Latin? No offense, but I'm twenty years younger than you? Nobody cares about that stuff? It has no commercial value? If anything, it has negative value? Why on earth would Kay Arbuthnot want to submit to a regime of patriarchal mind control? This isn't Gilead? The whole point of her degree is to break free of those mental chains?"

"That's Blake," I said.

"Blake who?"

"The phrase 'mental chains' comes from the English poet William Blake. Elsewhere he says 'mind-forged manacles.'"

"I don't see your point?"

"The title of Atwood's novel comes by way of Chaucer."

"I think I see what he means," Nick said soothingly. "I

suspect that in Moses's view we should be aware of these things—where our words and phrases come from. Is that correct, Moses?"

"A word's full power is rarely present to the conscious mind. The root of a word may be buried beneath its current usages, but that doesn't mean it's dead. Good writers will always be aware of the root. A good writer will be conscious of the past, because the past is with us in the words we use. It inhabits the words we are using in this conversation. It never goes away. It's your choice. You can be conscious or unconscious of the language you use. Of course, if you're unconscious, you're like the people who speak in nothing but clichés. You don't have to be conscious to use a cliché."

Ann Fitz sat gaping at me, but Nick persisted. "Give us another example regarding Osgood," he said.

"Sure. Osgood writes in his college paper, 'Learning ought to be an experience of wrestling with other minds.' It's clear and concise. The Latinate abstraction is brought to life by a good earthy German participle. He doesn't say, 'experience is reflected' or 'experience requires,' heaping up abstractions. He seems to know that the Latin verb *experior* means 'to test,' and that 'wrestling' gives it vigor. Arbuthnot, who is usually quite good, writes the following sentence in her college paper, 'A liberal arts education ought to teach human beings to identify more closely with others.'"

"What's wrong with that?" Ann Fitz said sharply.

"It's fine. Arbuthnot's grammar and syntax are flawless."

"Yes?"

"She never breaks through the wall of abstraction. I mean, 'teach' is fine, though it's an institution and not a person doing the teaching. 'Human beings' isn't bad in itself, but here it sounds like an academic circumlocution employed to avoid the matter of sex. 'Identify with' is, at best, uncritical. Arbuthnot knows this because she says, 'more closely.' The word *other*, like the phrase *human beings*, is how the parrots have been trained to sing."

As I finished my exposition, Ann Fitz passed through several stages of disbelief. Her chin tilted upward, her eyeballs bulged, and the wings of her nostrils flared. Finally, her face settled like fine pudding skin.

"Ann?" Nick said, restarting the Fitzian mechanism. "Ann?"

"Obviously Moses has a problem with brilliant young women? His prejudices are only too conspicuous? He sees what he wants to see? By his own account, Kay is an excellent writer? No doubt a female critic could heap abuse on Mal Osgood's writing just as easily? Look at Kay's writing? Flawless punctuation? Excellent paragraphing? An extensive vocabulary? As for the sentence in question, I have no idea why you're degrading the *other*? Possibly because you can't *identify* with the *other*? And as you yourself point out, Kay was perfectly *conscious* of what she was doing?"

During this spirit-stirring harangue, which expanded in my mind like an infinite chain of paperclips, the bust of the goddess Tanit seemed to grow larger. I could sense the displeasure of the *numen*. It seemed as if the goddess herself were speaking to me.

"Now I have one more thing to say about this...*situation*? Notice how Paris is rated *last*? Unbelievable? What this suggests in my mind is a complete lack of empathy on your part for human beings who are different from yourself?"

"Different from myself?"

"Hard to imagine, isn't it?"

"I liked his story about a world where you aren't permitted to call a corpse a corpse. The word has been officially suppressed. If someone in your household dies, you just have to live with the dead body and pretend nothing has changed. It could vote and watch TV, until it totally decayed, at which point the government would send in social workers to determine if decomposition was complete. I think the title was '*Esprit de* Corpse.'"

"That was the only one I didn't like?"

"Well, I thought it was his best work, by far."

"He won several writing prizes at Georgetown?"

"Academic prizes are exercises in political approval."

"When weren't they?"

"What I mean is, they have nothing to do with art."

"Paris has published his own science fiction? Outside of Georgetown?"

"I told you, I liked that story."

"At that level of accomplishment, I would hesitate to say that one writer is better than another?"

"Then why go through the hiring process in the first place?"

"I said 'at this level.' Think of all the stupid editors who rejected great writers, probably because they failed to recognize their own prejudices? How deep does prejudice go? It's an interesting question, if you ask me?"

Nick rapped his knuckles gently on the table. He kept it up until he had us in his grip, which he relaxed with the practiced smile of a billionaire diplomat who knows how to get exactly what he wants.

"An excellent dialogue," he said with satisfaction. "You've both made your points. I feel privileged to have sat in the audience. As Ann suggests, we cannot elude our...perspectives. What Carthage needs is to synthesize as many intelligent perspectives as possible. Bear in mind that's exactly what Hannibal is going to do."

Nick paused a beat and then began afresh.

"Our elephants will cross the Alps," he said. "Not only the Alps. They will cross the Rocky Mountains, the Pyrenees, the

Andes, and the Himalayas. They will climb to the clouds and astonish the world."

"What elephants are those, Nick?"

"Moses?"

"It's a metaphor from the Punic Wars. Nick and I were Classics majors."

"What are we going to do next, sell togas?"

"Ann, you are invaluable to this operation. I am well aware that you and Moses—how shall I say it?—represent different constituencies. I ask you both simply to keep it civil, and leave the civil wars to the Romans."

Thus chastened, we clung to our dignity like a pair of royal concubines crossing paths in the Forum. Nick was the boss, and, as matter of fact, the view at the moment was stunning. The spires of Midtown rose in glittering acres beneath us. The lordly Hudson flowed on beneath its icy sheath.

It seemed to me that, if Ann Fitz and I were never going to be friends, we could at least be intelligent about our differences. Where she equated language with politics, I did not. We could agree that language can be valued and appreciated according to its uses, be the use political, commercial, or scientific. But in my view, language should not be reduced to the status of an exploitable resource or an abstraction in an analytical field. There is always something more to it, something the cash nexus can't appropriate. Something more in the nature of art and religion. Possibly Tanit supplied the means to a spiritual elevation beyond the fatal obsession with excremental gold. But by approaching language in terms of numbers and instrumental reason, Hannibal would reduce the world to a marketplace. The machine would treat people like its fellow machines: a means to efficiency and profit. Man would become a Pavlovian dog walking on its hind legs. I am, I confess, a capitalist, a dull old capitalist, but even in the roil and toil of capital I prefer an opening for poetry—the musical phrase, the ambiguous question. I crave a touch of irony and humor, and machines don't do irony and humor. To my mind, we are better served by mystery and silence than by morally-minded logarithms. It's better, in the long run, both for people and for business. Then again—and this was Ann Fitz's angle—for the true ideologue, the logarithm was the best means to refashion reality.

As these deliberations occupied my mind, Nick gave us a move-in date. To acquaint me with the remains of Saint Malachy College before then, he was enlisting Mago. As if operating by telepathy, the Arcadian breezed into the room.

"Have a seat, Mago," Nick said, pointing to a seat. "I want you to record this. Do you want to use my phone?"

"Thank you but that's okay. I'll just use my own and send you the file when I'm done."

Mago readied his camera as Nick announced to his senior team a surprise treat, a motivational speaker in the person of former US Olympic soccer star Smack McCann. Nick hurried out to the hall to greet her, before returning to make elaborate introductions. As Smack displayed her gold medal for our benefit on the conference table, I observed her motivational outfit—a cable knit sweater and black yoga pants so tight they could have doubled as cling wrap. I have to say I was impressed despite myself. Those apple slices, or avocado slices, or watermelon halves, or what have you, would have lasted for weeks. Smack stood at the lectern, posture erect, golden hair pulled back, a clean, sculpted face worthy of medals and remuneration. The theme of her talk was teamwork. I did my best to ignore every word but I was outfoxed by her little girl voice. "You don't want to *kill* your teammates," she lisped. "You want to *skill* your teammates."

When it was time for questions, Ann Fitz's hand flew up. "What if someone has such a massive ego that they don't realize their skills are totally outdated?"

"That's an excellent question. The answer is you might not get the gold. You might not even get the bronze. But it's still your job to bring out the best in your teammates."

"What if someone is a living fossil?"

"The same principles of teamwork still apply."

"What if their entire worldview is extinct?"

"Perhaps the coach could get involved?"

Sensitive to this line of questioning, I looked up Smack McCann on my phone. I noticed Mago recording me on his phone as I did so. She was currently playing striker for a professional team called the Connecticut Coasters, owned by none other than N. P. Carty. I waved my screenful of data at Mago and mugged for his camera.

"What's that?" said Nick.

"Two ants on a mound of sugar," I said.

That night, another job offer came my way. It came from an aging veteran of the Fourth Estate named Tom Baldock. Years ago, Baldock and I used to rub shoulders in the elevator of a rent-controlled apartment building up on Cathedral Parkway. It was a fine bourgeois building with china vases mounted on Georgian mahogany side tables in a tiled and mirrored lobby. Beyond the elevator, close by the stairwell, there dwelled a Cuban supervisor who hated Castro with tremendous feeling. He would engage in fierce political arguments with the poets and painters who occupied the place, one of whom had a French wife named Renée. She treated me with kindness, refreshed my French, and dubbed me her Cyrano. Baldock in those days affected a guitar and could be heard now and then yodeling a Bob Dylan song to a paramour.

Professionally, my old pal was thriving. The new media environment brought out certain long-buried potentialities in his personality—potentialities that, in years past, had yielded place to the strict requirements of hard work. Maybe it's true that Tom Baldock was in his own unique way a victim. Imperceptibly at first, but more decisively as the last century receded, expectations changed and standards shifted. By the time the pandemic hit, Tom was practically a new man. He abandoned his earlier form of journalism for something freer and less restrictive, something closer to the modal improvisations of a third-rate electric guitarist. It remains to be seen whether New York's economy will ever recover from those front page headlines of his. They trouble my mind like an assassination that just keeps happening. "TERROR GRIPS APPLE!" "PANIC SPREADS!" "INCURABLE!!" "TOTAL PANDEMIC!" "BRAIN DAMAGE?" "DEATH PLAYS B'WAY!" "MASKS RUN OUT!!" "SUPERSPREADER H.S.!!" "VIRRRUS!!!" "KILLS IQ?" "DOCTORS DYING!" "SICK KIDS!" "CARRIED BY PETS?!" "STICKS ON MAIL!" "BABY DIES!" "DEATHS SPIKE!" "LIKE FLIES!!!" "MYSTERY SYMPTOMS?" "FOREVER COVID?" "STACK 'EM HIGH!!" "CITY AT BREAKING POINT!"

Baldock single-handedly achieved a level of devastation that a neutron bomb would have envied. Even so, I'll always wonder whether he was consciously sycophantic to the powers that be, or whether he was just going on instinct. I suspect the latter, because Tom was never really conscious of much. Looking back, I think that was the key to his success. Through all his years of feast and famine, he kept his position at the city desk of *The Village Void* until he became a fixture of the news landscape, like the desk itself.

He called that evening and asked, could we grab a drink together? Ten o'clock at The Dive Bar on 93rd Street? "Sure," I said. "Why not?"

Other than its serving glasses of alcohol to paying customers, The Dive Bar on 93rd was not an actual dive bar, not like the one on 52nd that W. H. Auden wrote about, which was like the ones the buyers and sellers in the old Garment

District patronized, back in the era of the four martini lunch, when those tireless alcoholics commuted on the L.I.R.R. five days a week, putting their kids through college and their livers through hell. Guys who, like Auden, wore jackets and ties, retired in their sixties, had the requisite heart attack, and, diverging a little from the great poet, left the comfortable suburban home to the widow along with a pension and the family pet.

At The Dive Bar on 93rd Street, the diving excluded hard-working sons-of-bitches, drunken bums, and other smelly persons as well. It was more like diving into the pools of streaming air on the planet Krypton, in the comic books of my youth, before gravity ripped the planet apart. Which is just as well. Tom was waiting at the door and we made our way to a table through the watchful crowd, through the eddies and currents of scents, vociferations swirling with laughter, splash of bass and beat of drums, the blood pumping, the liquor pouring, the web of lights, the custom of affluent men and women drinking expensive booze, testing and teasing, touching and repeating.

Baldock and I sat down and ordered a couple of scotches off the top shelf. He'd always kept himself in shape, jogging along Riverside Drive like they were going to put up a bronze statue of him. As we inspected each other for signs of decay, I could see that his stockbroker and his plastic surgeon had done wonders to preserve his boyish good looks. He hadn't changed very much, not outwardly, and he was still indulging his taste for designer brand street clothes. Tonight it was a leather jacket, so new it squeaked. The moment another riot broke out, he'd be there to cover it in style. Speaking of riots, he reported—actually, he kind of bragged—his only child was doing time in a federal penitentiary for torching several NYPD cruisers.

"Huh," I said as our drinks arrived. "I'm sorry to hear that, Tom. How long will she be incarcerated?"

"Another year," he said. "The D.A. couldn't have been more sympathetic. We've already got a job lined up for her at the *Times' Times*. That kid knows what she's doing. I tell you, she's going to have street cred. In some ways, it's more important than her Yale degree."

Baldock informed me that big changes were in store at the *Void*. He was broaching the subject when an intoxicated blonde jumped on his lap and shouted, "Hey! You're Tom Baldock." Her hair was freshly coiffed and she didn't notice me at all. I took the occasion to drain my bladder and when I returned she was perched leggily at the bar, surprising me with a dainty little wave of her fingers.

The waiter delivered our second round as Tom went on to explain that a number of the old guard at the *Void* were retiring. They were out of step with the twenty-first century. He was moving into cable himself, a hot new show called *Eyewitness Void*. His boss had asked him to find someone to revamp the paper's arts and culture section. Somebody with the experience to knock out feature articles while organizing a stable of young talent. Along with a highly competitive salary, the position included a boatload of perks—concert tickets, theater tickets, gallery openings, etc. It was a culture-vulture's paradise.

I said, "I'm flattered you would think of me, Tom. May I ask why?"

Tom stared at the puddle of scotch in his tumbler. He took a deep breath but it didn't help. The poor old jackass, he'd forgotten to do his homework. That's what happens at our age. You depend so much on lies that you forget they don't write themselves. I went ahead and tossed him a bone from our peanut dish.

"Just our friendship?"

"To be honest," he said, looking as honest as he could, "it was your body of work."

I noticed the journalism fan at the bar was eagerly thumbing away at her phone. Tom and I sure lived very different lives. I told him I'd think it over and left him to his erotic fate. After more than a year in the wilderness, I'd had two job offers in three days. Something was up, but I hadn't a clue.

Ambling down Broadway, I was bent on crawling directly into bed. But the minute I entered my apartment, force of habit got the upper hand. I logged into my iMac and clicked through versions of a story out of Washington, DC. It seemed that thuggish police had fired tear gas to disperse unarmed protestors who'd gathered to pray for racial justice. Then it seemed that the protestors had showered the police with frozen water bottles, bricks, and corrosive fluids that eat through riot gear. Then it seemed the police had incited this response by hurling racial slurs. I was weighing the merits of a third scotch when a bewildering email arrived as all emails do —just a blip out of nowhere. For the longest time, I stared at it like a bald gorilla who can't find the right button to press. Slowly, I began to see that I'd been sent an email forwarded by someone named scaevola21. The email was written by a.fitz and addressed to o.bright. This made no sense, since I knew of no connection between Ann Fitz and the editor of the *Times' Times*. The message, which was sent on Monday evening, ran as follows:

O,

He reminds me of your Uncle Dale. You should have seen how he stared at me. What a creep. Do you suppose I could be overreacting? Obviously, the man's an imbecile. He says he's writing a novel about a giant duck. I'm not joking!

The problem is Nick's insisting on this campus scenario. I could tolerate an occasional meeting, but the idea of having to work with him every day makes my skin crawl. This won't end well.

Bisous,
A

Chapter 3

The Old Hollow Discus Trick

Nick Carty's minor investments ranged the economic landscape in all shapes and sizes, from the Connecticut Coasters to a microbrewery called Hip Hops, from the Cowpoke Dude Ranch to the Flying Dutchman Ski Lodge, from a dog-training outfit called Semper Fido to a small limousine company, which he purchased mostly for his own convenience.

Image Limo operated out of a garage in Flushing, Queens, the town where I grew up. Architecturally, the Flushing of my youth was famous for Shea Stadium (no relation to us) and for the 1964 World's Fair. Shea Stadium departed Queens the same way the Polo Grounds departed Manhattan, the same sad way that Ebbets Field departed Brooklyn—under the wrecking ball. The World's Fair bequeathed to posterity a few somber memorials of the Space Age, mainly a colossal hollow steel orb, known as the "Unisphere," and the ruinous New York State Pavilion observation towers. These abstract-looking towers, notorious to veterans of the Long Island Expressway, are massive concrete cylinders topped with covered observation platforms, like layered discs, evoking purpose but frustrated in that evocation, their final cause unrealized, as if they'd never been completed in the first place. In my childhood, impressed by their refusal to conform to the shape of a drum, a water tower, a pagoda, or castanets, I came to think of these discs as spaceships in drydock, deserted by their race. The news from City Hall of their imminent restoration fed a fancy of their undocking, levitating over the old fairgrounds, and vanishing from sight like the ballparks of yesteryear.

The morning sky was the color of rubber cement when one of Nick's drivers appeared outside my apartment building in a long silver Benz, the Maybach S 600 Pullman. Waiting in the car's beige interior was young Mago, doubtless glad to have escaped Ann Fitz for the day. Not that he planned on paying much attention to the journey. He dug out an earbud to say hello.

"How are you?—big riot last night," he said. I sensed an excited flutter in this reference to another of the city's recent calamities.

"I hope nobody was hurt."

"Only a couple of pigs."

Mago extended an Arcadian smile and returned to his screen. The partition being down, the driver and I exchanged pleasantries. It wasn't until later in the day that he told me his story, with a depth bomb in the form of a mutual acquaintance. That morning, I was too distracted to say more than the few polite words needed to get us moving. His mentioning that the company garage was in Flushing, in a neighborhood I knew, jumpstarted my memory. The driver was on the Henry Hudson, but I was on the Long Island Expressway circa 1976 —driving with my father among the station wagons and the Volkswagen Beetles, talking with him about a book he was writing. He always drove a Benz. He always smoked.

"The Jesuits had such great imaginations," he said, waving a Camel. "*The Spiritual Exercises* is about exercising the imagination. Not just the sight, mind you, but every sense. I bet you never thought of your nose as imaginative!"

My father, John Daniel Shea, was one of the gifted theologians who stimulated the minds of young Catholics after the Second World War. As a graduate student in New York, he fell under the spell of that controversial Jesuit, Teilhard de Chardin, and visited him in the 1930s. Teilhard was a Christian humanist at a time when the oxymoronic effect of *Christian humanism* could not have been more pronounced. Some say that Teilhard's reputation has been resurrected, at least in certain quarters, but none would deny the fierce resistance he encountered during his lifetime. The great French Thomist Étienne Gilson was particularly hard on him. Teilhard was, after all, an evolutionary thinker, and Darwin is not to be found on the roll of saints. For that matter, I remain cautious about some of Teilhard's opinions, though I do not belittle his efforts to reconcile static and dynamic truth. What he inspired in my father was a devotion to nature, which included the usual testaments—taxidermy, mineral science, fossils—but expressed itself chiefly in extensive holdings in romantic mysticism and medieval theology, particularly Franciscan theology, all of which crossed the dangerous frontier between the natural and the supernatural.

The kerfuffle over my father's orthodoxy concerned, as is typical in such matters, the finest questions of emphasis. His enemies detected the sulfurous fumes of heresy at two crucial points. First, they thundered that he was downgrading the theological authority of reason. Second, and more insidiously, they claimed in a series of coordinated attacks that he was a liberal thinker interested neither in nature nor in Christ—that he was in reality waging a subterranean war against God's creation. On the first point, my father coyly replied that he took the theological authority of reason for granted. But the second point was stickier. To pursue the "Christ-generated" activity of nature might hardly seem heretical, unless, perhaps, you go into unflinching detail about what actually happens in the biological realm. In which case, what J. D. Shea called *stomaching the goodness of God* requires a hearty digestion. It was his most notorious phrase, satirized by rival theologians and not a few journalists to suit their envious purposes. It was intended to correct the sentimentalism of a modern, deracinated intelligentsia, who were ignorant of how the farmer and the midwife think and feel. Not that my father knew the first practical thing about farming or midwifery.

My childhood partook more of the *Traumsuche* of romance than of the hardware of realism. I don't regret my father's never having taught me how to change a tire or replace a washer. Not that I despise these things, not at all. My appreciation has only grown over time. But Christ bears his cross of pain and wonder, and that impresses us more deeply than hammers and nails.

I'm not sure what year it was when a New York gynecologist informed my mother that she would never have children. At the age of forty-five, she gave birth to a roly-poly baby boy. Cancer devoured her soon afterward. It went undiscovered until just weeks before the end. Had she lived for three or four more years, weaned me from her loving breast, cheered my first waddling steps, and called me to her in my mother tongue, doubtless I would have shipwrecked. I would have foundered in the whirlpool of my unconscious or crashed on the nearest rocks and gone down without a story. Instead, I survived her. She succumbed in the cancer ward while I was deep in the psychedelia that is an infant's first acquaintance with time and space. In my favorite picture of my parents, the one I keep to myself, she's waving an American flag. My father sports a pencil moustache that lends no distinction to his chubby face. She smiles like a lottery winner despite a beak that would have passed muster in a toucan nest. Yet I am sure they made passionate love. My father told me so. I can see it in their eyes.

My mother's maiden name, which she retained professionally, was Tauber—Miriam Tauber. She fled her native Pínsk before the war at her wise father's behest. Winding crazily through Europe before crossing the Channel and traveling steerage in a steam liner out of Southampton, she arrived in Manhattan to serve deli sandwiches by day, pound the typewriter by night, and, by the grace of God, to catch on as a teaching adjunct at the Union Theological Seminary, where she met Private J. D. Shea upon his return from the European theater, in 1946. Her family did not survive the war. Her father, Moses Tauber, my namesake and the dedicatee of her only book, had foreseen the catastrophe and made every effort to preserve the life of his gifted daughter. My mother saw a lot in her short life. Her intellect could be quite skeptical. But she loved this country as the last best hope of humankind. She revered its high democratic ideals, which she considered the greatest the world has ever known.

Following her untimely death, I endured an austere line of nannies. Never mind about them. It was a walleyed Dominican nun named Sister Mary Kanjia who restored the blessings of maternal affection to my life. As for my father's mother, she was inflexibly distant, with a studied politeness of manner that I can still imitate when I dislike a person. I remember she wrote for *The Catholic Worker* and was friends with the great Dorothy Day, whom my father called Doris Day in a private running joke between us. After he died, I discovered, buried under some military things, a shoebox crammed with letters. In one of these, postmarked two years after my birth, my grandmother confessed shunning her responsibilities for fear she might "accidentally on purpose" leave me on the express train. Sister Mary Kanjia was made of sterner stuff. She'd swing by the house to collect me in the 1949 Ford Tudor sedan the nuns had in common, and I'd follow her around the A&P, happy and safe in the shadow of her dauntless hips. I would remind her to buy plenty of eggs because I liked to cut up the cartons and make owls and penguins out of them. She called me "Mosey" in her warm Ghanaian accent, and "Nosy Mosey" when I stole off to the depths of the convent to view the Renaissance painting of Mary giving suck that fascinated me and corrected my prior assumption that women did not have nipples. She would lift me up now and then and squeeze me against her enormous bosom and kiss me on the cheek. One lucky afternoon she took me to a matinee to see *Duck Soup* on the premise that I needed to meet Harpo. I surprised her with my solemn pronouncement that I preferred Groucho "because of his words." But she remained forever dear to me. When on occasion I pray seriously—I mean when I work at it and face the struggle—it's often her memory that prompts me to do so.

My close relationship with my father determined the course of my life. It wasn't just that Dad owned an exquisite library that was mine to command, so long as I told him of my borrowings. The decisive factor was his marginalia, written in a fine, precise hand in hundreds of books he had studied and pondered. What especially attracted me was his commentary alongside a Greek or Latin text, often on a page facing an English translation. I soon grew accustomed to weighing these comments, and to puzzling through the words of a dead language. In sixth grade, just before Christmas recess, I snuck off to school with the *Antigone*, disturbed by my father's defense of the tyrant Creon, and added a few marginal comments of my own. But I somehow misplaced the book and we never recovered it. My father confiscated my licorice stash, revoked my movie privileges, and hired a tutor named Mr. Dobbins to initiate me properly into the mysteries of Greek and Latin. It seemed excessive. I drew myself up to my full height of four feet six inches and informed him (my father) with considerable dignity that I was already making progress in Greek, thank you, having deciphered the alphabet and identified words I already knew, like *paradox* and *irony*. Not much method to it, I suppose. But you'd be surprised what an enterprising boy can pick up on his own. In any case, I benefitted from the intervention of Mr. Dobbins, a retired schoolteacher who taught me both method and what method is. Method, according to the doctrine of Mr. Reginald Dobbins, is slow steady progress. A little bit done well, the next little bit done well, and so on, making one small patient step after another toward one's goal.

I was aware early on of trying to impress. I kept a tobacco pipe and on occasion could be seen walking the streets of Queens in a donnish display, blowing smoke and taking pulls of Virginia weed that refused to stay lit. Despite this flair for posturing and its cost in bouts of green-faced asphyxiation, my precocity went before me like a noble lion, protecting me against rambunctious classmates who were bored stiff by the glory that was G., the grandeur that was R. Most important, my father and I had great things to talk about. From the perspective of the theologian and widower J. D. Shea, a young son who could be left to read quietly on his own for hours, and who could engage fluently in the world of adult conversation within limits that were alternately humorous and absurd, brought unexpected rewards. In my innocent wisdom, I handed him a fresh start and a license to travel. In order to return to the international lecture circuit, all he needed to do was take me with him.

And that—to come back to why Nick hired me—is how I started learning languages. It was, as I think I told Nick, an accident of circumstance. Whether we breathe our first breath in Cape Town or Kalamazoo, we inherit an astonishing talent. It isn't even a matter of having to work for it. Children seem to have until puberty—that second Fall mirroring the first—to soak in as much language as they can. They seem to absorb it through the pores of their skin.

Our driver hurled a curse at a red Corvette snaking through the curves of the Merritt Parkway and I landed with a lurch back in the present. Secure in his headphones, Mago sat imperturbably, curled like a fetus in his corner of the backseat, angling his screen so that his window reflected it straight at me. At the moment he was consuming porn. He'd probably been on screens since before he could talk.

My father's friends and colleagues, when they noticed my love of words, encouraged and indulged me. A seven-year-old at home in Europe, I was already hopscotching skillfully through the Romance languages. These scholarly junkets, incidentally, relieved me of many a tedious school day. Following my dad and his succession of grants, I spent a year in Berlin and then a year in Moscow. I have fond memories of two summers in Tokyo, hobnobbing with the learned Jesuits of Sophia University. We also summered in Taiwan at Fu Jen Catholic University. At the ripe old age of twelve, I accompanied my old man to the Indian sub-continent—a ten-week sojourn. The inevitable hormones were massing on the border.

I knew little of comradeship at Regis High School, though the Jesuits were, as always, unfailingly kind. My nemesis was an insulting boy named Arnold Benedict Dopp, who once slapped a perfectly dissected frog brain from out of my open palm so that his imperfectly dissected frog brain wouldn't suffer embarrassment. Later in life he blended into the ranks of struggling authors until he emerged from obscurity with a prize-winning three-volume history of the USA called *How History Happens*. During one of the late brilliant presidencies (I forget which one), I sat down in a little café up by Columbia University with a copy of Dopp's middle volume, *Masters and*

Slaves. What I learned from the experience, while pacing myself through a series of cranberry muffins washed down with black coffee, was that America had fought no good wars and served no higher purpose. The traditional American story was nothing but an unusually grotesque lie, a European abortion without art or conscience, ending in pathetic jingoism. For A. B. Dopp, the older American historians wrote protofascist propaganda. At best, these writers with their warrior sentimentality were really kind of tacky. In fact, the familiar paragons of American virtue were evil. Davy Crockett and Daniel Boone, Abraham Lincoln and Walt Whitman, Lincoln Steffens and Samuel Gompers, Thomas Edison and Wilbur Wright, Ike and Omar Bradley, the whole star-spangled company, their reputations were ripped down like so many statues of Baphomet. Bad analogy. I got up for a refill and traded for Volume Three, *One Nation Under White Supremacy*. Sure enough, the KKK were in charge of the country. Executive Order 8802 had gone AWOL. Dopp framed the Civil Rights Act of 1964 as a recent, cosmetic departure from an ineradicable Jim Crow mentality. Affirmative Action? The Community Reinvestment Act? Not worth mentioning.

In a moment of what should have been paranoia, I looked around and realized to my growing horror that every kid in the café was reading A. B. Dopp. This impression mingled with his squadrons of perfectly ordered paragraphs, saturated with an essence that I knew in the bud, the tyrannical instinct masquerading as rebellion, the arrogance of a man whose every opinion had been cribbed from editorials in the *Times' Times*. It was as if a flying termite had landed in my mouth while I was gaping in puzzlement at the inventiveness of fate. It lost its way out, and died on my molars. It left a bituminous aftertaste. It seemed nothing could remove it. Gin and vodka failed. Only at last I discovered a cheap Kentucky bourbon called "Hound Dog '29" that seemed to do the trick.

So as not to take advantage of me, my father insisted we forfeit the long weekends in Europe when I started high school. He pushed me to join the track and field team, to realize the classical ideal of *mens sana in corpore sano*. The results were mixed. At the start of my labors with the discus, I was in danger of setting the wrong kind of records. But I worked hard and gradually improved. I had the support of our cheerleaders, the clever girls from the Convent of the Sacred Heart.

Moses, Moses, he's our alien!
Half-Jew, half-Episcopalian!

At an important meet I butted heads with a tower of fat named Ken Brinkerhoff. It was an unseasonably hot day late in the spring. Brinkerhoff and I were sweating buckets and finding it difficult to finish our throws standing up. As the afternoon wore on, we were increasingly layered and streaked with dirt. I could hardly see through my glasses. Had Zephyrus's sweet breath flung back our discuses and cracked both our skulls, Apollo wouldn't have sent flowers. All I knew was the relentless heat and the din of the spectators, cheering like soccer hooligans. After our final throws, Brinkerhoff and I were deadlocked. The entire meet was on the line. The field judge asked for one more throw—the tie-breaker—and Brinkerhoff suddenly beat me by fifteen feet.

"The old hollow discus trick," Coach Fletcher explained to the team. I was in a state of disbelief, but Coach wasn't on board for any dramatics. "Haven't seen that one for a few years," he said—and stepped on his cigarette butt. He discussed matters with the field judge and Brinkerhoff was disqualified. How could I have been so naïve? But it was my first taste of victory, and the clever girls from Sacred Heart went wild.

The one thing my father ever did that I found hard to forgive was to die. I was a senior in college. On an October afternoon when the sparrows were brawling in the Yard and the elms were paying their golden tribute to time and I was typing a Latin essay on a boxy computer, he suffered a fatal heart attack on the Long Island Expressway. He must have felt it coming because he pulled the Benz to safety on the shoulder of the road. He turned on the hazard lights and left a phone message the length of four breathless words, "I'll always love you." He paused for a few strange seconds between "always" and "love you." That pause—it never felt like a negation. It felt like he was giving me something. It felt like a gift. He was all of sixty-six, a fat man who smoked too much. God, I was angry. It pained me that he died alone. It pained me more that I had no one left to talk to. I'd come close with Mia, but Nick was already stealing her away. After the eulogies, after the obituaries, after the sympathetic letters, my freakishness hit me hard. I was orphaned in my freakishness. Only much later in life, spending time with a few young men who enjoyed my company because I could tell stories and dispense advice, did that emptiness begin to fill.

The onset of isolation occasioned a crisis in my theology. I maintained the mechanical routine of going to Mass, but I refused to beg heaven for drops of solace. My God was an absurdity, located only in violence and suffering. I lost contact with Jesus and his fishermen, despite my father's Ignatian lessons on imagining them as real people. The spring following his death, when I came into my inheritance, I made elaborate plans to squander it on debauchery. I would fly first-class to France, where the prostitutes can stomach anything, I said to myself, even the goodness of God. At the last minute, though, I cancelled due to an encounter with T. S. Eliot's poem *The Waste Land*. What I took from it was, in a sense, a memory of the future I had planned for myself, so that I no longer wanted to live through it. I sympathized with the Theban prophet Tiresias, doomed to observe the eternal recurrence—dead bodies and grinding bodies—of war and rape. To memorialize my mood, I wrote a large check to a Manhattan abortion clinic. It was a sick joke, the mental aberration of an impressionable young man, but it opened up the paths that led to my journalism career.

The driver called out, "Either of you guys need to take a leak? We're low on gas."

Mago was not available for comment. It occurred to me, not for the last time, that the rise of screens ought to breed misgivings, in the more evolved regions of the human brain, about the direction of our progress. The young man beside me was a case in point—superstitiously courteous, attached almost intravenously to the internet, and I'd yet to hear him make an original remark.

"Good idea," I replied.

The limo stopped and Mago sprang to life. The white-haired man-child peeled off his headphones, hopped out in his NYU tee shirt, and scouted the parking lot. The slower-moving driver was in his thirties, dark hair thinning on top, webs around the eyes of a solid masculine face, broad-shouldered, of middle height. His beard was closely shaved but thick as a steel wire brush. He wore a black livery that seemed more like a disguise on his person than a veritable uniform. Mago, ecstatic over the presence nearby of a rainbow-colored, hippie-era Volkswagen Beetle, wanted his picture taken alongside it. Obliging him, I aimed his phone as he flexed his biceps.

"Thank you so much," said the photogenic Mago, posting the latest versions of himself.

Then he needed to grab his jacket.

"It's cold," he explained.

"Oh, it's cold," the driver said, unlocking the door. "I guess that's why the fucking grownups are wearing their fucking coats."

Around us, the river of travelers was flowing fast and the

gas pumps pumping like mad. Snowflakes meandered downward in thin ranks through the wizened elms that bordered the sidewalk. In a fashionable gray coat and yellow scarf, a lady walked her black-clad white poodle on the stiff, frozen grass, close to where a man in a blue baseball cap stood smoking. The man and the woman ignored each other.

It happened that the driver and I both liked hazelnut coffee. "You've got to get it in the thermos," he said, pumping the thermos in the convenience store. "Those flavor squirts suck." I concurred. He stuck out a meaty hand and said, "I'm Manny, by the way."

"Moses. Pleasure to meet you."

Mago appeared on the line behind us with a can of Red Bull, some gum, a candy bar, and Swedish Fish in a bag. I put them on the counter, alongside the hazelnut coffees.

"Thank you so much," he said.

After that, we filled the tank and drove on to Massachusetts. Under the coffee's restorative power, Manny asked a few broad questions about my life. His interest spiked when I mentioned I'd been in the newspaper racket.

"Liars, Inc., huh?"

"Oh. A pun. Clever fellow."

"They punned on my life, those fucks. They drove me off the force."

"*La policía?*" I must have caught the hint of Spanish in his voice. If you get the accent right, people hear it unconsciously. He switched tongues like he was switching lanes.

"I was a lieutenant in Manhattan. I used to work with the kids in El Barrio. I coached baseball. I knew the little old ladies. Now I confess it's true—I accepted a few gifts. The kind of stuff you have to accept because, if you don't, you hurt people's feelings. Homemade bread, beef pies, jugs of homemade sangria. One day the father of a boy I coached wanted to give me box seats to a Yankees game. He owned a liquor store in the neighborhood. He

came to me full of gratitude, the son of a bitch. I took the tickets against my better judgment. Turned out his brother belonged to a drug cartel that was trying to extend its territory. I knew exactly who they were. I'd been keeping an eye on them and protecting my kids. In hindsight, I think it was all a setup. I think the liquor store owner was being squeezed. Dirty cops were involved. Somebody in the precinct tipped off the press. This pompous jerk who called himself an investigative reporter showed up one night knocking at my door. I was helping my children with their homework. He looked like a gigolo."

"What was his name?"

"Baldock. Tom Baldock."

"It's a small world."

"You know him?"

"I've known him many years. The devil was trimming his nails one day, and Baldock grew out of the parings."

"I thought maybe he took a shit."

Later I learned that Manny's last name was Murphy. He was on the skids, a twitch away from blowing his brains out, when the lucky call came in. His billionaire acquaintance was saving his skin with a job offer at a good salary—a salary you could raise a family on. Nick liked being a good guy. But he also knew that Manny would be a discreet and trustworthy driver. A disgraced cop understood the need for privacy.

He drove us past Hartford, past the Connecticut Coasters' stadium, and across the Connecticut River Valley—once a land of great spiritual fervor. Eventually, he exited the interstate on a long, elevated ramp that merged on a two-lane highway. We drove on past kettleholes and eskers, up and down evergreen slopes, around a hill where a white steeple rose above a sea of dark woods. At noon we passed through a juniper forest. Then I caught sight of snow in an ancient furrow near a rockpile claimed by crows. The road bent slightly and the campus opened up on our left. My first impression of Saint

Malachy College was of the charred ruins of a brick dormitory, a single wall still standing and, in its shelter, cinders pocked with snow. We made two lefts, the second one leading us under a cast-iron arch where two gold letters stood side-by-side, a nonsensical *la* proclaiming the entrance to the campus.

A stop sign brought us to a halt. To our left stood a temporary structure, a kind of long shapeless tent, grayish brown in color. It was repulsive to look at, like the cocoon of a man-moth. A right turn at this intersection would have led to the parking lot of the O'Connell Library, now under the management of the Commonwealth of Massachusetts. Just up ahead, engraved on the front of a marble bench, a golden C, pierced laterally by a spear, marked the turf that belonged to Nick. We drove slowly on, coasting an unraked greensward that engulfed an empty plinth. I was seeking the fallen statue when a flashing cruiser challenged our progress, and Manny pulled over muttering a string of expletives.

A fist banged on my window. Opening it, I came face-to-face with a tensely constructed female in a purple uniform, golden badge on cap, holster on hip. She removed her mirrored sunglasses to reveal a fortyish-looking face, expressionless as a parking meter. Her eyes scanned us for defects, and her angular nose thrust into the car and sniffed.

"Hello, Mago," she said.

"Hello, Sergeant Nachman. How are you?"

"Good. Thank you. How are you?"

"Good. Thank you. How are you?"

"Good."

Bolstered by this exchange, she handed me a purple lanyard with a photo ID clipped onto it. I saw my name and wondered at my shocked and frozen expression.

"Mr. Shea? I'd appreciate your wearing your company ID whenever you're out on the grounds."

"What?"

"It's not mandatory, but we strongly recommend it. You know, an excess of caution. We need to identify trespassers. Lawbreakers. They're out there in numbers, Mr. Shea."

"Lawbreakers?"

"Mostly from the old college. They've been infiltrating the grounds. You'll see."

"I won't be wearing it, in any case," I said, detaching the ID card from the purple lanyard, which I handed back to her.

"Please reconsider, Mr. Shea."

"Fine," I said, pocketing the lanyard. "It's been a pleasure. Can we go now?"

"That's your destination," she said. "Dido Hall."

She pointed to a red brick clocktower rising from a superior specimen of Victorian Gothic architecture. The placement of the clocktower was fantastically asymmetrical, which left room for a small central dome and a roof with tall chimneys, as well as balustrades and balconies on the walls, and an abundant variety of mullioned windows with leaded lights. I could imagine garden gnomes gathering on the spacious grounds before it, where a green and white sign announced "Virgil Hall."

"It says Virgil Hall."

"That's wrong."

Manny interrupted our colloquy by pressing his foot on the gas. He deposited me and my young companion under the roof of a porte-cochère, gave a quick honk, and exited the campus, flipping Sergeant Nachman a valedictory bird as he passed.

We climbed the steps of Dido Hall to a deep, arched doorway where Mago scanned his ID. The lock clicked open and our eyes adjusted to the dim atmosphere of a grand parlor. It was presided over by an oil painting of a smiling old priest, long gone to his Maker. The large paneled room was furnished with an assortment of chairs and antique-looking settees to accommodate the visitors who must once have been frequent. Pale light from the tall windows fell on unlit lamps. The gas burning in a black marble fireplace lent a lunar aspect to a white grand piano. We called *hello* and no one answered. We hung up our coats on a brass coat tree and tried again. This time a fine baritone responded from the interior, *Over here-ear*.

"Where are you?" Mago replied, spinning around and banging his shin on a side table.

We were met by the same four notes—*Over here-ear*—a major triad ending in a minor third. I took the lead and followed under an archway, across a perpendicular hallway where a grand staircase ascended on our right, and straight on until we reached a refectory with a domed ceiling and windows facing west. In this echoing space, leaning against one of several banquet tables, arms folded across his chest, the owner of the voice reclined. He was a large man of Asian extraction whose commanding presence suggested more of the djinn than the chef. Nonetheless, he was attired in a traditional chef's uniform, which took a dash of flair from a loose cravat, worn jauntily off-kilter and knotted with a sailor's hitch. A white hat or toque bloomed like a mushroom on his head.

Introducing himself as Gladstone, he disposed of me as a casserole dish not worth saving. Mago, on the other hand, sparked a certain interest. "We'll need to get to know each other," he said, his voice resonant and deep, "since we'll be meeting on a daily basis. Maybe I can show you around."

"Thank you so much," the ever-courteous Mago replied. "But it's actually Moses you'll be seeing every day. I'm just here to show *him* around."

"I understand," Gladstone said. "Aren't you free at all this afternoon? I can show you the new kitchen."

"Thank you so much but I'm rather busy."

"Just a quick tour? I've done a lot with the place."

"It's so kind of you but I'm afraid I can't."

"Half an hour?"

"I *really* appreciate the invitation. Maybe we can stay in touch. Do you have Snapchat?"

The aggrieved chef gestured toward a sumptuous array of soups, breads, cheeses, cold cuts, fruits, yogurts, pies, and custards. He directed our attention to an ample complement of beverages, as well as a colorful chalkboard that advertised gourmet salads and offerings from the grill. He recommended that Mago try the fresh dog.

"You're joking," Mago said. "I don't see any fresh dog."

"It just came in," Gladstone said.

His djinn-like powers prevailed at the cutting board, where he cored tomatoes and diced onions in a rhythmic blur. When he finished with a knife, he would swipe it on his apron and fling it across the length of the cookline at a manikin that hung from its collar on the wall. It was molded of synthetic cork, an ingenious material that permitted steel knives to penetrate to the hilt without damage to subject or object. He called it "Cowboy Joe." I asked if he worried that someone might accidentally catch a knife intended for Cowboy Joe.

"I never miss unless I want to," he said noncommittally.

I looked thoughtfully at Cowboy Joe.

"I'll call you when your lunch is ready."

"We'll just wait here, if it's okay."

"Cowboy Joe and I are having a talk," he said, conducting the grill with his spatula. "You boys go sit down."

We helped ourselves to big bowls of delicious lobster bisque. At our table the window gazed out on a leaf-littered field climbing to wooded hills beneath a raveled sky. When our sandwiches arrived, Gladstone delivered them with a salaam. Then he retreated into his kitchen with a ferocious slamming of pots and pans that didn't entirely let up for several minutes. Mago consumed a hefty tuna melt and I plowed through a massive Reuben on rye. Sometime later, when we emerged from our postprandial torpor, all was quiet in the refectory.

I wanted to walk off the extra calories at my leisure. The difficulty arose when I resisted Mago's idea of guiding us around with his phone. My perspective was not translatable to his perspective. No words would suffice to build a bridge between us. His phone and his worldview were one. Remove his phone and you created an evolutionary crisis. I told him I was going to the library to request a map. "A paper map?" he said histrionically. He straggled behind as I sallied forth in my overcoat to the O'Connell Library, mounted the steps like a tuba playing an ascending scale, and crossed the classical portico.

The desk worker smiled welcomingly. The instant her large eyes encountered Mago's Carthage ID, however, the smile ceased. The young lady went back to work in a depthless silence and pretended we didn't exist.

I trotted up to the desk and read the nameplate.

"Excuse me, Miss Phoenix. I was hoping you might have a map of the campus."

She lifted a book from the large pile on her desk, opened it, and typed at her computer. When she finished, her head swiveled in my general direction.

"May I help you?"

Her green sweatshirt proclaimed ST. MALACHY GRIFFINS in white letters. A Phoenix in the company of Griffins, the two birds being related, if I recall.

I repeated my request.

"This is a state library," she said primly. "We are not connected to the campus in any way. I would suggest you ask your employer for a map."

This was too much for Mago, who leapt up beside me and

spoke his vacuous mind. "Thanks," he said. "We don't really need a map, anyway."

"What *do* you need?" she replied.

"Come on," he whined. "This is pointless. I told you, we can use our phones."

"If you don't have a map I can borrow," I informed her, "I'll be at the mercy of this half-educated consumer of Twitter-feed and smut. I am here in the capacity of a stranger asking for your help. If you can spare the blessing of a map, I promise to return it."

She frowned at Mago, who froze in his Arcadian socks.

"Wait here," she said.

Presently she returned with a map of Saint Malachy College.

"Here," she said. "Keep it."

I bowed my head in gratitude. As for my young protégé, he was adding me to the list of things he didn't like about his job. We descended the steps to the parking lot in a raw silence. We skirted the grass oval, which framed another bare plinth, and faced each other, separated by thirty-five years and a technological muddle that had poisoned the roots of things.

"What are you? Some kind of Nazi-Puritan?"

"I don't think of myself in those terms."

"You have no right to judge me."

"I wasn't judging you. But you're playing with forces you don't understand."

"So that's why you embarrassed me in front of that girl?"

"She probably thought you were cute."

"She was wearing a cross."

"A crucifix."

"What's the difference?"

"You don't know?"

"I don't care. It just means she's stuck."

"Stuck?"

"She has no space to change."

"Why would she need a space to change?"

"Forget it. Text me if you need something. Good luck with your map."

He sauntered off at an easy pace, confident in the extinctions of the past.

The original campus was a hundred fifty acres of arable land surrounding low wooded hills, with a broad path running along the perimeter, into which narrower, tributary paths flowed. This path, which remained in good shape, led me past the ruin that we'd seen from the road—Dante Hall, as my map informed me. Once upon a time, it boasted a cartouche with a laughing gargoyle. It must have been carved on some other wall than the one standing before me, its empty window frames staring eerily at nothing. A little further on, concealed from the road by a copse of lichen-splashed oak, Aquinas Hall lay in its final desolation. Not a single brick remained in place. A withered row of six dogwoods had suffered the scorching heat from the fire. It would take unusual bud hardiness for them to blossom again.

Venturing off the main path, I toiled up a slope where lustrous laurel leaves stood out among the pale browns and grays of the dominant oaks. Here and there growths of pine and hemlock rose above the forest floor, and when I came across a cluster of black birches I remembered how you can break off a twig and catch a strong scent. Wintergreen.

A moment later, for the first time in my solitary walk, I glimpsed another soul. On this low frosty hill, where the remains of Newman Hall stretched out like a bomb site, a woman in heavy work boots appeared to be swinging a large thurible back and forth. A visionary impression, to be sure, but as I soon learned, it wasn't so far off. For some unaccountable reason, she was combing the rubble with a metal detector, the kind you see at the beach sometimes, where lonely men probe the dunes with them like dowsers. I slipped behind a tree but she'd noticed me already and scampered off in the opposite direction. She was so surprised and alarmed, however, that she dropped her instrument and had trouble extricating it from the dangerous debris.

"What is it you're looking for?" I called, clambering up the hillside. "I doubt there's much here of any value."

The overall effect of my glasses, double chin, and balding pate has been known on occasion to put people at ease. I summoned a homely smile and she started to cry. She was close to me in age with the usual blessings—crow's feet, wrinkles, sagging skin. We were standing on two crumbly islands in a sea of shards and broken brick. I reached across to her with a tissue. She accepted it and blew her red fleshy nose.

"Will you tell me what you're looking for? I really am curious."

"But who are you?"

"My name is Shea. I'm in the advertising game."

"Well, Mr. Shea, my name is Donna Ramella. If you really want to know, my son used to live here. He lost a Saint Anthony's medal that's been in our family since before we came to America. That's what I'm looking for."

"*O Sant'Antonio prega per me!*" I responded, my breath white from the cold.

She wanted to cry some more but checked herself. As she blew her nose again, I inspected our situation. Newman Hall was a disaster area. It was an open invitation to a case of tetanus. I wondered why Nick hadn't hired a demo crew. Someone could get badly hurt.

"*Come on,*" I said in Italian. "*This is a dangerous spot. Where's your car? I'll walk you over.*"

"*It's way over there,*" she said, pointing southwest.

"*Tell me about your son,*" I said, as we started walking.

"*Are you a priest in disguise?*"

"No. I swear. I'm in advertising."

She told me about her boy in a voice trembling between pride and anguish. His name was Fabio. He'd been a very affectionate child. She was afraid she'd spoiled him. But he worked so hard in high school. The college had awarded him a full scholarship.

"Where is he now?"

"He joined Antifa."

"He what?"

"He's a terrorist. He's living with his former professor in New York. She just had an abortion. She's a whore. They want to destroy the country. They say Saint Malachy's was just the beginning."

This poor woman was trapped in a nightmare. Some instinct told her that if she could just return to the source, if she could recover what had been lost, things would come right again. I wondered how many hours she had devoted to her impossible quest.

"I never used to pray," she said, switching back to English with a sob. "My mother—she came from Foggia—she was so disappointed in me. But now I think she was right. God left us here and we have to get back to him somehow."

I said, "I feel the same way." Then I said it in Italian, feeling the words, the plangent o's. *"Mi sento allo stesso modo."*

Her road-weary green Ford Taurus with the rosary beads hanging from the rearview mirror waited on a dirt driveway off the east-west highway. Hoping to elude detection, she'd trekked with her metal detector across half a mile of trees and open field. We reached the car and she put the instrument in the trunk. The leafless woods around us were hushed as patches of afternoon sunlight came and went. A few brown oak leaves still clung to their stems. She searched my face like I might know something.

"What do you say to a boy like that?"

"I suppose you say what his teachers should have said. That civilization is slow hard work. That we're all seriously flawed. That knowledge is hard to come by and you have to sweat for it."

"I wish he'd studied with you," she said. "And not with that whore."

I said some gentle words and waved encouragingly as she drove off. I was still waving, but it was too late when I remembered what I forgot to tell her, that she needed to keep a sharp eye out for Sergeant Nachman.

Consulting my excellent map, which unfolded all kinds of local lore, I devised a short cut through the field sinking gradually toward swales and wetlands. I'd opted for the right shoes that morning, the same magnificent mall walkers I'd worn in Las Vegas. I was committed to the amphitheater and the chapel, at least. As for other sights—the gym, the science building, the three surviving dorms, etc.—they would have to wait for another day.

A blur of color began emerging from the landscape. It was a row of yellow witch hazels, marking the way to the amphitheater. Their wispy blossoms, exempt from winter's neutral tones, reintroduced the idea of beauty to my surroundings. They dispatched the ghostly tentacles that had been coiling around my mind ever since I passed the remains of Dante Hall—the choking sensation of chaos in the ascendant.

When I reached the earth and marble amphitheater, I recited aloud what I could recall of a Sophoclean chorus:

He is an exile who, in his blind rush, betrays love and duty.
Not by my hearth, he who does such things!

Generations of students must have recited those lines, young people breathing the air of a great civilization, while, among the reeds, an audience of bullfrogs pondered the performance, eyes bulging with life and death.

I was determined to visit the chapel even if it meant a salt bath for my feet before bed. Skirting the frozen marsh, I crossed a slender wooden footbridge with no railing, and propelled myself uphill. I could see the statue Nick had mentioned as soon as I crossed the bridge. According to my map, it was a cast bronze sculpture of a Civil War hero, one Corporal Brian Patrick Walsh, who served in the famed Irish brigade and died defending fugitive slaves on the grounds of a Maryland church. The building behind him came to be known as the "Civil War chapel" because it was built so close to the statue.

Later I read Walt Whitman's account of Walsh's demise in *Specimen Days*. In 1862, the Confederates had been crossing the Chesapeake in a series of daring raids, a diversionary tactic prior to the attack on Chambersburg. Rebel spies had tipped off the raiders about runaway slaves in the area. Corporal Walsh had just walked five miles to make his confession. His priest explained to him why Johnny Reb was intent on the stables. He advised the young corporal to hide. Instead, Corporal Walsh exited the church with a Colt Model 1860 in each hand. He entered the stables, slew three of the raiders, and sent the rest of the pack flying back into the woods. A musket ball pierced his neck and he received final unction in the shadow of the belfry.

It was through a number of curious anecdotes that I came to hear how Walsh's statue survived the worst of the student rioting. Three hundred aging alumni, veterans of Korea and Vietnam, arrived to form a phalanx. A Latino guy, one Rodrìguez, had fought at the Chosin Reservoir and the other veterans revered him. To a man, they knew their duty. With multiple dormitories going up in flames, the President of Saint Malachy College arrived on the scene. In her left hand she held a megaphone. In her right hand she gripped a mysterious object and pointed it at the noses of the chapel's defenders.

Some said it was a cigar, others a flute; some a banana, others a fig; some a wedge, others a stake; some a spike, others a prong; some a ruler, others a dagger; some a ferule, others a pointer; some a fly-swatter, others a spatula; some a crayon, others a drill bit; some a carrot, others a maraca; some a spyglass, others a squash; some a curling iron, others a goad; some a sheath, others a scabbard; some a popgun, others a popsicle; some a blackjack, others a bodkin; some a windshield wiper, others a chopstick; some an arrow, others a dart; some a bottle, others a bottle rocket; some a toy submarine, others an umbrella; some a truncheon, others a nutcracker; some a fasces, others a crowbar; some a baton, others a pool cue; some a snow cone, others a lollipop; some a mushroom, others a harpoon; some a Snickers, others a snake; some a pike, others a pickle; some a glasses case, others a bar of soap; some a chile pepper, others a Philly cheesesteak; some a rook, others a queen; some a handle, others a spout; some a candle, others a candlestick; some an AA battery, others a flashlight; some a monkey's paw, others a mummy's foot; some a Berkshire pork tenderloin, others a rectal thermometer of American manufacture; some a bicycle pump, others a grenade launcher; some a volumetric flask, others a poodle balloon; some a crab's claw, others a corn cob; some a gyro, others a gyroscope; some an iron poker, others a skeleton key; some a cricket bat, others an oar; some a rolling pin, others a screwdriver; some a blaster, others a blintz; some a baguette, others an éclair; some a saltcellar, others a pepper shaker; some an egg-whisk, others a Panasonic remote; some a squib, others a stick of dynamite; some a kaleidoscope, others a refracting telescope; some a candlepin, others a can of Reddi-Wip; some a sausage, others a lance; some a whipstock, others a pizzle; some a boomerang, others a tailor's clapper; some a nozzle, others a cruet; some a catkin, others a peapod; some a gator tooth, others scrimshaw; some a strigil, others a fan; some Ken, others Barbie; some a peace pipe, others a lead pipe;

some a cattle prod, others a straw; some a tusk, others the jawbone of an ass; some a lobster, others a harmonica; some a right circular cylinder, others an oblique cone; some a crystal, others a pestle; some a frankfurter, others a shish kabob; some a roll of Buffalo nickels, others a roll of Mercury dimes; some a stalagmite, others a stalactite; some a thyrsus, others a distaff; some a syringe, others a fountain pen; some a cane, others a marotte; some a brickbat, others an ingot; some a cactus, others a crocus; some a gewgaw, others a gimcrack; some a vacuum hose, others a vacuum tube; some a mace, others a parade stick; some a voodoo doll, others a philosopher's stone; some a shillelagh, others a shofar; some a crozier, others a stage hook; some a dingus, others a grail; some a totem, others an idol; some a scepter, others a rod; some an Oscar, others an Emmy; some Circe's wand, others Moses's staff; some a 6.5 mm Mannlicher-Carcano cartridge, others a booster shot; some Pinocchio's nose, others a satirist's head; some a lightsaber, others Gaudier-Brzeska's Torpedo Fish; some a golden bough, others a vial of dreams; some a diploma, others nothing. My personal theory is that these accounts are all true, quite true, but true on a hermeneutic level, unlike the Miracle of the Sun at Fatima, which I have always taken literally.

Her name was President Eudora White-White and she denounced the men as fascists. She decried their patriarchal logic. She condemned their toxic masculinity. She demanded they check their privilege. She said she didn't mean counterargument. She lectured this crew of war-torn, working stiffs about the overriding importance of wealthy women who had enjoyed every benefit afforded by an advanced and tolerant society—that is, the society the men before her had defended to the hilt—in order to be celebrated and professionally pampered because of historical injustices that were cynically exploited by beneficiaries of the system like herself. President White-White digressed from her lecture to bust a few moves to

"The Power" by SNAP!, which blasted from a nearby loudspeaker. She went on to advance a number of strategic initiatives and to say she was very optimistic about the future, as well as to solicit donations for a new, thirty-million-dollar mental health facility intended to "unite the campus." Then she commanded the men to do the right thing by shutting up and getting out of the way.

When the rioters rushed the hill, intent on toppling the statue and burning the chapel to the ground, the three hundred old guys endured cuts, bruises, and one or two heart attacks, but they held out until some local skunks, provoked by the ungodly racket, hosed down the belligerents with a fine artisanal spray. Skunks are basically peaceful animals.

The chapel pre-dated the campus and to my eye it seemed stranded in time. It was a plain structure of warping wood, white and dry and hollow as a shell. Most of the windows were boarded up, including the windows on the tower, which resembled a dwarfish lighthouse. A border of rosebushes added to the challenge of gaining a glimpse of the interior. At one of the remaining windows, though, I noticed the red sanctuary lamp was burning.

Twenty minutes later I was back in Dido Hall. Mago had mentioned my rooms were on the north side, so I made my way to the corner suite on the first floor and turned the knob. Inside was a handsome sitting room with a leather chesterfield sofa fronted by a low glass table, along with a brass-studded club chair entrenched in the thick white carpet, and a gas fireplace on the far wall. Under the window—which looked out westward on a possible garden—stood a semi-circular console table with red cyclamen on it, and a couple extra chairs occupied the wall to my right. The first room communicated with a reading room that had a white built-in desk, wall-high bookcases, and an Eames chair by the window. A box of newly minted business cards sat on the desk. In the bedroom I found a set of dark, solid furniture with an abstract painting on the wall above the king-sized bed. A yacht of a marble tub awaited behind one last door.

I was puttering about, trying out the blinds, examining the framed map above the chesterfield, and testing the fireplace, when a gray-garbed cleaning woman entered carrying a plastic watering can. She introduced herself in a solemn manner as Tatiana Kuznetsov. From the moment of our first encounter, she struck me as a strange bird. Her platinum hair swept to her shoulders with a kind of studied recklessness. She wore scrupulous makeup and her almond-shaped glasses in their pale green frames would have passed muster in Hollywood. She retained a grip on good looks that must once have been formidable.

She was watering the flowers on the side table when she turned to face me. "Your zipper," she observed, pointing scientifically at my trousers. Placing her can on the rug, she leaned over and zipped me up to the top in a single, swift motion. "There," she said, with a hint of maternal pride. "That's better." For some reason—whether it was age, middle-class complacence, or human inertia before deviant circumstances—I excused this behavior. I went ahead and thanked her in Russian. Speaking in her native language, she smiled for the first time and expanded. She grew up in far-flung Vladivostok. She followed her husband to Moscow where they lived a quiet life while he pursued his studies. During the "Era of Glasnost," he was invited to teach at M.I.T., an arrangement that lasted five years. But when Putin rose to power he fell afoul of the new regime. He died under mysterious circumstances in his lab. She retrieved a feather duster from a closet in the reading room and recounted all this while giving the furniture a few unnecessary flourishes. Then she returned the feather duster and, watering can in hand, departed saying it would be nice to have someone to talk to.

I found Mago in the recesses of the parlor.

"I thought maybe you were having sex," he smirked.

A few minutes later, Manny came by to collect us. He'd been doing a crossword puzzle. "'Poetic villain,'" he said. "Six letters." As we drove off, the snow, after having let up for hours, began to fall in the dusk, like the memory of snow, like the refrain of an antique ballad.

Chapter 4

Office Hours

Under the old dispensation, the Victorian mansion known as Dido Hall went by the name of Virgil Hall, as testified by the green and white sign that maintained its lonely post on the front lawn. But much had changed. The poet's shade, assuming he is on call for further visits to our *selva oscura*, would have been pained by the marble bust of the goddess Tanit in the new conference room. She wore a necklace made of sea snails, of the type known as *murex*, boiling vats of which produced the resplendent Tyrian purple consumed in vast measure by the Romans as well as by their Carthaginian enemies. If ghosts can blush for shame, the ghost of Virgil might have done so, surmising that Carthage had risen from the ashes, that the world had witnessed a Fourth Punic War, and that Rome's defeat had neutralized Jupiter's magniloquent prophecy of *imperium sine fine*—empire without end.

It can be debated, however, whether our distinguished revenant would have noticed the recent absence of images and symbols that were venerable and Roman, yet not quite as old as he. As for the new residents of Dido Hall, they had no way of detecting such things. None of them had seen the refectory windows before the stained-glass panels were smashed and replaced by clear acrylic, so that, on a clear night, when the moon's rays scoured the high refectory wall, they traced a peculiar blankness, like the faintest cicatrix on the forehead of Apollo. In a small room devoted to a large, tightly sealed aquarium, where a single octopus watched visitors come and go, the careful observer could discern the outlines of a private chapel. Numerous changes to the parlor could likewise be discovered, if one knew where to look. Above the antique mantel was displayed a yellow crescent with its tips pointing upwards. A herd of shining terracotta elephants populated the mantelshelf. Newly acquired paintings, the exotic canvases of nineteenth-century French painters, hung throughout Dido Hall, extending the afterlife of ancient Carthage. A witty American instance resided in the upstairs lounge, a poster from *Citizen Kane*, advertising Susan Alexander in the operatic role of Salammbô. In his renovations, Nick spent lavishly on changes no one thought twice about, not knowing they were there. But every curator requires an audience—and I suspect Nick made use of me in that respect. We ought to consider, though, that he was never among the crass individuals who derive pleasure from defiling the Christian past. He was, in his sophisticated and knowledgeable mind, removing a stain and permitting the effects of beauty to shine through.

The new team was gathered on campus now, with our first meeting scheduled on another of life's Mondays. The transport of personal items had been accomplished. Carthage deployed its own colossal truck throughout the operation, which ran with military precision. The truck appeared outside my apartment building at twelve sharp on a frigid Thursday, as a biting breeze caromed off the river and swept along sidewalks. The movers stowed my clothes and boxed about a thousand books. When they were done, I packed up a few things and drove the Mercury to Massachusetts. On Friday morning, I was installed in my Eames chair, deep in the hallucinations of the *Times' Times* and nursing a fine caffeine buzz. At the peaceful hour of nine a.m., my concentration was jolted by the *beep-beep-beep* of a heavy truck lumbering in reverse. The wheeled colossus had caught up with me.

The movers were the same silent, uncomplaining men who had loaded my belongings in New York. They laid down carpet runners, hung up my shirts, stocked my new drawers, unboxed my books, and shelved them like they were reassembling the London Bridge—all in the time it took me to eat breakfast. They advanced tactically from the first to the second floor, hand trucks at the ready, elevator shuttling up and down, executing their task with planning and precision. Ann Fitz and I were lodged in suites at opposite ends of the building. The young folks resided in smaller suites upstairs, furnished in a style closer to a luxury hotel than a barracks, off a carpeted hall that flowed into the grand staircase. It was during those first days that I became aware of a tech crew operating inside a fortress of machines in the basement. Dough-colored men with drab moustaches and glazed eyes, they were tending to the needs of Hannibal, the most advanced supercomputer on the market. They operated according to their own cryptic schedules.

We were all present for our first meeting in the conference room: Ann Fitz and I, Paris Allan, Kay Arbuthnot, Sophie Liu, Mal Osgood, Ricardo Quinones, and Kiki Sinclair. The burgundy chairs, table-top cartography, conference lectern, and aquamarine carpet evoked the conference room in New York, an impression confirmed by the presence of the glowering goddess. Here, however, the windows faced east toward the classical façade of the O'Connell Library, not west to the Hudson River. Also, the hallway wall was transparent glass.

Ann Fitz, sitting at one head of the table, with the young

people between us chattering and laughing and getting to know each other, surveyed the scene and cleared her throat.

"Have we all met by now? Let's go around the circle and formally introduce ourselves? As you know, I'm Ann Fitz, the Project Director?"

Seated to Ann Fitz's left and right, respectively, Arbuthnot and Sinclair exchanged diplomatic glances. Arbuthnot wore a brown pullover sweater and ripped jeans. Her flaxen hair curled luxuriously down her back. She cultivated an expression of refined boredom—her characteristic expression, as I came to realize—despite her intimidating brain power. Sinclair, who always fussed with her hair, chose braided pigtails for the occasion. Pert and conspicuous, she'd tucked her pink turtleneck in at the slender waist of her camel-hair skirt.

"Kay, would you like to speak first?"

But like identical twins too polite to be born, Arbuthnot deferred to Sinclair, who deferred back to Arbuthnot. We could hear the drumming of the cold rain outside, which beat on without interruption until Mal Osgood said, "I'm Mal Osgood and I'm not the Project Director." The man of the hour wore a yellow tie. His hair was a bit mussed. He looked at me encouragingly.

I introduced myself briefly and awkwardly, still adjusting to the beauty of my co-workers. As an aging bachelor, I'd grown lax about my wardrobe. I could tell that gimlet-eyed Ann Fitz had noticed this defect. A decade earlier, stretched out on the rack of celibacy, I'd hired a pricy Italian tailor with a terrible cough. He accoutered my body in endless bolts of black—double-breasted jackets, pleated trousers, overcoats, turtlenecks, scarfs, robes, pajamas, you name it. He kept assuring me that black made me look thin. Often, he would hack up tablespoons of sputum into his handkerchief as he did so, addressing himself to his expectorations while he was talking to me, and then meeting my gaze with forlorn sadness. The wags in the newsroom were amused by my new style. "Eight ball in the side pocket!" they cheered. "Bankshot off the water cooler!" When they asked about my tailor, the inside joke was, of course, that they wanted to be sure to avoid him. At the moment, though, my chief concern had only marginally to do with style. It was simply this. If this young whippersnapper Osgood was going to keep wearing ties to these meetings, then I needed to wear one as well. For the moment, I was in luck. Out of sheer habit I had packed a few ties and it turned out I was wearing one. I dropped my chin to examine it. It was a kind of peach, with a faint coffee stain.

We'd worked through our introductions back to Ann Fitz, who was focused on her tablet. A deformed silence yielded by degrees to a fumbling and flourishing of phones from pockets and purses. We were turning our attention to the meeting agenda. The marketing items suggested that Nick had been reading my "Daily Wares" column.

(1) Introductions
(2) Marketing items and discussion
a) Sleep On
b) Edge Off
(3) Assignments, coordination of linguistic proficiency
(4) Creation of teams

"I'm excited about these new sleep trackers made by Sleep On? They're small and attach to the forehead? The question I see is, do we want to market sleep or do we want to market the device?"

"Both," Arbuthnot said immediately.

"Agreed," Liu said.

"Sleep is attractive," Quinones said.

"Some people seem to live for it," said Sinclair.

"Like they're dying for it," Quinones said.

"And when they get it...." Sinclair tilted her head back and snored. "Zzzzzzzz."

Amidst the laughter and an infectious giggle that I think belonged to Liu, Ann Fitz aimed the longbows at me—as if I were at fault. She had hired them separately, but now she was surrounded by bright young things, brimful of life and high spirits. What did she expect? I utilized my glasses as shields and stared straight back at her. The tactic worked.

Meanwhile, Allan picked up the thread. "Sleep is the image of death," he said.

"And death is secretly desirable," Quinones added.

"But hard to sell," Arbuthnot checked him. "You have to approach the unconscious mind indirectly."

"So don't call it death," Quinones answered her. "Call it sleep."

"Okay? It's a global strategy? We're looking mainly at American and European consumers for this product, but we're ready to expand? The largest Asian market is Japan?"

Ann Fitz kept talking as she consulted her tablet. "My Japanese writers are Sophie and Mal? That means extra work for the two of you? This week the Tanit Team will be Sophie, Paris, and Kiki? The Baal Team will be Mal, Ricardo, and Kay?"

"You can call me Rico," said Quinones.

Ann Fitz unglued herself from her screen and pondered him like he was a fuse box. Then she went back to her screen.

"We have access to Hannibal 24/7, but let them know you're coming at least thirty minutes ahead of time?"

Sinclair quipped, "Let's play Baal." The others groaned.

"I believe Moses has some knowledge of Japanese? Sophie and Mal should feel free to consult with him? Moses, are you alive? Shall I run through the agenda again?"

"He's sleeping with his eyes open," Osgood explained.

"He hasn't tried Sleep On," Allan put in.

"Maybe we should all try the devices we're marketing," Liu said sympathetically.

Sinclair placed her lily-white hand on her cherry-red lips.

"Oops," Liu commented, inciting another chorus of laughter.

"Our other marketing item for the week is the new Edge Off smart vibrator? We think this is the wave of the future? You know? Now that women are outperforming men? In addition, studies indicate a negative correlation between long-term demographic decline and the demand for Edge Off products?"

An iffy silence.

"I think the men can be helpful?"

"I have a question first," Arbuthnot cut in. "Do we want to go with *vibrator* or is *dildo* a viable option in your opinion?"

The Project Director hesitated.

"*Sir* Dildo," Arbuthnot continued. "Some women might get a kick out of that 'Sir.'"

"Please, *sir*, I want some more," Sinclair said in a fainting English accent.

"Paris, that wonderful story you wrote about alien love-making? Some of that descriptive language might be worth revisiting?"

"I stole most of it from a gay romance novel. I hate it. It sucks."

"I'm sure it doesn't suck?" Ann Fitz persisted. "At least you know how the other feels?"

"Whatever," Allan said. "I'll see what I can dig up."

"And Ricardo?"

"Rico."

"The Latinx community—"

"What the hell is that?" Quinones objected, looking around.

"Is so richly...*erotic*? More erotic than...?" In the act of avoiding whatever mysterious comparison she had in mind, Ann Fitz outdid herself. A political chasm had evidently opened before her, and she overleaped it like a lunar astronaut. She achieved escape velocity and thrust herself into the cosmic riddle of space...?????

"What about the Kama Sutra?" Quinones said, eyeballing Sinclair, who eyeballed him right back. "It still resonates in India."

"It's very philosophical," Sinclair replied. "I don't think of dildos as philosophical. Do you?"

"I'm intrigued by your suggestion, Ricardo?" commented the Project Director, returning from her voyage. "Let's see what you can come up with?"

"It's Rico."

"That leaves Mal? Any thoughts?"

"No, ma'am. Not at present."

"Well, you might construct a list for us? Five reasons why a smart vibrator is better than a man? That would be very helpful?"

"Make it ten," Arbuthnot said languidly.

"Nick wants your Research and Algorithm reports by ten a.m. next Monday? I'll need to see the drafts by ten a.m. Friday? Keep it short and to the point?"

Neither Nick nor I anticipated the social difficulty of my fitting in with a much younger crowd. Ann Fitz, of course, was not friendly or supportive. She seemed pleased to watch me flounder. I appeared in the hall for coffee runs. I stared at the portrait in the parlor. I sat down to solitary meals. While others chatted in the refectory—even the Project Director and her kale salad had a lunchtime companion—I was visited by memories of schoolchildren, minor monsters like myself, caged behind invisible bars. I thought of the fragile boy who lisped, the smiling boy with carious teeth, the pretty girl who broke out in a bright rash and blubbered over her Scooter Pie. Strange, to be among them again. I am not given to self-pity, but you can't escape these things, even if you have the strength and good fortune to outgrow them.

I had arranged for my mail to be forwarded from New York and now it was starting to arrive. Along with an urgent bill, I received a letter from a Catholic publishing house called Amor Christi Books. I was struck by their logo, which featured a silhouette of Christ on the Cross (spraying blood) in place of the letter "t." Amor Christi Books was advertising "ONE HUNDRED CLASSICS FULLY EXPURGATED AND IMPROVED FROM ARISTOPHANES TO SWIFT." Blurbs from Saint Thomas, Saint Catherine of Siena, and Saint John Henny [*sic*] Newman caught my eye. "Our books have been through Purgatory so you don't have to," the publisher explained. To judge from the handsome images, the cloth-bound volumes of Amor Christi Books were solidly manufactured. You could collect the entire set for a thousand bucks. Plus, if you acted today, you'd get a bonus: an improved edition of the Catholic classic *Wheat That Springeth Green*, by J. F. Powers. The third chapter, which the author had originally titled "Looking Up Skirts," had been redubbed "Looking at Skirts," and *the content completely deleted!* A picture showed the new title beautifully printed on a page as white as Mary's little lamb.

I wondered if Liu and Osgood would approach me about advertising in Japan. It was an excellent topic. I remembered a Jesuit priest in Tokyo explaining to me that the Japanese don't obsess over sleep the way our health gurus do. It has a different place in their culture. To explain the difference, what I needed was a middle ground between East and West, and it seemed to me Homeric Greece had potential in just this respect. I wanted to discuss the matter, but there I was, not wanting to impose and unable to connect.

As for those magical vibrators, their manufacturers knew they'd hit pay dirt. They were employing us to polish and refine their image with a coating of prophylactic wit. To boost sales, they needed us to shield the product's unimaginative function from unprofitable feelings of modesty or shame. For the Elizabethans, who invented the clever word *dildo*, the comedy of sex found expression in stage antics and bawdy double entendres—a medieval vein of humor the theater-hating Puritans detested. The older English writers owed much to the French, who inherited their comedy in these matters from the ancient Romans.

My recent conversation with a sales rep in Las Vegas came back to me.

"It's what automobiles were a hundred years ago," she explained.

"Why automobiles?"

"It's what everybody wants. Independence. Freedom."

"Wave of the future?"

"Tidal wave. You should see the balance sheet."

To my way of thinking, her flashy exhibit of sex toys proclaimed no less clearly than the furthest abstractions in the Museum of Modern Art that body and soul had divorced in America—they were splitsville, file the papers, sayonara baby, see you in my nightmares. But it was worse than that. We had nearly succeeded in enslaving the body, minimizing the inconveniences of corporality, while riding the flesh for all it was worth. I was talking to the sales rep—it turned out she owned the company—when my father's line about *stomaching the goodness of God* crawled out from under a rock in my mind and nodded at me with serpent eyes. It seemed the serpent wanted me to say something. Finally, I answered the sales rep, but I don't think she understood me. "You have to keep a sense of humor," I said.

Tuesday morning, I exchanged a few unnerving pleasantries with Mrs. Kuznetsov, who materialized to help me with my coat and tossed in a free shoulder massage. My first order of business, now that the weather was more favorable, was to visit the grounds of Dido Hall. I was particularly curious to inspect the patch of garden outside my western windows. Gladstone surprised me, though, or I surprised him, standing on the stairs that led to the basement, in conversation with one of the Subterraneans. What surprised me at the time wasn't Gladstone's acquaintance with one of these nameless techies, but the fact that he smiled amiably when I wandered into view, in a spot where foot traffic was rare.

Northwest of Dido Hall, the road leading to the gym was flanked on either side by a procession of tall black oaks, their barks ridged and tough. High up in one of these trees, a red-crested woodpecker was drumming for grubs. The bare branches fanned out overhead and interlaced in multiple directions. Come spring, they would form a green canopy. A mature, tawny-coated chipmunk was studying me from atop a small boulder, and a pair of gray squirrels bounded and scurried in no discernable pattern, fussing over their acorn hoard.

I became aware of a strobe light approaching me from the rear. It grabbed my shadow by the scruff of the neck and flung it repeatedly against an oak tree. When I accelerated my pace, Sergeant Nachman availed herself of her vehicular PA system.

"Mr. Moses Shea. Are you wearing your ID, Mr. Moses Shea?"

The chipmunk scrambled below deck and the squirrels escaped to their vertical world.

"Mr. Moses Shea."

I continued to ignore this invasion of my privacy for as long as I could. But when I heard her vehicle door slam shut, I had to admit reality: Sergeant Nachman was the only person on campus who seemed interested in talking to me at all. Her low-riding gun holster hung unobtrusively from her duty belt, along with a flashlight, steel handcuffs, a radio, a pepper spray canister, a magazine pouch, a knife, and a telescopic side-handle baton. Her sunglasses blazed like furnaces.

"I told you, Sergeant, I'm not wearing my ID."

"All right, Mr. Shea. It isn't absolutely required. Besides, I see that you and I are getting to know each other."

A thin smile bent her leaden lips. On some remote level, she appeared to find the fact of our acquaintance amusing.

"I was going to ask your assistance."

"What were you going to ask them?"

"Mr. Shea, you exhaust my patience."

"Sorry, Sergeant Nachman."

"If you catch sight of two elderly gentlemen, I need you to alert me by using one of the red security phones."

"May I ask why?"

"They're the illegal infiltrators I warned you about."

"Illegal infiltrators?"

The phrase was new to me. It seemed the copper-plated coinage of a low-grade military mind adjusting to civilian life in a society educated by totalitarians.

"This isn't funny, Mr. Shea."

"Sergeant Nachman, may I speak frankly?"

"Of course, Mr. Shea. What is it?"

"That day when you pulled us over, weren't you wearing the same glasses?

"Probably."

"I see. Well, you really do them justice. I wish you a good day, Sergeant Nachman."

I am just so dull in appearance it's practically a superpower. When they cross my path, most women find themselves at something of a loss. They see a bland talking head bobbing on a marshmallow body, but male, recognizably male. If I try to sympathize with their position, it usually makes matters worse. Sergeant Nachman nodded uncertainly and returned to her Beloved Vehicle without a backward look. Finally, as she drove off into the distance, not sideswiping any trees or injuring any pedestrians, I waved like a proud father watching his problem child go off to torture herself and others in the sad affairs of life.

A few hours later, I was settling into my big tub, observing how my body displaced precisely its volume of water, which gushed like a jet through the fleshy fork of my legs, leveling off around my hairy belly as I reposed on my plump buttocks, when the solution to my social difficulties presented itself.

"Eureka!" I cried, like old Archimedes, whom the Romans accidentally murdered before erecting a monument in his honor. Cicero writes about it, in case you're taking notes. The upshot was this: I recalled what my professors used to do—and how you might go by and talk with them about a problem in Greek grammar or what Sophocles meant by a particular phrase or, now that it was all coming back to me, why Cicero was called "chickpea" by the French.

I was excited to give my new idea a try.

First thing after lunch, I sent out a group email to announce what I called my "Office Hours." They were to be Monday through Friday, two p.m. to four p.m., and by appointment. I would be holding them in my rooms.

The "Office Hours" twist got off to a slow start. No one knocked on my door, and I continued to dine alone in the refectory. But at two p.m. on Ash Wednesday, I opened my outer door to find Osgood sitting there with ashes on his forehead. He'd taken a chair from the parlor and set it by the entrance to my suite. I pondered it for a moment: the beauty of a simple Windsor chair. The armrests and back rest were smoothly curved. I decided it should not be removed and made a mental note to tell Mrs. Kuznetsov. Inviting Osgood inside, I asked where he attended church.

"Waterbury, Connecticut."

"Latin?"

"High Mass. You?"

"Local parish. Saint Anne's. Bad homilies. Good choir."

"You should come with me to the Latin Mass. It's great."

The Latin Mass stirs a host of feelings among Roman Catholics, from gratitude and reverence to derision and mockery.

"I started going in college," Osgood continued. "It feels larger, more spiritual."

I felt no need to dampen his enthusiasm. When celebrated by devout and capable priests, the Tridentine Mass harmonizes more levels of human experience than are easily articulated. The perennial problem was Catholic in-fighting, the Church as a human institution prone to folly and faction. I said to Osgood, "Look at *Catacomb*. Their ideal reader died liberating Jerusalem from the Turk. They think this country's an irredeemable failure. No wonder they prefer the Latin Mass." Osgood, to my surprise, sensed an authoritarian threat coming from the Vatican. I was mystifying him with my ambivalence toward lace surplices when a knock at the door announced another visitor. It was Sophie Liu, fresh from the shower and shouldering a leather backpack. Seeing Osgood had claimed the chesterfield, and leaving the club chair for me, she grabbed a chair from the wall and placed it near us, enthusing, as she did so, about the fireplace, which glowed all the more cheerfully for her words.

I had on hand a small green book, old and well-thumbed, from which I read aloud a short passage of about twenty lines. A weary Odysseus is sailing home to Ithaka. He's in a Phaeacian ship when he falls asleep so soundly that he all but departs the world of the living. Osgood listened attentively and then recited the entire passage from memory—in Greek. Liu, who smiled at the mnemonic fireworks, opened her laptop and asked for a moment to locate the text on the internet. We went on to discuss it at length, noting how sleep comes only after the hero's magnificent feats of endurance, and how, when Odysseus comes to consciousness, his voyages are finally behind him. He's back in his homeland.

Then I directed our attention to Akira Kurosawa's 1954 epic, *The Seven Samurai*. Liu cued it up in the original language. We visited the scene where, exhibiting Odyssean wiles, the warrior Kyuzo returns to the village with an enemy musket. At that moment, his task accomplished, he sits on the ground and drops to sleep over his sword, inspiring no end of awe from the hero-worshiping young man, Katsushiro. The parallel between the episodes was striking, and both Liu and Osgood followed the lesson eagerly. I explained that Japanese business culture is a heroic endurance test, in which one must stay vigilant against "the sleep demon." Because the Japanese fear ever being caught asleep on the job, or even being suspected of not constantly giving their all, they practice a form of impromptu napping known as *inemuri*. The word itself is constructed from two Chinese characters, the initial *i* that means being "present" to the situation at hand, and *nemuri*, signifying "sleep." It's the paradox of being present *and* asleep that assuages the Japanese conscience, so that a person who is exhausted can sleep almost anywhere, like Kyuzo. By contrast, the westerner Odysseus awakes with the dawn—the natural rhythm that is alien to *inemuri*. But here was the payoff: the idea of heroically earning one's sleep by serving a noble cause joins both cultures. Japan and Ithaka were both islands that needed defending. What we needed to consider, I suggested, was how to create a heroic aura for Sleep On products in Japan. If we could sell a hero's sleep that was richly deserved and devoted to the greater good, then we could justify a sleep like death— even to the Japanese.

Liu absorbed the lesson in her usual sympathetic manner.

She moved the chair back to the wall and slung her backpack over her shoulders. "Thanks, Prof," she said. "See you later."

Prof?

Then she paused on the verge of going.

"Do you want me to leave your door open?"

I said, "Just a little. Thank you, Sophie."

I hadn't counted on Osgood's sticking around. But the tie-wearing wonder was still occupying the sofa, in fact looking rather comfortable on it. He didn't appear to be going anywhere.

"So what do you think happened to this place?" he said.

"Saint Malachy College?"

"A bit like *Lord of the Flies*."

"It would seem the kiddies were left without adult supervision."

"But they had their teachers with them," he said slyly.

"And President Eudora White-White."

"That woman would tell Jesus Christ how to behave."

Osgood roused himself and walked over to inspect the fireplace. "But to actually destroy buildings," he said. "That impresses me."

"It doesn't surprise me that much. It's in our nature. Wars break out for any number of reasons. Plus, you've given everyone a cell phone...."

I excused myself to fetch another one of my little green books. It opened like the *Sortes Virgilianae* to exactly the right page, from which I read aloud: "'Those who have sufficient reason to obey, but not to think, are slaves by nature.'"

"Aristotle."

"The two key words are *reason* and *nature*. Technology has, if you will, altered the nature of people under thirty, making them suspicious of reason. The process started when they were small so that now they don't even think about it."

He asked to see the book. After a moment or two, he

returned it and said, "They have a glass case in the library with books from the Aldine Press. Real *Aldines*."

"You're making that up."

"They have Plato, Aristophanes, Theocritus, Iamblichus."

"In a glass case?"

"The books don't circulate. But you can sit down in the library and read them."

"Show me."

"All right. I'll meet you by the stairs."

After putting my shelves back in order, I slipped into my overcoat and waited by the newel at the bottom of the grand staircase. When Osgood reappeared, he was sporting a Greek fisherman's cap to go with his pea coat.

I said, "John Lennon used to have one of those."

"John Lennon," he replied nonchalantly. "Wasn't he in a band?"

We fell into step together and crossed the way to the O'Connell Library. Working the front desk, Miss Natalee Phoenix firmly ignored us. We turned into the main Reading Room, where a peristyle of white Ionian columns supported a high ceiling above a fine sculpted entablature. Spacious wings led to winding staircases descending to the stacks. In a quiet corner, in a Victorian glass case, a dozen books from the Aldine Press rode out the centuries on a plain wooden shelf.

Drawn as if by adamant, I gave the antique knobs on the bookcase a gentle tug and delicately extracted the *Poetae Christiani Veteres*.

It weighed about a pound. The spine was faded brown leather with pale traces of gilt lettering. I opened the cover of the book with my left hand and inspected the printer's device, the famous dolphin curled around a wide-fluked anchor: AL to one side, DVS to the other. It was the anchor of hope, anchoring the soul. I turned a few pages as gently as possible. Latin on the left page or verso, Greek on the recto.

Being in a state of astonishment, I forgot about Osgood entirely. If you had asked me the year, I would have mumbled incoherently.

The book rested in my right hand to display the manually typeset poetry of Saint John of Damascus. What was on the mind of Saint John of Damascus?

> *The Son of God born on the grief-stricken earth*
> *for the grace of men,*
> *Absolving the sins of this heavy world.*

Feeling that slow, clear music, so alien to the busyness of our lives, I put the book away and closed the doors with reverence.

Osgood said something I missed. He repeated himself more loudly and an ash-marked old bird emitted an indignant "Ahem!" Lowering his reading material, he frowned in our direction. I thought I recognized him from Mass. He had a florid complexion that climaxed at the tip of his nose in a stain like dried lees. He perfected his scowl until the turkey wattles on his neck trembled above his Windsor knot. He was on the verge of a cardiac moment, or I'm no judge of vermilion. Osgood and I were at fault not only for talking, but, to make matters worse, Osgood was unintentionally flaunting his Carthage ID.

We departed on the double and the apoplectic gentleman went back to his book. As we were skirting the front desk, though, we heard what sounded like a firecracker from outside the building or possibly backfire from a passing truck. It was a bad noise, piercing the atmosphere at a fluky angle and threatening general dissolution.

"That's a pistol," Osgood remarked.

Then I became aware of a dull metallic creaking, followed by rivets popping in rapid succession, accompanied by a tearing sound of a weighty and ominous character. The front of the building started to vibrate.

Natalee Phoenix and I made eye contact through the invasion of dust. "Look out!" Osgood shouted impressively. A light fixture of great bulk was coming loose. Dust and debris were pouring down on the front desk. I saw Osgood vault over it and in a single continuous motion haul the librarian by the arm as he flew to shelter. The next instant, a huge basin of stippled glass plunged in free fall, only to stop, suspended by four fraying wires, an inch from the floor.

As the dust gradually settled, the old gentleman arrived in the vicinity with a party from the Reading Room. Their general instinct was, I sensed, to suspect Osgood of some untoward act. But the sight of the art deco basin gave them pause. Osgood and Miss Phoenix appeared together in a doorway, looking like they had risen from an ash pit. The general silence was comical and should have been social, but when the others stepped around the suspended basin to comfort her, Osgood joined me without comment.

We exited the O'Connell Library and beat the dust from our clothes. In front of Dido Hall, the Beloved Vehicle stood parked, its light bars flashing like it was high mating season. We advanced in its direction. At a range of about ten yards, a window lowered and the inscrutable driver inspected us.

"Good afternoon, Mr. Shea. I suppose it's Ash Wednesday?"

"My dear Sergeant Nachman," I said, waiving the point. "Fancy meeting you here. Tremendous. I was wondering if you might be able to satisfy my curiosity regarding an unusually loud noise in the area, some five or ten minutes ago."

"I fired my gun."

"You fired your...*gun*."

"I popped ol' Sam."

"May I ask why you popped ol' Sam?"

"Infiltrators."

"Did you kill someone, Sergeant Nachman?"

"It was a warning shot."

"I see. May I ask who or what provoked you to fire this shot?"

"Some old lady sniffing around the dorms. She had a doohickey."

"Oh, God. Did it look like a hockey stick?"

"Yeah. Kind of did. Only it had a whatchamacallit at the end."

"A large disc."

"That's what I said."

"You do wonderful work, Sergeant Nachman," I said.

Sensing it was time to say goodnight, Osgood waved cheerfully.

"That's the local sheriff," I explained, taking him by the arm as we turned toward Dido Hall, conspirators of ash and dust. "She's all that stands between us and the illegal infiltrators."

"I know some illegal infiltrators."

"You do?"

"Let me see. Simón, Andrés, Santiago—

"That's James."

"Juan, Felipe, Mateo—"

"Pablo."

"*Sí, Pablo. Muy mal infiltrado.*"

"*Muy mal.*"

"You couldn't resist that, could you?"

Chapter 5

A Russian Winter

Because the movers had reshelved my books in order, I could indulge my longstanding habit of inspecting the troops. On one such occasion, while reviewing a row of French books, I detected a wrinkle. My hand hesitated before seizing on a leather-bound volume, thick and weighty, the dustcover long since gone. Horizontal rows of gold and faded emerald ran up and down the spine. Set off by a gap in these alternating rows, the gold lettering of the title square remained mostly intact. Gustave Flaubert. *Oeuvres*. A sash held the reader's place amidst the thin, densely bound pages. I was looking for the opening page of *L'éducation sentimentale* when a sheet of stationery slipped loose. As it pinwheeled down to the floor, so strong were the feelings it occasioned, it might have been a white bird circling above a drowned man. Then a prayer came to mind, like a rope ladder tossed from a window in the sky.

> *Virgo virginum praeclara*
> *Mihi iam non sis amara*
> *Fac me tecum plangere...*

There was a time when the *Stabat Mater* strengthened my grip on reality. Since then, my prayers had lost their medieval freshness. They were chastened, modern prayers. They knew about the void. Back in my youth, whenever my passions slipped the leash, my response was to fall to my knees and call to Mother Mary. I wandered the streets of Cambridge and Manhattan like a mystical rabbi combing the desert. I was searching for God's love in human form, but I found that love was hard to come by. I hope you understand me. The more I searched the human heart, the more distant grew love and desire. I pored over the *Spiritual Exercises*, but every time I made progress, every time I felt my soul raised toward my Creator, I soon found that things were no easier, that holiness receded like a mirage.

As regards the ways of the world, I was slow of study. I resisted the painful lesson that the fair sex never noticed me unless they wanted something. When I gave them what they wanted, they had no more to say. The pattern repeated until it focused my attention like a deep bruise where you don't remember getting hit. At last I put two and two together. I was a dupe, a sucker, a sap, a stooge, a chump, a pushover, a soft touch, you get the idea. Four years of college, a dozen languages, money in the bank—and I was still a dewy-eyed innocent.

One evening I raised the price for a special favor. I had in my possession certain clues, pieces of a valuable puzzle, so that the value of what I was selling became more tantalizing to the buyer with every scrap of information she could get her attractive claws on. At twenty-four, I lost my virginity to a bottle of bourbon, a late night, and an aging beauty who'd survived multiple abortions and wrote a column called "Street Smart." My career was taking off. I was carving my niche—the flora and fauna were getting used to me. But all the while, it was cold fear that kept me in the pews, that guided me to the confessional, that had the power to delay but not derail the same sins, the same penances, the same diurnal round of heat and exhaustion. It took many years, but little by little I started to glimpse the truth, to see myself as the fool I am, and that was a step in the right direction.

I always wondered if Nick knew about Mia's note. An impartial judge of these sentimental matters, admitting the note as evidence, might have awarded the prize of her affections to me. And that would have irked old Nick, who never liked to lose, certainly not to Moses Shea, of all the schlumps this side of the funny pages. On the outside, at least, the divorce didn't seem to faze him. The biographers agreed—he never looked back. His marriage to a pious and beautiful Catholic was just a youthful glitch. It lasted little more than a year, a slim fraction of a long and adaptable life. There were no children. If Nick's conduct cost him his standing in the Catholic church, no one seemed to mind—though I suspect a few of his old-fashioned relatives either disapproved on principle or hinted at the benefits of decorous hypocrisy. Nick was a great admirer of JFK, but Mia lacked Jackie's tolerance. I'm sure she drew the line very hard, very fast. She believed in the efficacy of the sacraments. She never granted Nick an annulment.

I reread the handwritten note.

MIA MAZUR CARTY

Ash Wednesday, 1984

Dear Moses,

Nick and I are separating. I didn't want you to hear the news from somebody else.

Now I must live like a nun! I am such a fool.

I told Nick my happiest times were with you. I shouldn't have said it but at least it wasn't a damn lie. Why is it so hard to tell the truth?

Please write from time to time. Let me know how you are.

Love,
Mia

How's that for brevity? I refolded the slip of paper and returned it to the pages of Flaubert. I was thinking now of Frédéric Moreau and Madame Arnoux. The needy young man from nowhere and the luscious married woman trapped in a bad marriage, they survive their passions, in part by sheer luck, but also by his maturing and by her instinctive virtue. Moreau was no genius but his life always seemed to me worth living. The author conducts a great survey of France, from the visionary dullness of Nogent-sur-Seine to the Paris of the barricades. Most of all, he details the passions. He studies and pursues them from backward country nooks to the smoky purlieus of the Paris demimonde. He dissects the insane lust for power among those with no connection to anything larger than themselves. He illuminates the whole with his sublime encyclopedias of the natural world. But it was Flaubert's grasp of Moreau's erotic fate that I valued most, because it offered some perspective on my own.

A knock on my outer door dispelled my reverie. It wasn't Moreau's ghost. It was, in fact, Paris Allan, very properly attired. He'd mentioned that he wanted to talk about Vonnegut. We were chatting at dinner and it came up that I met Vonnegut years ago, at a George Plimpton fundraiser in

New York. As I ushered him in, a flock of bluesy chords arose from the piano in the parlor.

"Do you know who that is?"

"No idea."

We sat down and he got to talking about two of Vonnegut's most memorable characters, Howard W. Campbell, Jr. and Harrison Bergeron. Campbell is the American Nazi in *Slaughterhouse-Five*, and Harrison Bergeron is the eponymous hero of a short story in *Welcome to the Monkey House*.

"I get the thing with Campbell," Allan said. "He's a rightwing fascist and Vonnegut hates his guts, though he captures him very well. Vonnegut was a liberal and he's attacking fascism. That's how I was trained to write. The problem is Harrison Bergeron. There it seems to me Vonnegut is attacking the idea of equity—that everyone should be absolutely equal with no individual advantages. The Handicapper General, Diana Moon Glampers—"

"The one with the shotgun."

"Right. She reminds me of the far Left. Do you see my point?"

"How could a good liberal like Vonnegut write a satire of the far Left? Are you asking this because it goes against your training, as you say, or for more personal reasons?"

"To be honest, I've been writing more satire. I start with my usual science fiction and it bores me. Then, thinking I'm not doing my homework and playing hooky, I go down this other road. The shit makes me laugh."

"I liked '*Esprit de* Corpse.'"

"I don't even know where that came from. I wrote most of it at one sitting. A few days later I polished it and sent it off. Actually, I used a pen name."

"May I ask?"

"Jupiter Jefferson."

"I like it."

"All my satires are by Jupiter Jefferson."

"Sounds promising."

"But who the hell is Jupiter Jefferson?"

"Now I see where you're coming from. The way I understand these things is that the ego wants to conform, to be a good citizen, but the monster in the cellar needs to break out now and then, or the patient will go insane."

"So Jupiter Jefferson is the monster in my unconscious?"

"No and yes. I don't think all art comes from the unconscious. The ego no doubt is better at polishing. But they're intertwined."

He sat at his ease on the sofa and regarded me through half-shut eyes. His silk tie had tiny red and yellow flowers. I recognized the music of Gershwin on the piano.

"What about things like race?"

"Things like race?"

"What does the unconscious think about race?"

"It thinks it's a dangerous topic."

"Because people make it dangerous. People who can't write."

I swallowed down the dregs of my morning coffee. It was pleasantly bitter.

"You want my opinion."

"Go ahead."

"Rule Number One. Art, not graft."

"Graft?"

"Politics—same thing where art is concerned."

"Be it Shakespeare or be it Eminem?"

Against his subjunctives I retained a perfect mask of tutorial blandness but then he collapsed in a shoulder-sagging chuckle.

"I'm just kidding," he said, evidently amused. "I don't even listen to Eminem. What's Rule Number Two?"

"Rule Number Two? Go where the Muse takes you."

"I never got the Muse."

"Like the memo?"

"No, I never got that, either."

"I'll tell you something funny about the Muse."

He gave me a shy, serious look, like a turtle peeping out of its shell.

"She's promiscuous."

"What do you mean?" He hoisted his eyebrows, indulging a turn for comic slyness. "She a slut?"

I had to laugh.

"If you like."

"How so?"

"Artists are promiscuous. There's a lot of crossing over."

"I follow you."

"Aretha Franklin went down to Muscle Shoals to work with a bunch of white guys who resembled grocery clerks at the A&P. Everyone who heard the record thought they were black."

"Where is Muscle Shoals?"

"Alabama."

"Never been there."

He glided off the couch as if free of gravity. "I appreciate your time," he said. I pushed myself upright and shook his hand as he continued. "Maybe we could work together on next week's agenda? Belizean chocolate?"

"Don't forget funerary urns."

"Nobody said it was going to be easy," he answered with cheerful irony. It was clear why he'd been appointed team captain at Georgetown. He was charismatic. He was taking the time to boost my morale. That's fine, I thought, as I shut the door and lay down on the chesterfield. Just so long as he doesn't ask me to throw the discus.

The piano was quiet and the purple dusk of twilight time

was stealing across my windows when Tatiana Kuznetsov came bearing gifts.

"I thought you might like some nice medovik," she said by way of rational explanation. As I've mentioned, she'd been attentive, helping me with my overcoat, prancing about with her watering can, chatting gaily in Russian as she dusted and spritzed. Now she was standing before me with a large cake in her hands. She was increasing her power over me, though I wanted nothing to do with her, as she probably knew, except, as she also probably knew, I couldn't cancel her animal attraction and must have betrayed signs of interest whether I wanted to or not. My working hypothesis was that she wanted to marry me and get out of the cleaning lady business.

"Come in, come in," I said, holding the door the way men hold the door.

She deposited the cake on the console table by the cyclamen. "There!" she said happily. Then she pressed a finger to her lips, inviting me to share in whatever conspiracy was afoot. Without her glasses, her dark eyebrows impressed me more than usual. But something else was up. Gradually, as she went in and out, it struck me that her uniform had grown more expressive of the Kuznetsovian figure. In retrospect, I suspect it wasn't the same ho-hum gray dress at all. It was cut with a lot of pizazz.

She'd brought a canvas shopping bag. *"I hope you don't mind,"* she said, placing the bag by the cake. Like a magician in a cabaret act, she reached in and extracted a green bottle. *"I thought a little champagne might be nice."*

While I fetched glasses and a towel for the cork, she bent over the medovik with a big knife that looked like one of Gladstone's. *Pop!* I poured the bubbly. "Sit down here and let me serve you," she said, patting the sofa. She made several little trips, dispensing silverware, dishes, paper napkins, before sitting down snugly beside me.

Then she proposed a toast.

"To life!"

"To life!"

"Bottoms up!" she said, winking.

We clinked glasses, so close that our knees touched. The situation was ludicrous, but she had me figured by now. She knew she could rely on my manners for at least twenty minutes—plus a grace period in honor of who knows what.

"You are a kind man."

Having arranged things on the glass coffee table, she admired my progress with the medovik like a mother watching her baby learn to feed itself.

"Every day is so hard....I think of Moscow in the spring....Life used to be so promising."

"I'm sorry."

"Tell me about your week? How is your work going? Do you like your coworkers?"

Her blue eyes sparkled and expanded as the room went a bit wobbly. I paused to get a handle on my condition but the handle was disintegrating into a mishmash of mental fatigue and lechery.

"The cake is delicious. You made it yourself?"

"I haven't made one in many years. Not since my husband died. I haven't lost my touch?"

As she said the word *touch*, she polished the knob of my knee and smiled. Her teeth seemed gigantic.

"Not at all."

"Eat."

My mind had slowed to a snail sprint. I tried focusing on the cake, a creamy mélange of honey and walnuts. The cargo on my fork seemed stuck in space.

"I'm thirsty!" she exclaimed gaily. She was at the table refilling her glass, she was sashaying across the room, she was nattering about climates—Boston, Moscow, Paris, New York.

When I made a determined effort to stand up, she rushed to my rescue in a white welter of cleavage and sat me back down. I felt warm and woozy, as if nothing in the world would be more satisfying than a long nap.

"How I love champagne!" she said, twirling in a fairy circle. *"It makes me feel young."*

I had the impression of her bolting the outer door. She stood with her back to it and her hands on her hips, studying me where I sat on the couch limp as a marionette.

Whether she dragged or carried me into the bedroom, that's where we ended up. It seemed that Mrs. Kuznetsov and I were lying naked together and she was trailing her fingers up and down my hirsute trunk.

"Are you comfortable, Mr. Shea?" She continued to use the respectful form of address.

"This is very nice, Mrs...."

"You must call me Tatiana." Her warm soft flesh skimmed my side as a feeling of bliss came over me. The bed seemed to have become unmoored and we were gliding through the heavens.

"I will tell you a secret and then you will tell me a secret. That's how we'll get to know each other. My secret is that I don't like America. It's a big capitalist lie. What's your secret?"

"I'm going to fart."
"Shh. What's the worst thing you ever did?"
"I hated God."
"You don't believe in God?"
"But I do."
"Do these young people?"
"Some of them."

. . . .
"What is your address, Moses?"
"250 West 85th Street."

. . . .

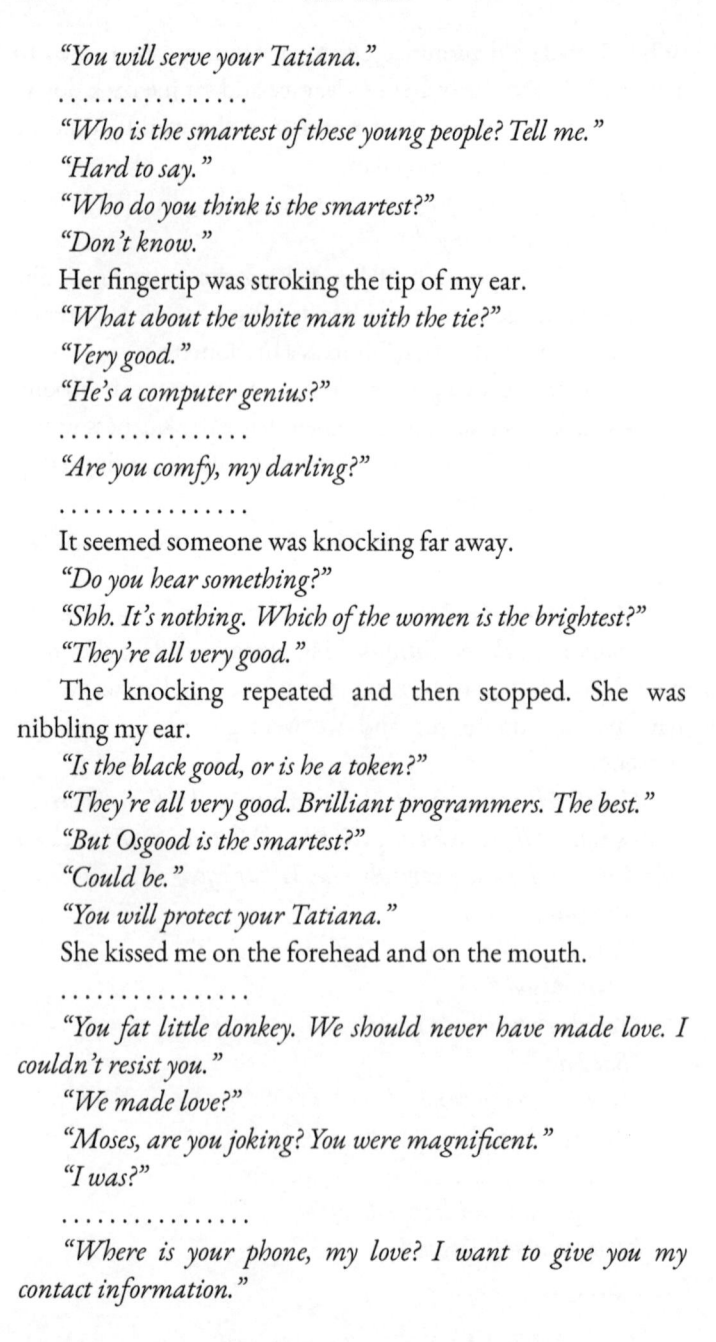

"You will serve your Tatiana."

....

"Who is the smartest of these young people? Tell me."
"Hard to say."
"Who do you think is the smartest?"
"Don't know."

Her fingertip was stroking the tip of my ear.

"What about the white man with the tie?"
"Very good."
"He's a computer genius?"

....

"Are you comfy, my darling?"

....

It seemed someone was knocking far away.

"Do you hear something?"
"Shh. It's nothing. Which of the women is the brightest?"
"They're all very good."

The knocking repeated and then stopped. She was nibbling my ear.

"Is the black good, or is he a token?"
"They're all very good. Brilliant programmers. The best."
"But Osgood is the smartest?"
"Could be."
"You will protect your Tatiana."

She kissed me on the forehead and on the mouth.

....

"You fat little donkey. We should never have made love. I couldn't resist you."
"We made love?"
"Moses, are you joking? You were magnificent."
"I was?"

....

"Where is your phone, my love? I want to give you my contact information."

"On my desk."

. . . .

She pressed my thumb like a corpse's thumb to the touch ID. It took a few tries. She was propped up comfortably topless in my bed with my phone in her hands.

"I have to go," she said. *"But you can text me now. Just look in your contacts."*

"Okay."

"You're a good little donkey. You must serve your Tatiana."

Through an exhausting medley of dreams, scored with desultory snippets of Gershwin and Aretha Franklin, I slept through the night. When I came around again, my brain felt like a bucket of mud. It was past nine. Mrs. Kuznetsov had vanished after tucking me in. My rooms were in perfect order. My dirty clothes were in the laundry hamper. Even my drinking glasses were clean—on the shelf where they belonged. Not a trace remained of the evening's festivities. It might all have been a midwinter night's dream, but, when I checked my phone, I found her among my contacts, under K.

The breakfast kitchen closed at ten sharp—which meant I needed to hurry. Operating under foggy conditions, I arrived at the refectory at the last possible minute. The room was empty except for one table where Allan and Gladstone sat with their coffee mugs between them. Allan was wearing a Beatles tee shirt.

"Hey, prof," he said. "I came by again yesterday. I guess it was after hours."

"Forgive me, Paris. I was indisposed."

They laughed for no reason and, again, for no discernable reason, Gladstone was charming. "Can I rustle you up some eggs?" he said, his coal black hair combed back and glistening. "The notorious chef's special." I'd seen him only once before without his chef's hat—when he smiled unexpectedly at my appearance in the garden area. I passed on the offer and shuffled off towards the buffet. "Lots of fresh fruit!" he called after me.

I sat down at a polite distance to juice, coffee, and a bowl of fruity oatmeal. Soon I was absorbed in the *Times' Times*, a long, convoluted story about a controversial editorial decision at the *Times' Times*, with a hundred quotations from anonymous sources who worked at the *Times' Times*. I was polishing off my bowl when Allan came by.

"Aren't you going to the emergency meeting?"

"What emergency meeting?"

"Didn't you get Ann's message?"

"I'm not sure," I said. "When did she send it?"

"Last night."

"I'm afraid I've been out of commission. When's the meeting?"

"We're late."

Why had I given Tatiana Kuznetsov my phone? I checked my email. Sure enough, Ann Fitz had written the entire group.

Dear Colleagues,

At Carthage we stand by the values of our diverse and inclusive community. Therefore, I am saddened to report that, during our first week together, our cleaning lady, Tatiana Kuznetsov, found the phrase "Algorithms aren't racist" scrawled on the floor under the octopus tank. It is unclear when this malicious vandalism occurred. Nonetheless, I have contacted Public Safety, and DPS has opened an investigation.

I want to thank Tatiana for her responsiveness and urge all of us to defend our community. If you encounter acts of hate, don't be silent! If you see anyone damaging property, please contact Sergeant Nachman.

This is not how we want to start our important work together. If you are unaware of racism in recent world history or its use today by Christians and other White Supremacists, take the time to learn. Let us join in our determination to end acts of hatred in the community we aspire to.

The experience of hate can be traumatic. If you would like one of our counselors to visit you, please reach out to Human Resources.

Finally, please attend an emergency meeting in the conference room tomorrow at 10:30 a.m.

With hope for our future,
Ann Fitz
Project Director

So Tatiana had discovered a bizarre phrase. In a bizarre place. She sure hadn't mentioned it to me. Later I learned that the originator of the phrase was none other than Nanolith CEO Holden Crawford. It was an offhand remark he'd made in an elevator at the Waldorf Astoria in Beverly Hills. Overhearing him, a junior high school student condemned the remark on her Twitter account, and soon it was trending.

The moment I entered the conference room, I experienced a kind of epiphany. Ann Fitz sat enshrined, basking in an emotional aura that left the rest of the room in spiritual darkness. So inviolable she seemed, that I hesitate to describe her. She sat exalted in an atmosphere of moral transcendence that my unregenerate pen cannot begin to fathom, can only degrade in a display of my own unholy degradation. As she spoke, we bowed our heads in shame.

"I hope you understand the seriousness of this act?"

Silence.

"Is our community falling apart?"

More silence.

"I ask again, is our community falling apart?"

Peak silence.

"How big was it?" Sinclair squeaked.

"The actual writing? The actual writing was small?"

"How small?"

"I don't know what you're talking about?"

"I'm with Ann," Arbuthnot said. "It's deliberately insensitive."

"It reminds me of college," Liu said. "Are there any college kids around here?"

"Or deans?" Quinones said. "Deans love this kind of shit. It's what they do."

"I knew a guy named Dean," Osgood said. "Dean James. That was his name. He was a strict Thomist. A cause without a rebel."

"You're not making any sense?"

"Maybe it was there before Carthage bought the campus?" Allan suggested.

"I don't think that's possible?"

"Personally," Osgood said, "I've got my head full of algorithms—whether they're racist or not. You'll have to excuse me."

The same chisel that had carved Tanit's bust might have carved Ann Fitz's face, which seemed to harden to a white, metamorphic density. I thought the silvery bob might go porcupine, winged porcupine. The others filed out behind Osgood like the English Ambassadors exiting the stage at the end of *Hamlet*.

I went back to my rooms and lay down on the chesterfield. It struck me that Tatiana Kuznetsov desired something other than my hand in marriage. What did I have that she could want? It was a strange business and I needed to call Nick about it. I was contemplating how to accomplish this feat without the use of my phone when a fresh concern announced itself like a nova in the Ptolemaic heavens. What if Tatiana was an industry spy?

My mind stopped. For a long while, I lay motionless, staring glassily at the ceiling and incapable of action. At last, by way of a chance association with Mia, whom I remembered talking on a payphone years ago on one of our youthful rambles, the thought occurred to me of finding a nearby town and calling Nick from a payphone, if one existed.

The clear twilight lingered as I started the Mercury. I drove south past the cluster of low buildings where Clifden consolidates its existence. Soon an old forest surrounded the road, where fantastic silhouettes of gnarled and twisted trees jabbed at my overstretched nerves. The farther I went into this wood, the more I experienced the inexplicable feeling of committing a mortal sin. I drove on, with no traffic to contend with except one car curving along behind me, flash-flashing in the mirror. My lower jaw started throbbing as my blood raced through its tight circuit. Then, on the other side of a small lake, I bumped into a sleepy little hamlet with a ma and pa grocery store, a Zippo station, and a rundown cinema that was showing *The Lord of the Rings*.

Stepping onto the poorly lit street, I was overtaken by a dream-sensation of moving towards a forbidden door. I took a deep breath and reassured myself that I was fully awake and that the ground under my feet was not a deception. No one was manning the ticket booth, so I passed under the dilapidated marquee in search of a payphone. The short young man who labored over the popcorn buckets directed me at once to an isolated section of wall where an old-style payphone kept its lonely counsel. My conscience was now in high rebellion. And yet I knew it could be in error. All it took was one false premise among many true. Wasn't Tatiana a poor widow? Didn't she feel affection for me? Was it right to jeopardize her job? I dialed the operator to place a credit card call. But the effort kept setting off painful sparks in my head. I was ensnared in a slow-motion juggling act with card and wallet and payphone, when someone or something in a green parka entered the premises. A big bald head, cauliflower ears, a nose that had been broken once or twice, wet meaty lips—not a reassuring sight. I went back to the popcorn counter to solicit a pen. The young man's cornflower blue eyes and curly brown locks—tucked under his food service worker's hat—seemed, in the face of an existential threat, more than a little absurd. Regarding me in a curious but friendly manner, he passed the pen from his shirt pocket. I was using it to copy Nick's number onto the palm of my hand when baldy sauntered by and knocked it onto the red theater carpet.

"Oh, excuse me," he said mockingly.

"What the hell do you mean, 'excuse me'? Who the hell are you?"

He started to say something when the young man shouted at him.

"Hey, mister!" he said. He was recording the action with his phone, which seemed to shine like the phial of Galadriel. The vicious oaf staggered blindly back and retreated to bursts of music and laughter from inside the theater. When he was gone, the little fellow snuck up on me, cool as a cucumber. "That guy was a real monster. Would you like me to call the police?"

"I still need to use the payphone."

"You go ahead. I'll give them a buzz."

"Thanks. I'm Moses, by the way. I appreciate your help."

"I'm *Frr-ed*," he said with a mischievous smile.

The police arrived in five minutes. In the meantime, I managed to reach Nick. Through a staggering headache that tortured every conscious second, I explained the situation as well as I could. He said he'd take care of it.

When I hung up the phone, a wave of relief swept over me and my head cleared. I thanked Fred once more and then the local cop walked me to my car.

"You're a lifesaver," I said to the man in blue. "I appreciate it."

"It's what we're here for," he said. "Have a good night."

The next morning, before the screaming started, I discovered that two more emails had been forwarded to my account by scaevola21. They were dated the night before, about the time I was making my visit to Middle-earth.

O,

I'm more convinced than ever that we need to simply destroy him. His influence on these young people is appalling. He is encouraging their worst prejudices. The problem is he's a master of patriarchal lies and racist fantasies. He writes racist graffiti and thinks it's funny. If I were an angry person, I'd cut off his you-know-what and shove it right down his lying throat.

A

The reply.

A,

Never fear, my dear! This is a little tricky but I'm on it.

O

P. S. Tom loves the dildo you recommended!

Chapter 6

In-Betweeners

To the best of my recollection, it was Saturday morning around seven-thirty when the screaming started. I'd awoken at seven to the previously mentioned emails, as well as a short story in the science fiction genre, written by a new author named Jupiter Jefferson. "The In-Betweener" began as follows:

Orbited by seven moons, the planet Ur floats in a pearly atmosphere. Its great continent, Oomaguadaland, is home to an inland sea and three vast mountain ranges. On the west coast, the Klowk people inhabit their winding megapolis, Logarium, which twists and turns above and below the earth through coastlands linked by supersonic trains. Their hated rivals, the Kleek people, live in colossal fortress-towers called Ataloo and Buliabin, Queeo and Zwark, that illumine the eastern seaboard with the light of small suns.

Centuries ago, the green-faced Klowk captured and enslaved the blue-faced Kleek. The prophet Bandwin came from the Great Southern Desert warning the Klowk to free their slaves. If they failed to do so, he said, a bloody civil war would break out between North and South. He was tortured and burnt to death.

When the Klowkian Civil War erupted (known among the Kleek as the War of "Umlagada-Dudadane"), the Kleek gained their freedom, but they never forgave their brutal captors. In the reign of the hated Klowkian monarch Tor-Hump III, they embarked upon an exodus and crossed Oomaguadaland to build their mighty strongholds. But one day, two blue-faced Kleek parents gave birth to a green-faced baby boy....

I was absorbed in this imaginative vision when an unaccountable shriek scattered the morning quiet. At the moment, I was wearing nothing but backless slippers and a full-length black kimono. I opened my outer door and peeped out. No one in sight. Then a second shriek made my duty clear.

Adjusting the sash around my waist, I hurried off in the direction of the screams, which seemed to have originated in the part of the mansion farthest from my own. A third shriek, more terrible than the others, nearly unmanned me.

Fortunately, as I went waddling through the long hall past the kitchen, the mighty figure of Gladstone rushed out, carving knife in hand. We plunged ahead, side by side, I in my black kimono, he in his chef's uniform, until a series of quick turns brought us within sight of the Fitz suite. Gladstone wasted no time. He beat twice on the door. He opened it and flung his weapon.

What I saw was this. Gladstone's knife had impaled a good-sized octopus, puncturing its scrotum-like head as its tentacles writhed in futility. The monster had been toying with Ann Fitz who, having been cornered by the beast, stood shivering in a large bath towel that protected her modesty. Her face was green as pale seaweed.

The chef retrieved his knife from the floor as the sand-colored creature sagged upon the blade. "Excuse me," he said. "I'm going to put this sucker on ice."

He strode off to the kitchen as Ann Fitz skirted the foul puddle on the carpet and retired. Scanning the room, I was impressed by many things—cane chairs with striped pillows, white bookcases devoted wholly to women writers, a massive Georgia O'Keefe lily, a signed photograph of Oprah—but most of all I was impressed by the bubbling of a spacious fish tank against the wall, mounted on a cast-iron stand with delicate scrolling. What intrigued me about the thirty-odd gallons of water inside the tank was not the charming arrangement of shells and coral. It was the absence of fish.

Ann Fitz reappeared wrapped in a black silk kimono not unlike my own. She hurried to the tank and peered into its depths.

"It ate Nemo!"

"Nemo?" I inquired.

"My clownfish, you idiot." She was practically in tears. "Nemo!!"

"I'm terribly sorry. These things happen, I suppose."

"No, they don't, you moron."

"I mean, in the wild, in the sea."

"How on earth did that octopus get in here?"

The question sucked us out into the hallway, where a trail of slime led down a stretch of lacquered hardwood. It was about forty feet of hallway—evidently not an impossible feat for the now deceased cephalopod. When we got there, however, the door to the octopus's room was shut. On the other hand, as we soon discovered, the seal over the octopus's tank had been breached. The clamps still held, but a hole the size of a silver dollar compromised the integrity of the clear mesh top.

"That's all it needed to get out," I commented. "A tiny little hole like that."

"You seem to know a lot about it?"

This was patently unfair, and Ann Fitz soon changed her tune.

"It must have slipped under my door?" she said. "It isn't flush with the floor?"

We pivoted in tandem to examine the door to the octopus's room. When Ann Fitz closed it, the space at the bottom was plain to see. We stood side by side, contemplating the unforeseen effects of poor workmanship.

"The problem is—"

"I can't believe it?" she interrupted me.

"But how did it know your fish was inside?"

"I wish I knew?"

"And who cut the hole? I don't think an octopus could have done that."

"Probably the same person who vandalized the floor? This is very troubling?"

The door swung open and Arbuthnot and Quinones entered in their pajamas. I noticed that even Quinones's striped pajamas were pressed to perfection. Keep your eye peeled for a man in a black jacket and waistcoat, I said to myself. They were staring as if their tongues were paralyzed. I struggled to gather what had struck these two highly articulate persons speechless. The reason was not the octopus tank. It was that Ann Fitz and I were wearing identical kimonos.

"I can't believe you and I are both wearing kimonos!" Ann Fitz blurted out. "What a strange coincidence?"

"Good morning!" I said. "Did Gladstone show you the octopus?"

"He's going to grill it," Quinones reported.

Having grown accustomed to our kimonos, the new arrivals proceeded to investigate the crime scene.

"Is this how it escaped?" Arbuthnot inquired, poking her finger around the hole in the top. "Can an octopus do this?"

Quinones circled the tank. "It's a suspicious hole," he said.

They were an unexpected pairing, Arbuthnot and

Quinones. Beneath his unimpeachable tailoring, Quinones was a serial prankster. Rumor was he'd hacked Neil Young's homepage to announce that Neil had won the Nobel Prize for Literature.

> *On the shore lay Montezuma*
> *With his cocoa leaves and pearls.*

I suspect he was the one who taped the CUSTODIAN sign on my door—naturally I insisted on its staying put. Arbuthnot's snow-elf complexion did not obscure a sensuous, brooding spark. Were they a couple?

"Excuse me?" Ann Fitz said. "I've got to talk to Nick? I just hope I can get that report done on time?" She trudged off like Atlas resuming his solitary station.

Arbuthnot and Quinones explained that they were having coffee in the upstairs lounge when they heard a screech or two, so distant and indistinct they thought it was a barn owl. They came downstairs and Gladstone filled them in on the morning's mayhem. Was the timing a coincidence? First the incendiary graffiti and now this. Forces were on the move. The Project Director seemed overwhelmed.

"It's mysterious," Arbuthnot said in her flannel jammies.

"Very," Quinones concurred.

They craned their necks to inspect the sculpted light fixtures on the high ceiling. They examined the window and the noisy steam radiator below it. Finally, Quinones squatted on his powerful hams to examine where the phrase "Algorithms aren't racist" had been scrawled on the tile floor beneath the tank. There was no sign of it.

"It could be industrial warfare," he said, peeling a blonde hair from his neat pajama cuff.

I said nothing. The problem confronting us, from my point of view, was unsolvable: how does anyone train an octopus?

"Maybe one of us is a double agent," Arbuthnot proposed, delighted at the prospect.

"I'd put my money on the Project Director."

"A lot of people have access to this place, Rico. The cleaning lady, Public Safety, the laundry people. Gladstone practically lives here."

"And that crew in the basement. Talk about weird."

I said, "What do they do?"

"All I know is they log us into Hannibal."

"Probably just maintenance technicians," Quinones said.

"Hmm," Arbuthnot mused. "How big is Public Safety? Is it just Sergeant Nachman?"

"I hear they're expanding," Quinones replied. "Her husband's joined the force."

"Should we contact them?" Arbuthnot said.

"No doubt Ann Fitz already has," I said.

We studied the tank, which rebuffed our attempts at comprehension.

"Maybe it *was* the octopus," Arbuthnot said. "Don't they have beaks or something?"

"I've got it!" Quinones cried. "The gun was taped to the bottom of the tank. All the octopus had to do was acquire it on the way down."

"What about motive? Did the octopus even know Ann Fitz?"

"Maybe Gladstone was in on it."

"In other words—"

"The octopus was a patsy!"

"Time to get dressed," Arbuthnot concluded their dialogue. "See you," she said to me, and Quinones followed her lissome form out the open door.

I looked around and confronted the vestiges of the private chapel—a gothic niche in the wall, a holy water stoup, a faint nameless residue—and was left to ponder whether the room had been deconsecrated. Nothing about the campus seemed fixed. To the contrary: everything seemed in flux. Exiting the premises, I recalled a conversation with an arthritic French gentleman in Louvain when I was six or seven. We were conversing in simple French. I had asked why Athena participated in the Judgment of Paris. He said it was a good question and was quite earnest with me, in the way that the very old can be with the very young. He spoke in a kind of sing-song. He said the wisdom of this world was folly in the eyes of God.

Later that morning, when I got around to facing my phone, I found that a pair of text messages had arrived, both of them in Cyrillic. Tatiana continued to address me in a formal manner. *"Greetings!"* she exclaimed. *"Are you mad at your Tatiana?"* This was followed by, *"If you don't write me, I will shoot myself."* "That would be a waste of a perfectly good bullet," I replied. She quoted Akhmatova, *"I'm not asking for your love...."* This leap into poetry offended me. Akhmatova was about the most serious person that ever lived. So far as I know she was a Russian Orthodox Christian—a deeply religious woman, though you'd never know it from reading Wikipedia, the Great Eraser. "Whatever," I replied. A minute later: *"Shall I come by tonight?"* This drew no reply, but it gave me a terrible headache.

After breakfast I went out walking. The weather was dry but not too cold, and the sun didn't seem to mind the extra work. I strolled down the path to the gym, not remotely suspecting that Sergeant Nachman was lying in wait—operating without the BV. With the benefit of hindsight, I'm sure that's what left me vulnerable to her flanking action.

"Mr. Shea!" she called, breaking cover. It seemed unquestionable that, with or without amplification, she had succeeded in training me to stop whenever she called my name.

"What can I do for you, Sergeant Nachman?"

"Mr. Shea, I'm afraid those older gentlemen are back."

"Sorry to hear that."

"I hate these people, Mr. Shea."

I didn't like the sound of this but I preferred to shrug it off. "Why on earth do you hate them?"

"Because I grew up Catholic." She said it emphatically, as if nothing more needed to be said. I could only hope she wasn't a victim of child molestation or some other trauma. Could be. Then again, people with fairly normal upbringings come to hate their parents and clutch that hate like a piece of heaven to their hearts. I wanted to recite Yeats to her.

> *Come away, O human child!*
> *To the waters and the wild*
> *With a faery, hand in hand,*
> *For the world's more full of weeping than you*
>   *can understand.*

But I decided to play it safe. "You want me to use one of the red security phones."

"Thank you, Mr. Shea."

Soon afterward, I discovered that a couple of elderly gentlemen were in fact lurking in the vicinity. I was circling the gym when I caught sight of their fugitive figures. They were tall and dressed almost identically, in fedoras and trench coats. They saw me first, however, and nipped around the corner.

While I have never mastered the running motion and therefore lack the feel for running, I had a hunch as to where these two fellows had disappeared. On the far side of the gym, a stone's throw into the field, there stands a hedge maze, a highlight of Saint Malachy College's annual Renaissance Fair. I'd explored it a few days earlier and found all it needed was a good pruning. The journey to the center took twenty minutes. The trick was to stay calm and to remember the dead ends. Eventually, the anxiety about losing your way in the high hedge will be overcome by the satisfaction of solving the puzzle. Such mazes are a beautiful form of play. Mimicking mortal danger, they are a means of facing down fears and keeping your wits about you in preparation for the day when your life really is a feather in the wind—as it must be someday for all who inhabit this windy planet.

I suspected that the objects of my pursuit were hiding within the maze's cunning passageways. I crept like a fat old cat around to the far side, where I could keep tabs on the maze's entrance. I also had a wide-open view, about fifty yards away, of the back of the gym—a strategic advantage in case Sergeant Nachman made an appearance. To the west, the field's distant expanse towards the brow of a hill was interrupted only by a culvert pipe and a thin stream that spilled into the frog pond.

As I'd anticipated, the two elderly gentlemen—I was sure now that one was black and the other white—showed themselves at the maze's mouth. I adopted as unconcerned a manner as possible and made my approach. The pair was deep in hostile territory, vigilant but not frightened. The black gentleman studied me from under shaggy eyebrows. His face seemed carved in his brown flesh. It was a hard face, hawk-nosed and long, with high cheekbones, and heavy sacks under the eyes.

"Fine weather," he said.

"Sure is," I replied. "But there's a cop in the neighborhood who'd like to make your acquaintance. I'd be wary if I were you, because she just might be crazy enough to shoot somebody."

My words made no visible impression. And this indifference confirmed in my mind that something was off-kilter about the pair. To begin with, their nearly identical style of dress extended from their old-style coats and hats to gray woolen trousers and track shoes—and this superficial likeness was reinforced at a deeper level by their angular bony frames and by their identical height. I would have guessed six four, maybe six five. They stood rooted and remote like an expedition of tall skinny aliens. The reality they inhabited wasn't the one that Carthage inhabited. Nachman had enlightened me. They were the enemies of Carthage. They occupied the same plane of existence as the amphitheater and the sanctuary light burning in the chapel.

I said, "The thing I don't understand is why Carthage just leaves those ruined dormitories lying around. Someone could be badly injured."

The black gentleman nodded. "We were wondering—do you work for Carthage?" His relaxed voice and easy manner belied his severity of countenance.

I said, "I'm in the advertising game."

"That's why you're here?"

"I'm here because I'm fluent in tongues."

"Like the Holy Spirit?"

"More like the Vatican Bank."

Their muffled asides led me to suspect I'd stumbled on some form of code. The other man's voice sounded gruffer, with a memory of South Boston before gentrification smoothed out the grit. "Well," the black gentleman said, turning to me, "it's nice standing here talking, but if as you say we're being pursued, we had best be on our way."

"I'd like to hear your side of the story."

"An interesting proposition," he replied. "But why should we talk to you?"

"I'd like to compare notes. If you're nervous about being discovered, we could go inside the gym."

They debated the matter in their fashion.

"Okay," the black gentleman said at length. "Lead on, sport."

We crossed the field to the back of the gym without incident. I scanned my ID and the doors swung open into the broad daylight. Trading looks, the two men proceeded to move at a sober pace down a good-sized corridor, triggering fluorescent lights overhead as I trailed behind. The gray floor was concrete and the corridor was lined with gray metal doors. It ended in a dark gap into which my companions disappeared entirely, as if they were entering a portal between worlds. Next the lights on the gym ceiling came on with a series of faint clicks. I found myself on the edge of a basketball court. At its center they stood side by side. Their heads were tilted back as they focused on a row of green basketball jerseys hanging high up in the rafters.

"Who are you guys?" I said, stepping onto the court.

"I'm John Phoenix," the black gentleman replied. "This is my associate, Tom Carlucci." They were together up there as well. PHOENIX and CARLUCCI. White letters on green jerseys. Number 13 and Number 7.

"Right. My name is Moses Shea. Never played much ball. What I mean is, who are you guys? Why are you here?"

Mr. Carlucci politely excused himself, saying he needed to make a brief inspection and leaving Mr. Phoenix to handle my questions.

"The reason for our being here," he began, moving to the bench to rest his lanky frame. "You ask the reason." He removed his fedora and thumbed the rim, revealing thin kinky hair, ash-white and high on his wrinkled forehead. I sat down on the bench and waited to hear him out.

"This was a great place. The Pope Pius XII Gymnasium. Our team was the Griffins."

"Glory days."

"It's always a dangerous crossing from one time to

another."

He spoke now with a touch of weariness.

"When I look back on it, I think what I liked best was the occasional hour of leisurely meditation, to which the beauty of the place lent a quiet blessing. I think that's what I really miss. You see, Mr. Shea, everything we'd achieved came under relentless grinding attack. Truth is, we were never stupidly loyal to the country, but we tended to like it. We knew there were a lot worse places on earth. We knew the Church could be corrupt, quite corrupt, but it was the best light we had. Don't let them tell you our problems had to do with science. We were doing fine. Science was integrated into the curriculum from the start. But there's a difference between being addicted to useless gizmos and studying real science.

"For twenty years they sold us down the river—that's an American phrase, by the way. You can look it up. They hired a bunch of insolent tomfools who tore down everything Saint Malachy College used to stand for. As for minority students, the new faculty never wanted them to succeed, because, in order to succeed, you need to work inside the system. A flawed system, like I said, but not systemically racist. I do not propose to discuss the challenges of thinking through history with you. But this is certain and my old brain hasn't forgotten it yet: the idolatry of race in the national discourse is a disastrous development. Doesn't history teach us anything?"

"What does it teach us?"

"That life is many-angled and complicated and you better do your damn homework, Mr. Shea."

"But what exactly happened? How did you lose the school?"

"Last year around this time, a student group smuggled a theologian onto campus. She was originally scheduled to give a public lecture, but the administration revoked the invite. Her subject was 'The Laws of Nature and of Nature's God.' She gave a good talk and things ran smoothly until the Q and A. Then the atmosphere grew hostile. Her response to the hecklers was to put up a chart showing that, after 1776, slavery went into worldwide decline. It was the American breakthrough. The herald of reforms that would have happened faster in Heaven, and never would have happened in Hell."

"Well said."

"Following the lecture, faculty started preaching revolutionary violence. Windows were smashed and the president said she was listening better. Fires broke out and she said she was learning a great deal. Students were mugged in their classrooms and she said she was profoundly moved. Troublemakers arrived from out of state—anarchists, terrorists, gang members. I've never been clear who funded that. On the last day of classes, we defended the chapel and the library. We couldn't save all the dorms. Our Honors students pulled down the statue of Flannery O'Connor. It's in Carlucci's garage along with a statue of the Little Flower—but the peacocks' tails were broken. During exam week, President White-White received an award for the college's anti-racism curriculum. The media were lavish in their praise but parents were now paying attention, and, as the glass shattered and the graffiti thickened and spread, White-White could no longer depend on slick advertising to gloss over the wreckage. She doubled down, of course. Her kind always does. She posted videos and excoriated her critics, but no serious Catholic parents wanted to send their kids here. The place was known for turning students against their families. The next year's enrollment dried up."

He paused in his account, content to sigh through his long nostrils and to run a fingertip along the top of his hat. Then he gazed at me with fire in his eyes.

"But the thing you need to know is this. It isn't over. Nicholas Carty knows it isn't over. Because of the two chapels on campus, there's a restriction on the title deed. It forbids a sale to non-Catholics unless—this is what it says—'a reasonable period of time is allotted to finding a Catholic buyer.' The board of trustees sold the campus to Carty without honoring the restriction. It was easy for a local judge to stop all development on the property until the issue was resolved. And that's why the dorms haven't been cleared."

"Who's the judge?"

"I am."

A smile wrinkled his wooden features.

"Now I have a question."

I waited.

"Is there a boy named Osgood working with you?"

"What if I said there was?"

"He's a relative of my wife. She'd like to see him."

Out of the architectural recesses of the Pope Pius XII Gymnasium, Tom Carlucci emerged with a loping gait. "Looks good," he called out. "They've got the pool up and running and there's a new weight room in the East Wing. But nothing much has changed that I can see."

The judge awaited my reply about Osgood.

"I'll see what I can do," I said. "Do you have a business card?"

"Tommy," he called. "Can you give us one of those cards you had printed up?"

Friends of the Griffin, it said. We were all standing now. We exited the gym and the two companions disappeared into the west side of campus, blessedly undetected, like Saint Peter escaping Herod's prison.

It wasn't until Sunday morning that the mystical thread resurfaced of a story that continued to exceed my powers of comprehension. Sometime in the night I developed a painful cramp in my leg. It persisted after my efforts of stretching and hydration. I went out early, determined to restore my leg to health. A cold mist saturated the air, though that in itself cannot explain why I took the path to the amphitheater instead of my usual route around the gym. As I approached the footbridge that straddled the frog pond, a small boy stood watching me from the other side. He wore a blue scarf and a puffy white coat. He regarded me with the delicate perception of a rabbit. Then he ran off. That was it—except for the fact that my cramp went away.

I didn't see Osgood until Monday, when I found him in the refectory, hard at work while wolfing down a plate of eggs. He was deep in the final details of his R&A report. I waited patiently until he finished. "There," he announced, closing his laptop and pushing away the remnants of his breakfast. When I handed him the business card, he studied it and said nothing. But when I recounted my adventure with the two old gentlemen, he flipped the card over and scribbled something on the back. It was then I noticed he was left-handed.

My first ever visit from Sinclair occurred during Monday office hours. We hadn't spoken at the morning meeting, which she attended in a very short skirt and thigh-high boots—her response, I gathered, to Ann Fitz's setting the boys against the girls for the week. It was classic Nick. I'm surprised he waited until Week Two. In any case, Sinclair's hair was now blue as a Nereid. Unnerved by her raffish splendor, I recalled my night of love with Tatiana Kuznetsov, who, by a curious coincidence, appeared in the hallway dragging her vacuum cleaner just as I was greeting Sinclair.

"Did you see Mal's five ways a dildo is better than a man?" Sinclair said for openers.

"No. I missed that."

"It's brilliant!"

She sat down, cued up her phone, and passed it to me, rising as she did so to admire Osgood's handiwork by hanging gregariously on my shoulder. I could scarcely believe my eyes.

How could Mal Osgood—that good Catholic boy—have written such an unholy thing?

*FIVE WAYS AN EDGE OFF DILDO
IS SUPERIOR TO A MAN*

*1. You come first.
2. Ready when you are.
3. No miscommunication.
4. Nine-hour battery.
5. You can share it with a friend.*

"I love that!" Kiki said, returning to her seat. The air was now entangled with the scent of perfume—cinnamon and musk. I swallowed hard and stared with creeping terror at my outer door. To open it was to be at the mercy of the merry widow, whose vacuum cleaner was battering away at the wall. To leave it closed was to be at the mercy of the slender-thighed Nereid. My imagination filled the breach. It surprised me, to tell you the truth. Why? Because my imagination is never reasonable. It only pretends to be reasonable. But maybe this time it wasn't pretending. It said, in effect, imagine being a liberal arts professor at Saint Malachy College. Not some living fossil like yourself, but a solid piece of a man who fit the bill whether he wanted to fit the bill or not. Then think of a class of undergraduates on an April afternoon when the charms of spring are everywhere, and of trying to do literary justice, not to Roth or Updike, giants though they be, but to good old *Romeo and Juliet*.

*Oh, Romeo, that she were, oh, that she were
An open-arse, and thou a pop'ring pear!*

In my mind, I could hear the ghosts of Nietzsche and

Freud quarreling over the rubble. "The patient died of resentment," said one. "No, no. The patient died of repression," said the other.

Sinclair sat patiently with her chin saddled on the back of her fingers and her elbows propped on the tabletop. She was waiting for me to marshal my thoughts. The subject before us was the selling of Belizean chocolate, and she wanted to discuss *taste*. Her idea was that something could taste so good that it would no longer be in good taste.

"Are there any more rules to break? I wish I could find some."

"Transgression has become a bore. It's a problem in aesthetics."

"Let's see," she said. "We studied aesthetics in my Beckett class...I've got it, 'The chocolate that's better than nothing!'"

"How about this?" I countered, thinking hers was actually pretty good.

You've lost your taste for fashion
You're sick of social action:
If love's belief's old hat,
Try Belizean chocolate.

"That's absolutely terrible," she said, looking pleased. "Did you just make that up?"

"No. It's by Rudyard Kipling."

"Rudyard Baloney. Let's see...." She tilted her eyes toward her forehead—always a gesture with her. "What about going meta? A chocolate bar about a chocolate bar."

"That'll sell."

"What about race?" she said, firing away. "Dark chocolate and white chocolate. Ebony and ivory?"

"Too eighties."

"Well, back to the drawing board. You ought to have a drawing board in here, by the way. It would be inspiring."

The vacuum cleaner had rolled onto the next stretch of

carpeting. I could barely hear it singing now. Sinclair was ticking away with pursed lips through items on her phone when suddenly her face brightened.

"What about their gods?"

"The Belizeans?"

"No. I was thinking of the...what were they?"

"I know what you mean. Not the Aztecs. The Mayans."

"They practiced human sacrifice."

"So?"

"We could stamp the Mayan gods on Belizean chocolate bars. They must have had some beautiful gods. You're holding this beautiful god in your hand, and, instead of your being sacrificed to the god, the god is sacrificed to you!"

"Huh."

"Pretty good, isn't it?" she said excitedly.

"I fear someone in California might take offense."

"True. But it would depend on how we market it." Her thumbs danced a jig on her phone. Then it was "Thanks, prof," and off she went, drenching the air in a Nereid spray that made my balls ache.

To escape the wake of her perfume, I went into my reading room, shut the door behind me, and checked my email. Ann Fitz had sent the team an update.

Dear Carthage Community,

I write to report two more disturbing incidents. As you may know, the octopus escaped this morning. It traveled from its room to my suite, where it slipped under the outer door and made its way to my aquarium, in order to devour my clownfish. I hope none of you will see the humor in this. I contacted Public Safety, and DPS has opened a second investigation.

A little over an hour ago, Tatiana was cleaning the upstairs lounge and found the Pi symbol (π) written inside the storage cabinet. It is unclear how long this malicious vandalism had been festering. I contacted Public Safety again, and DPS has opened a third investigation.

I want to thank Tatiana again for her responsiveness and urge all of us to defend the community we love! If you encounter acts of hate, don't be silent! If you see anyone damaging property, please contact Sergeant Nachman.

We will always stand by our values at Carthage. If you are unaware of systemic racism and its long, devastating impact on this hateful country, take the time to learn. Let us join together in our determination to end acts of hatred in the community we aspire to.

The experience of hate can be traumatic. If you would like one of our counselors to visit you, please reach out to Human Resources.

Finally, please attend an emergency meeting in the conference room this afternoon at 4 p.m.

With hope for our future,
Ann Fitz
Project Director

I was simply out to sea. Had to look it up. To my dismay, "π" was a symbol of "Western math." It was a construction of "Whiteness" on par with the swastika. As for the source of these bizarre disruptions, there I was on solid land. Indeed, the fact that the cleaning lady knew the rules of a language-game designed to infantilize a nation pointed well beyond the tactics of industrial espionage. The question was, whose secret war, devised by which spy-masters, was Tatiana fighting?

When I arrived, I found the meeting already in progress, but not getting very far.

"I'd like to know who arrived here first?" the Project Director said icily.

"What does that have to do with anything?" Osgood said hotly.

"Who put the baseball cap on the goddess?"

The offending cap was nowhere to be seen. A skein of geese emerged over the O'Connell Library, gray clouds at their backs.

"The R&A report was good? Nick was happy with it? But we're obviously failing as a community?"

"I don't think we're failing as a community," Liu pushed back gently. "Sorry about your fish, though."

This drew sympathetic nods all around.

"That was weird," Allan said. "Gladstone says he's worried about serving the octopus because it ate your fish and...."

Quinones could not restrain a galling snort.

"That's not funny?"

"When is Nick coming?" I asked.

"He'll be here tomorrow? He's going to meet with each of us individually?"

"Are we done with this stupid meeting?" Osgood said.

"We're not done? I need to know what's going on with us? Who do you think is responsible for these racist acts?"

"Well, I don't think we can accuse the octopus of racism," Quinones remarked in a voice that mingled cynicism with dementia, like a ham actor playing the detective part in a surrealist film noir. "And we can't blame the vandalism in the upstairs lounge on the octopus, either. Frankly, I just don't see how it could have climbed the stairs. You can only ask so much of an octopus. Maybe I'm missing something here —Paris?"

Allan suffered a coughing fit.

"Maybe we're the octopus," Sinclair said, her face a pitch-perfect blank. "There's eight of us."

Arbuthnot came to Ann Fitz's defense. "Look," she said, reddening. "It's easy for us to make fun of the situation, but the United States has a long savage history of slavery and oppression and our generation agrees on that. As for pi, or algorithms, for that matter, these things are no more racist in themselves than a field or a stone. The question is, what does society do with them? Does it build equal housing on the field or a jail to incarcerate innocent black men? Does it let the stone rest in peace, or does it use the stone to destroy the dreams of poor black children in Birmingham, Alabama? I think Ann has every reason to be concerned."

"Thank you, Kay," Ann Fitz said.

"We need more racial sensitivity, not less," Arbuthnot resumed. "It isn't enough to be non-racist. Not nearly enough. We need to be anti-racist. We need racial consciousness." Gone was the witty young woman whom I saw exchanging quips with Quinones. Gone was the brilliant programmer. She commanded the stage like a psycho-diva whose lover lies dead at her feet, slain by the vilest villain ever to walk the earth. "We need to hunt out racism everywhere, in every film, on every canvas, in every space of whiteness, every book, bulletin, and blackboard. We need to hunt out whiteness in every room of every house, in the attic, the kitchen, the cellar, the den, under the rug, in the bathroom, and in the plumbing. In the crawl space and the air ducts. We need to search our cars, our trucks, our furniture, under our beds, in our closets, in our socks, and in our underwear. We need to pry into every nook and cranny, every crack and every hole, to leave no stone unturned, to try the guilty, sentence them, and dance on their graves. We need to purge our mailboxes and pick through our garbage. We need to probe the laboratories and break up the boardrooms. We need to visit the ends of the earth. We need to apologize constantly and seek therapy. We need to grovel in the dirt like guilty collaborators who aren't worth the weight of our own shit. Because, honestly, we're not. We need to chain ourselves to justice." Arbuthnot paused briefly to consult her phone. (Imagine, I suppose, the phrase "This must change" on her screen, affixed to some tweet expressing a blanket condemnation of the West.) Then she continued: "We need to keep constant vigil, to stand guard on the streets, to mind our museums, to heal our hospitals, and police our parks. We need to march through the valley of the shadow of death and climb the highest mountain. We need to dredge the rivers and excavate the earth. We need to plumb the oceans and monitor the moon. Does anybody ever ask, why are there no African-American astronauts?"

"Actually, there are a lot of them," Allan said.

"We need to think before we speak, to listen to others, to re-educate ourselves, to recognize our complicity. We need to put an end to the legacy of slavery once and for all."

"Thank you so much, Kay," Ann Fitz said, her eyes misting over.

"It's about fighting for truth," Arbuthnot concluded, exhaling scarlet steam.

"That's your narrative," Liu said calmly. "The reality is you don't know what you're talking about."

"How dare you?!" Arbuthnot thundered. She scooped her phone off the tabletop and departed in a fury.

Sinclair hiccupped into the silence. "Sorry," she said.

"Okay!" said Osgood, "I've got a case of good beer in the fridge upstairs, if anyone wants to join me."

The emergency meeting had ended in an emergency. Only Ann Fitz and I remained, sitting apart like an old married couple who've been divorced for thirty years. "Let's go up and have a beer," I suggested. "It's been a long day."

"No?"

Chapter 7

Getting Even

Nick and I hadn't spoken in days, not since I called him from the payphone in the movie theater. According to someone in his office, we were slated to meet late in the day Tuesday. Early that morning, though, my phone rang.

"There's a secure line in the conference room," he said. "Call me back at this number."

"The conference room?"

"Go in there and lock the door behind you. Make sure you're alone."

I was calling him as instructed when the cleaning lady appeared, pushing her trolley down the hall. In place of her drab vesture of gray, a new housekeeping outfit of candy-stripe pink adorned her person. It was cut tight upstairs, short-sleeved and double-breasted, with white cuffs and lapels. Her hemline to her heels showed white stockings. She knocked on the door like an Oedipal nightmare and I repulsed her attack by waving the phone at her face. Then she went to work dusting a large oil painting by a minor French master named Guzac, who converted to Islam and kept a harem. It portrayed a gauzily attired Salammbô stretching her arms to the crescent moon. It hung in the hallway, where Tatiana dusted the elaborate gilt frame while I spoke with Nick.

"Hello again," he said. "Where's the Russian, do you know?"

"I'm looking at her right now."

"Can she hear us?"

"No. She's out in the hall."

"Look, Moses. We've got a situation on our hands. Your girlfriend is a Russian spy. No doubt about it. The story she's peddling about her husband is fake as the Steele Dossier."

"The Steele Dossier had legs."

"I imagine she does too."

"No doubt about it."

"It would be simple to tip off the feds and walk away."

"But you're not going to do that."

"No. I think we'll play a little game of cat and mouse. I've got her under complete surveillance. Her apartment. Her car. I'd like to see if I can find a use for her."

"Where are you, by the way?"

"We're on the Merritt."

"How's the traffic?"

"Never mind about the traffic. Here's what I want you to do. Tell her we know she's a spy."

"She's dusting Salammbô."

"Wait till you get off the phone, Moses. Tell her we know about the Cyprus connection."

"The Cyprus connection. Got it. What good will that do?"

"We'll see." I was busy watching Tatiana mount a stepladder and start to flick the top of the frame with her duster. Nick continued: "She's thirty-five, you know. The gray hair's a ruse. I've seen photographs. She's a most attractive woman."

"Why don't you ask her for a date?"

"Her code name for you is 'fat little donkey.' Here, let me read you something. 'I have the fat little donkey eating out of my hand.' She sent that three nights ago. Here's one from last night. 'My fat little donkey rides well. He'll give us everything we need.'"

"She's delusional."

"She almost had you, Moses. From what I gather, you showed considerable resilience getting to that payphone—where did you say you were, a movie theater?"

"They were showing *The Lord of the Rings*. The whole trilogy. But I'm still trying to follow the grand scheme here. Why wouldn't she flee to Russia when she realizes her cover is blown?"

"It's like I said. The Cyprus connection. A woman like that will go to surprising lengths to avoid being murdered."

"I'm lousy at blackmail, Nick. I lack the element of personal charm."

"Blackmail's an ugly word. Think of it as poetic justice." After a lengthy pause he added: "You were too strong for her."

"Thanks." The truth is the "fat little donkey" line had gotten under my skin. It hadn't gotten far yet, but it was making its way from the high road to the low road to the mud. It didn't help matters when she met my eyes with a guilty look over her shoulder. If there's one thing humans are good at, it's guilty looks.

Nick was wrapping up the conversation. "I'll see you after I've calmed down Ann Fitz. That's going to take some doing. Now listen to me, choirboy. Whatever you do, don't start feeling sorry for that woman. She knows the rules of the game. She'd just as soon skin you as do her nails. You hear me?"

"All right, Nick. I think I have something in mind. See you later."

Tatiana was descending the stepladder as I exited. She

slipped, dropped the duster, and banged the back of her head against the glass before coming to rest in a sprawling heap on the carpet.

"Why are you wearing heels?" I said, whisking back to my suite.

But I left my door ajar. Soon she announced herself with a timid knock.

"Come in, come in," I said, waving my hand impatiently. "Close the door behind you."

"May I sit down?" she said, rubbing her skull. Having established a comfortable position on the chesterfield, I leaned back and clasped my hands behind my head. Had I been a smoker, now would have been the time to light up.

"No. You may not sit down. Stand up straight."

She stood up straight. Her eyes went to the conversation piece on the wall—a map of the ancient world according to Plutarch. Naturally, it included the island of Cyprus.

"We have a situation, Mrs. Kuznetsov."

"What is it?"

"Actually, you're the one with the situation. It was in Cyprus. See, it's just south of Cilicia."

"What do you mean?"

"On the map in front of you."

"What do you have to say to me?"

"Now of course we both know you're a Russian asset. We know you're thirty-five years old and you dye your hair to make yourself look older. You're a spy, Mrs. Kuznetsov. A ruthless spy who's going to pay the price for her insolence. Do we understand each other?"

She said nothing.

"Nicholas Carty said you were very attractive, by the way."

She made an inarticulate sound in her throat.

"Tell me, Mrs. Kuznetsov, do you ever feel like a seedy actress who's lived a despicable life—a private chronicle of the

most sordid and nauseating sins—who couldn't resist the allure of one last role on the stage? So you put on your greasepaint and rouge and get out in front of the audience one last time. You wiggle your hips and flirt with the men and dispense all your charms. On a good night you might even forget who you really are."

"*What is it you want from me?*"

"*You drugged me, didn't you?*"

"*So what?*"

"*You thought you could control me? Steal my secrets—make me your pet?*"

"*What do you want?*"

"*First, I want a complete confession. Who are you working for?*"

Her eyes narrowed with contempt.

"*You're a phone call away from being neutralized, Tatiana, or whatever your name is. I wouldn't take too long replying. I asked you a question.*"

"*The Foreign Intelligence Service.*"

"*What kind of drug did you use on me?*"

"*A drug called Recorder.*"

"*What does it do?*"

"*It lets you plant suggestions in the mind. It works best if the drug is accompanied by an intense emotional experience.*"

"*But you couldn't arouse me?*"

"*No. You lack a sufficient sex drive.*"

"*Your story about your husband was a lie?*"

"*Yes.*"

"*You were responsible for the incident with the octopus?*"

"*Yes.*"

"*But how did you get the octopus to enter Ann Fitz's rooms?*"

"*I left a sardine under her door.*"

"*Clever. And the graffiti? 'Algorithms aren't racist' and the pi sign?*"

"The 'Algorithms,' yes. The SVR RF recommended it."

"And the pi sign?"

"No. Someone else did that. I honestly don't know who."

"I don't believe you. What was your next little message going to be?"

"Exterminate all the brutes!"

"Heart of Darkness."

"Yes. Conrad would have approved. The horror of your civilization. Your phony diversity is your fatal flaw, Mr. Shea—it is so easily exploited for political purposes."

"Because human beings are naturally envious."

"You Americans, in particular. You take the cake. No pun intended."

"I see. But now you're trapped, Tatiana. You know the rules of the game."

"What do you want me to do?"

"Turn around. I want to have a good look at you."

She regarded me with razors in her eyes. *"I see you desire women only when you're holding the whip,"* she said. Then, without my so much as handing her a ten dollar bill, she put her hands on her hips and twirled on the Kuznetsovian axis.

"Very nice. Do it again, slowly."

"Pig," she sneered. Then she did it a second time, slowly and with a slight sway.

"Where is your gray polyester dress?"

"That ugly rag?"

"Yes."

"I keep it in the broom closet."

"Go put it on—and lose those heels."

"Now?"

"Yes."

"What do you want me to do with this dress? It fits me so much better."

"Hang it in the broom closet."

"Next to the Windex and the Lysol?"

"Yes. Be back here in five minutes."

I took advantage of the interim to keep up with my dental hygiene. When she returned in her gray polyester uniform, I again instructed her to stand at attention.

"You prefer me in this?"

"Chin up. Look straight ahead. Keep your eyes on Cyprus."

She stood upright as a caryatid as I paced up and down the room with my hands behind my back, shaking my head with a blistering air of rebuke. The fire in the grate burned a steady blue.

"This is some fantasy of male power."

"I suspect a lot of women would enjoy this situation, Mrs. Kuznetsov. Human beings are such perverse and dangerous creatures. They can easily revert to the most savage and primitive state of mind—which is one reason I like a good Catholic Mass. But that's hardly the point."

"What is the point?"

"The point," I said sternly, *"is that Dido Hall looks like a dump. The dust is out of control. Practically every trash receptacle in the building is overflowing. My bathtub hasn't had a single cleaning all week. The soap scum is starting to accumulate."*

A bolt of illumination electrified her from top to bottom.

"You want me to clean?!"

"You're going to clean this place good. And you're going to like it."

"Frankly, I'd rather be raped."

"Not going to happen."

"You sick man—what's wrong with you?"

"You wear your gray polyester dress to work. You leave me the hell alone. And you scrub Dido Hall like a professional cleaning lady. Let me tell you, you're going to have to pass the white glove

test. I see any grime or dust on that glove, and they'll be hearing about the Cyprus connection at the SVR RF, I can assure you."

"You heartless bastard."

"Not as heartless as you are, Mrs. Kuznetsov."

"Don't call me that."

"Why not? It's a perfectly respectable name. Now get cleaning!"

After a hearty New England breakfast, I paid a visit to the O'Connell Library. My purpose was to do some research on funerary urns. Thanks to a wealthy startup called Hydria Technologies, urns were competing with Belizean chocolate for our time that week. I had a good idea about where to get started. Unfortunately, though, I'd left my copy of *Hydriotaphia* in New York. It remained with the bulk of what I call my "Silver Collection": a thousand minor works of lasting significance, originating in sundry times and places, ancient and modern. My "Silver Collection" was infinitely more valuable than my "Contemporary Collection," which was devoted to highly lauded works of the twenty-first century. To be fair, among the thousands of books in my "Contemporary Collection," two or three might have tried to give, and succeeded in giving, a high order of intellectual and emotional pleasure to the reader, untouched by political posturing, so as to be rewarded with a place in someone's "Silver Collection" at some future date, when we are all of us shelved away in urns, graves, and other repositories of dead matter. I suspect it was a disturbing sense of all this dead, dead contemporary matter that prompted my remembrance of *Hydriotaphia*.

And yet, if I may elaborate, what I was conscious of *on the day* when I left the foxed volume behind me in New York among my Silvers was a potential lapse of judgment that could come back to haunt me, as such lapses often do, especially when you sense that they will. And maybe it was that haunting awareness that inspired me now, as lack leads on to lack.

The historical setting of *Hydriotaphia* was the discovery somewhere in seventeenth-century England of ancient Roman sepulchral urns, which survived not only the names of their dead, but all the topographical changes that the unimaginable touch of time could effect. Here, excellent reader, is the long-dead author of *Hydriotaphia*, Sir Thomas Browne, ruminating on urns and the ironies of human existence: "Time, which antiquates antiquities, and hath an art to make dust of all things, hath yet spared these minor monuments." And "Oblivion is not to be hired: the greater part must be content to be as though they had not been, to be found in the register of God, not in the record of man." One more sparkling jewel of language: "Life is a pure flame, we live by an invisible sun within us." Browne's work was, in short, a treasure trove of the most excellent advertising copy. His gorgeous language was ripe for use—so long as one dispensed with his ironic framing of human vanity and negated everything else the author believed in. Sitting in the library, I scribbled down a few notes. "Don't be dust!" "Pay off oblivion!" "Don't be content to be as though you hadn't been!" "Go on record!" "Rest in an invisible sun!"

The Hydria concept was to place a person's incinerated remains inside an urn-shaped tablet equipped with a solar panel. The screen would endure as long as any columbarium on earth. It would last a geological age underground. When the screen was exposed to sunlight, the deceased would appear to share his or her achievements with the living. The people at Hydria Tech considered the worldwide academic market a potential goldmine. Professors could store any kind of information: groundbreaking academic publications, glowing letters of recommendation, adulatory readers' reports, prize-winning memoirs, manuscripts, performance art, conference videos, novelistic essays, essayistic novels, one-hundred-page professional résumés featuring epic catalogs of committee work—you name it. Thanks to Hydria Technologies, what Doctor Browne called "the iniquity of oblivion" was a thing of the past. All one needed to do was purchase "A Well-Wrought Urn." I was anticipating office hours with pleasure.

On my way back from the library, I noticed Manny Murphy parked in the silver Benz limo under the porte-cochère. I strolled over to say hi.

"Hop in," he said. "Let's go for a spin."

"Only if I can sit in front."

"Door's open."

I slid my trousers' seat onto the warm leather surface and shook hands with the driver. Manny seemed all right, the same webs around the eyes, but he was keeping himself in fighting condition. He looked the part of a plain clothes detective in his black gabardine jacket and gray hoodie.

"Nick said to lose the uniform," he explained. "It's because things have changed in New York. You see a lot of beefed-up chauffeurs these days. The suits want people to know they have protection."

"Do you carry?"

"Of course I fucking carry. I'm not an ex-con, you know. The rap against me was poor judgment."

"The poor judgment of blocking a criminal cash flow. That really was poor judgment. So where are we going?"

"There's a little coffee shop down the road."

Manny steered the big Benz past the four-way, where Sergeant Nachman studied our progress from her bizarro fortress. Exiting the ruined gate, we drove south until, just past the east-west highway, the place appeared on our right. A sign rose up on a yellow column streaked with rust, announcing a comatose establishment called the Griffin Café. Somehow I hadn't noticed it before. The Zippo station, the P.O., the burger stand, the bank, and the convenience store were a little further down the road.

Despite effects of age, the Griffin Café was a charming relic of bygone days—brown clapboard and yellow trim, a wraparound porch with columns, and plenty of elms and maples to burst into flame every October. Ours was the only car in sight, a luxury limo parked in the shadow of the mythological creature that resided atop the column.

The atmosphere within seemed depleted, as if it had exhausted its supply of life-giving elements years ago. This impression was confirmed by the stale smell of burnt coffee and the starved appearance of tables and chairs whose best years were obviously behind them. And yet the walls were curiously alive. Their crowded surfaces were home to a gallant host on pennants and in frames: pugilistic Griffins, basketball-dribbling Griffins, golfing Griffins, gridiron Griffins. I saw a plunging diver in a one-piece swimsuit, black-and-white photographs of men's sports teams, the blueprints of the Pope Pius XII Gymnasium, a letter from Éamon de Valera, and a picture of our first Catholic president. The panorama was so intense in its collective reality that you had the feeling it might *do something* once you turned your back. I've thought about it many times since. The Griffin Café was a cultural fossil, but the student of psychological history might have taken away some valuable lessons from a time when the quest for dignity was more important than the quest for status. Here, the American ground had not yet shifted. The Griffin Café still had a foot in the American past, and, so long as the Griffin Café survived, that past had a beachhead in the present. And while I felt summoned to be respectful, I noticed that much of what survived the deceased was their humor. In one photograph, a mortarboarded old coot in a billowing graduation gown stood lecturing the young, pointing his index finger at the sky like Raphael's Plato. In another, a soberly dressed female professor diagrammed *Oedipus Rex* in chalk lines on the blackboard. You could see the glistening ducktails on the backs of the boys' heads. In a third, a bespectacled priest posed with a football. He had his arm cocked back as if he really meant to chuck it. I sure hoped he did. But the picture that finally riveted my attention was a photograph of a basketball team. The guys in front were holding a banner that said "1962 Eastern Conference Champions." Three of the hoopsters were black guys and one looked Hispanic. Standing in the middle of the second row, side by side, were John Phoenix and Tom Carlucci. Phoenix was palming a basketball and holding it out to the camera. All the boys were smiling like they were watching the Jerry Lewis dance scene in *Cinderfella*—the one with Anna Maria Alberghetti.

We took the table by the bay window and sat patiently. The aproned woman who eventually emerged from the swing door was not welcoming. "Only pie and coffee," she said. Her bunned-up hair was drained of color, and sunspots dappled her forehead. She stationed herself between a tall stack of trays loaded with dusty water glasses and an equally tall stack of ancient coffee cups. I glanced at the barren shelves inside the display case and looked back at her.

"What kind of pie?" I asked.

"Just pie," she said.

Outside our window, a blue Subaru pulled up and doubled the number of cars in the area. The driver, it turned out, was the florid fellow from the library. He sat behind the wheel while the passenger door opened and out sprang Natalee Phoenix. That's when I first made the connection. Natalee wasn't especially dark-complexioned but she wasn't a fair-haired daughter of Albion, either. No doubt they were related, she and Judge Phoenix. She entered the café and hesitated at the sight of us, but then she smiled and said hello. Then she chatted with the lady at the counter and paid for a good-sized box of lunches—enough coin to keep the establishment afloat for another day. Manny hurried over to open the door as she carried out her load.

The coffee and mystery pie were not coming any time soon. Then the phone rang and we overheard one side of a conversation from somewhere in back.

"Oh hello, Natalee."

"He is?"

"That's fine, dear. Thank you for letting me know."

A minute later, our coffee appeared, along with two slices of berry pie.

"Sorry to keep you boys waiting. The coffee's fresh and I baked the pie this morning."

Manny thanked her with his handsome-dog grin and she winked back at him before leaving us to our conversation.

"Did you hear what happened to Baldock?"

"Something happened to Baldock?"

"You didn't hear about it?"

"When did it happen?"

"Like a week ago."

"It's been busy."

"He got caught with his pants down."

"Really?"

"I'm serious."

"What was he doing? Skinny-dipping in the Hudson?"

"He picked up this chick at a place called The Dive Bar."

"The one on 93rd?"

"You know it?"

"I live in the neighborhood."

Manny loaded some pie on his fork and washed it down with hot coffee. I did the same.

"Delicious."

"Wow."

"That berry flavor."

He lowered his voice.

"So one of the things I didn't know about Baldock is he's a switch-hitter."

"I never knew. All these years."

"He and the girl went back to her place and her roommate joined them for, you know, a three-way situation."

"No kidding."

"They got out the UV body paint and went to work. Very intimately. They painted the word 'Newsprick' on Tom."

"Where?"

"Where do you think?"

"That's a lot of letters."

"Baldock is pretty well endowed."

The proprietress returned to check on us. I got the feeling she'd been following every word. "How's the pie?" she said amiably.

We couldn't have been more enthusiastic.

"I've been baking those a long time," she said. Then she hoisted her eyebrows and departed.

"Like I was saying, he's a man with an outstanding paint job. Now it turns out this roommate guy was something of a joker. If I understand correctly he's known to run in reactionary circles. He's been linked to this smartass playboy who used to shoot his mouth off in the press. Flamboyant type. Fake blond hair."

"Oh, that guy."

"This pie is unbelievable."

"Sensational."

"Where was I?"

"Newsprick."

"Oh, yeah. They had a blacklight and a camera on Baldock —I won't go into details.

"Better not."

"The roommate gets him to read one of his masterpieces

from the start of the pandemic. You know, death and panic, shoot yourself in the head and jump out the window kind of shit."

"Yeah, I remember."

"The guy is pushing Baldock to keep on reading. Baldock's doing a great job. And the girl's down there doing everything she can to help."

"I won't ask what that means. Please don't tell me."

"I have the video right here."

"I wouldn't watch it if you paid me."

"The next day, someone hacks the *Eyewitness Void* website. A subtle piece of work—no one even noticed. Among the menu items is a link to a well-edited little clip called 'Newsprick.' And there's Tom Baldock in his glory—the way God made him. You know, that voice of his is one of a kind."

"I would call it a fruity baritone."

"I like that—fruity, just like this pie."

We finished our plates with a feeling of deep satisfaction.

"So how's old Tom been doing?"

"I hear they fired him at the *Void*."

"That's too bad."

"Sad, isn't it?"

"What's he doing to put bread on the table?"

"I think he's washed up."

But I wasn't so sure. Baldock had a long history of sticking around. He was in a different class from your usual, garden-variety, priapic menace of a newsman. He was more like the god himself. Something in my gut told me we hadn't seen the last of him.

On the way back to campus, we fell into silence and Manny mentioned he'd brought a book to keep him company while he waited for his boss.

"I didn't know you could read."

"I can read your forehead. It says, 'Room for rent.'"

"So what are you reading? A novel?"

"My wife reads novels."

"What is it?"

"You want to know?"

"You brought it up."

"It's there in the glove box."

I opened the glove box and out tumbled the book. It was called *A Hidden World of Wonder*, by a man named Trey Lumpkin. It had mountains and clouds on the cover. To tell you the truth, I was fairly taken aback. Manny was a tough guy. I never expected him to be interested in *wonder*.

"Do you know how high birds can fly?"

"No."

"Guess."

"A half a mile?"

"Way off. Some birds can fly over the Himalayas. I mean, that's five, six miles in the air. Way up there. Canadian geese fly very high."

"Why is that, do you think?"

"Stars, magnetic fields, navigation. But the author has a theory I agree with. He says the animals enjoy themselves. He says it's fun for a bird to be way up in the sky like that. They like it."

"So it doesn't boil down to natural selection?"

"It plays a role, but it's not the whole story. Animals can get depressed, even when they've found their survival niche. Food and safety aren't enough. They need something more."

I was never close with his breed of iron men, but Manny and I seemed to hit it off. He had a sensitive streak and he seemed to trust me. I sensed something was up behind that tough exterior. "Manny," I said, "everything all right?"

"What do you mean?"

"I don't know."

"I don't know, either, but the days go by."

"Sunrise, sunset."

"Same old, same old."

We were back on campus, sitting in the limo with the motor running. We were gazing out the windshield at the grass, which the winter winds had littered with brown oak leaves from the west side of campus.

"Why don't you join me for a walk? I'll show you the sights. There's a story here but I haven't quite figured it out yet. I could use the help of a good detective."

"A story?"

He checked his phone. "Okay. Let's go for a walk," he said, cutting the engine.

We headed to Dante Hall, along the route I'd taken on my first visit. Without going into detail about Judge Phoenix, I explained what had happened. The campus, which he praised for its beauty as we strolled along, had sold cheap because of damage from student rioting. I mentioned that some alums were hoping to take the college back, but Nick would do everything in his power to disappoint them.

"It's sad," Manny said.

We came to the wreckage of Dante Hall with its wailing wall. Colonies of black and green mold competed on the brick. The scattered heap of black cinders had an oily appearance. Nature would have a lot of work to do before her calm oblivious tendencies prevailed.

"Looks like God didn't come through for old Saint Malachy," Manny commented as we skirted the ruined dorm and continued along the path.

"I take it you're not a believer?"

"Me? I believe in the miracle dump."

"What's the miracle dump?"

"It's when you don't even need to use toilet paper."

"You're good to go."

"No fuss, no muss. It's a miracle."

Soon we were passing under bare branches to where the remains of Aquinas Hall lay moldering under the winter sky. We halted and stared solemnly at the withered dogwoods.

"They're not coming back," he said.

On we went, up the mild slope into thicker woods. I was telling him about the amphitheater and the frog pond when he cut me short.

"Who's she?" he said.

On the low hill where the grave of Newman Hall crowned the landscape, Donna Ramella pursued her absurd quest. The instant we became aware of her, she stumbled almost comically on the debris. We'd startled her, and I sickened at the thought of her being injured. But Manny hurried his pace and helped her to her feet well before I arrived on the scene.

"Oh, Mister..." she said upon my arrival. "I was just telling your friend here about my son's medal."

"It's Shea. Moses Shea." I handed her my Carthage business card. "Are you all right?"

"A bit bruised."

"No cuts?"

"I wear a lot of padding."

Manny was studying the ground with keen attention.

"That's the one area I can't do very well," she said, pointing where she fell.

When he volunteered to spell her, she relented and handed over the metal detector, urging him to be careful. He went off like a firewalker and soon he was sweeping the area. More than once he struggled to retain his balance as he maneuvered and squatted and kneeled, retrieving here a coin, there a spoon, and there a rusty key.

As Mrs. Ramella and I watched him work, she updated me on her son. She told me Fabio was having doubts about the direction his life was taking. His professor was sleeping around with various other Antifa members. She always seemed to be attracted to the most violently insane. Anonymous donors were flying them to different cities around the country, but Fabio didn't see much good coming from it. He'd witnessed the accidental shooting of a child in Chicago and it upset him. He was reading a lot and spoke of trusting a man named Gandalf. Gandalf wouldn't be a big Antifa supporter, he texted.

"Is Gandalf Italian?" Mrs. Ramella asked.

"No. He's a wizard in a fictional world."

"I don't believe in wizards."

"He's a type of Christ. I like Fabio's comment. It's hopeful."

Manny was standing motionless in a remote corner of the rubble, holding up a silver chain with a medal dangling from it. The sunlight paused on the scene as if the sky were taking his photograph. Then we heard a tremulous male voice exerting itself from the woods below us.

"Stop there! Stop there!" These vociferations heralded the appearance of a strange figure inside a purple uniform, like a man stuck in an eggplant.

"Help!" the eggplant man cried. "It's Deputy Nachman."

"Do you mean 'Stop?'" Manny asked politely.

"Stop!" he cried.

The eggplant man held at arm's length a weapon, which seemed to fight him every step of the way. It swung around, veered maniacally from high to low, tugged him in two directions at once, and levelled off before sweeping the distant horizon. One suspected that it and Deputy Nachman were long-time adversaries and the day would soon come when one of them went bang for the last time. Nonetheless, a polished leather holster hung from the deputy's duty belt, along with the customary flashlight, handcuffs, radio, pepper spray canister, magazine pouch, knife, and telescopic side-handle baton. When Mrs. Ramella reached for a large white handkerchief, Deputy Nachman responded by radioing for backup. From the east side of campus, a siren flared up.

"I'm putting my gun away," he announced as if to an army on the east-west highway.

The deputy holstered his service weapon without incident. He extricated the handcuffs from his duty belt and approached us.

I said, "You've got to be kidding."

"This is none of your business," he said unconvincingly. Then he addressed Mrs. Ramella. "You've been apprehended for trespassing on private property. Please turn around and put your hands behind your back."

The desperado in question, having had a good pull on her handkerchief, did not turn around as requested and put her hands behind her back. Instead, she started cursing the deputy in Italian, a language that houses a magnificent collection of swearwords, unparalleled in history when it comes to cataloging the anatomical grotesqueries of our oversexed species. I must say I was surprised and gratified by Mrs. Ramella's soaring eloquence. I deeply appreciated the operatic style of her delivery, which owed more to *opera buffa* than to *bel canto*, that is, more to the unrestrained, sunny lands of the south than to the refined, law-abiding regions of the north. Then she kicked Deputy Nachman in the nuts.

The deputy being thus occupied, ex-NYPD Manny Murphy slipped off undetected. He stepped behind a tree and watched Sergeant Nachman arrive in the BV. She rocketed into view at warp speed before screeching to a halt, burning rubber up and down the length of the parking lot. Her light bars and siren swirled and blared in monstrous anticipation. Next, the siren ceased as the lights went on flashing, the driver's door opened, and a black boot gripped the pavement. Sergeant Nachman had arrived on the scene, a grim-faced soldier of the law, armed and ready behind her inscrutable shades.

"Good work, Deputy Nachman," she said, jerking her chin at Mrs. Ramella. "This one's been on my list for a long time."

Crumpling to the ground in a fetal position, the deputy was unable to reply.

Fortunately, Sergeant Nachman was a woman who knew her duty. She didn't let her devotion to her husband interrupt her important work. A moment earlier, when Mrs. Ramella resisted arrest, the handcuffs had gone leaping from Deputy Nachman's hands like a trout. Sergeant Nachman retrieved them and ordered Mrs. Ramella to turn around. Just at this crucial juncture, however, the light bars on the BV unexpectedly stopped flashing.

Manny stood calmly by the driver's door, dangling a loaded key-ring from between his thumb and index finger. In his other hand, he held a Glock 19, pointed muzzle down.

"Wow," he said. "This is some high-end Navy Seal shit."

"Uh, uh, uh, uh—" The sound was coming from the grass.

"You're Mr. Carty's driver! What do you think you're doing?"

"Uh, uh, uh, uh—"

"You have no right."

"Uh, uh, uh, uh—"

"Hey, meatball!" Manny called to Deputy Nachman. "What the hell's wrong with you?"

"Can't move," the deputy gasped. "Uh, uh, uh, uh—"

Deputy Nachman lay stricken beside a few dead leaves. The daylight fell apathetically on his abject, eggplant body. It seemed that nature wanted nothing to do with him.

"Look," Manny said considerately. "What you want to do is squat and get your breath back. Like this."

"Uh, uh, uh, uh—"

Manny waited patiently but Deputy Nachman was out of service.

"Now take off your duty belts and leave them on the ground. Come on. We don't have all day."

The sergeant's hand twitched above the holster that held ol' Sam. I couldn't see her eyes but I'm sure they were glued to Manny's Glock. Her draw would need to be extraordinarily quick. At last, the peeling of Velcro announced that Sergeant Nachman was surrendering her duty belt. The deputy complied on his end by lying on his back, undoing the belt, and, after several failed attempts, rolling onto his belly. The sergeant scowled and glared. "What are you going to do with us?" she snapped. One moment she'd been in peak form. The next she was shown up like a rookie, checkmated in one, humiliated in front of an infiltrator. Behind those mirrored shades, I sensed that dangerous gears were spinning. Someone or something had pushed the wrong button.

"I was looking around for a suggestion box," Manny replied.

Gathering their belts, he returned to the BV and dumped them in the trunk. He took a snack bar from the front seat and tossed it underhand to Sergeant Nachman, who was in no mood to play catch. It sailed straight past her and smacked her husband on his plump purple duff. Making sure the car doors were locked, Manny dropped the key-ring in after the belts. Then he slammed the trunk shut.

"Okay," he said. "You're free to go. Have a nice day."

Mrs. Ramella helped Deputy Nachman to his feet. "Sorry I kicked you in the balls," she said. "I guess I lost my temper."

"That's okay," the deputy said affably. "I don't like being handcuffed either." His gaze fell significantly on the sergeant, but she wasn't looking at him.

"Mr. Shea."

Once more, she succeeded in stopping me dead in my tracks.

"You have aided and abetted an infiltrator."

"I wouldn't get too beat up about it, sergeant. As a matter of fact, I don't think you'll have to worry about this particular infiltrator ever again. Manny, what was it you found over there?"

Donna Ramella's face took on a quizzical expression. Then her old brown eyes lit up. Manny replied by pulling the chain and medal out of his pocket and passing them to her. He seemed embarrassed when she sank to her knees. She was clutching the medal to her bosom and rocking back and forth in inarticulate prayer. She stood up and hugged Manny. She hugged me too. She hugged Deputy Nachman and they started sobbing.

Sergeant Nachman hung her head in shame.

"Mr. Shea?"

"Yes, Sergeant Nachman?"

"You had best be going. I consider this only a truce in our ongoing—"

"Dalliance?" I suggested.

"Battle. I ask you to call Triple A and depart forthwith."

"Forthwith? I always liked forthwith. The suffix does a lot of work."

"She's very smart," Deputy Nachman said loyally.

"You disgust me," Sergeant Nachman replied.

"Here," I said. "You can use my phone. Just return it when you're done."

"It'll be in the Public Safety office, on the desk."

When Nick and I met that evening, my overdetermined phone was back in my possession. The hour was six o'clock. It was suppertime but the refectory was eerily dim and quiet. Nick, on the other hand, was full of life and dressed to the nines. His bespoke English suit fit him beautifully. His jacket was unbuttoned so that his carmine tie sprawled indolently on his lap. He bounced to his feet as I entered the conference room as if it were his first meeting of the day.

"Moses, Moses, Moses," he said, as we shook hands across the table.

"We meet again, Colonel Ming," I said.

He raised a masterly forefinger while he speed dialed a contact on his phone. "I said six o'clock." Then his lips curled into an invincible smile. "You want to hear the good news or the bad news?"

"Always the good."

"I've smoothed out the differences between Arbuthnot and Liu. They're back on speaking terms and they've promised to keep working together. Also, the first week's A&R report was excellent. That's the good news."

"Great. What's the bad news?"

"Ann Fitz is threatening to quit and we have two spies on the payroll."

"Two? Who's the second?"

"I have to hire a new chef."

"Gladstone?!"

"He absconded this afternoon along with one of the tech guys who worked on Hannibal. Buford Blandings. Buford came with the start-up. Acne, bad moustache. Anyway, I had a chat earlier today with FBI counterintelligence. They were just about to contact me, they said. Can you believe those clowns? I don't think they have a clue about Tatiana Kuznetsov. As for Gladstone and Blandings, they're halfway to China by now."

"Can't they catch them at the airport?"

"No. They'll go through Mexico. That border exists only on maps. Look, it's right over here, by my elbow."

Mago entered looking freshly cut out of the white radiance of eternity. White hair, white shirt, white suspenders, white trousers, white shoes. He himself was white. He was balancing a bottle of white wine and two glasses on a little white tray.

I said, "Hi, Mago. I like your outfit."

"Thank you so much," he said, depositing the wine and glasses on the table-top. "How are things in the twentieth century?"

I had underestimated Mago, who left with the wreath of victory on his brow.

"I don't want to lose Ann," Nick said, pouring the wine—a Château Cheval Blanc. It had a knockout bouquet and it tasted like money. Satisfied, I placed my glass in the Indian Ocean.

"Why not?"

"Because Ann is smart. She understands systems analysis. She keeps up with the tech. She's an advertising pro. You follow me? She writes great reports—I'll come back to that. She stays on budget. She's a superb communicator."

"That's funny, because I can hardly understand a word she says. It always ends with a question mark. I'm Ann Fitz? I live on planet Earth?"

"I'll tell you something else and I ask you to please listen. Ann is extremely well connected."

"You don't say."

"She suspects you're a total reactionary. But the fact that Kuznetsov was behind the recent incidents gives you a second chance."

He scrutinized my non-response.

"Did she confess about the octopus?"

"Yes."

"How on earth did she get it to go under Ann's door?"

"A sardine. The door wasn't flush with the carpet. There's a narrow space, and that's all an octopus needs."

He nodded in appreciation and we sipped our Château Cheval Blanc, two clubbable men catching up.

"What did you do with our lovely Russian?" he asked at length.

"I put her to work cleaning the place."

"You what?"

"She hadn't been doing it—cleaning, I mean."

It's hard to surprise Nicholas Percival Carty, but I had succeeded. He shot a warm gust through his nose hairs and sank back in his burgundy seat. He reached for his wine glass and tossed it down. Then he tilted his head back and meditated.

"I'll find a use for her," he said.

"Whatever you do, don't forget to hire a new cleaning lady. This place is starting to look like a dump."

"All right, old boy. I'll make a note of it. Now here's a couple things you can do for me. First, will you please tell Ann you like her poetry?"

"You think Ann Fitz writes poetry?"

"Here we go."

"I'll tell you the one thing I found out about her and poetry. She took out the editor of a prominent poetry magazine with a single tweet. Ruined him like that. They replaced the guy with a political consultant."

"I'm sorry to hear that."

"Who cares?"

"You know, you're right about things, Moses. Often you are. But you exhaust me. I hear Mia isn't well, by the way."

"I didn't know you two were still in touch."

"Do you still have that note she sent you?"

I passed that one up.

"She mentioned it to me."

I poured the wine and we took our time with it.

"Too bad there are no female popes," he said. "She'd have made a good one."

"You could be Joan of Arc."

"What the hell is that supposed to mean?"

"Just a thought."

I stared out the window. The lampposts outside Dido Hall cast a faint light but did little to illuminate the scene. I wondered where everybody had gone.

"Now here's something else we need to go over. It's a little sensitive."

"Ann Fitz is a little sensitive."

"Will you shut up and listen? That last report—Sleep On and Edge Off—was more than excellent. It was over-the-top sensational. Just so you know, Ann included you in the report. That was some fine work you did."

"Thank you. I enjoyed it."

"Good. Now as I say, this is a sensitive issue. The fact is all six of these workers are highly valuable employees."

"I agree."

"I suspect Mal Osgood is unusually talented."

"I do too."

"You and he seem to get along."

"Honestly, Nick, we haven't spent that much time together."

"Well, Ann's jealous."

"I think she has a problem with boys."

"Maybe. Maybe not. We have an opportunity here, Moses. Osgood's family history is—how shall we say?—more than a little peculiar. When he was a small boy an older couple named Osgood adopted him. I've looked into it. His real name is Malachi Knott. His adoptive father died three months ago. The man spent four decades at Langley. A case officer. Highly respected by his colleagues."

My mind raced to place this information alongside what I'd gleaned from Judge Phoenix. Also, the realization came to me, right at that moment, as his image floated up before my mind's eye, that Mal Osgood was somewhat less physically attractive than his co-workers. He wasn't a bad-looking boy, not at all, but with his eye teeth and that mole on his cheek he paled in comparison to the others, who really had no physical imperfections. As regards sheer brainpower, though, he was likewise the outlier. I nodded along to show Nick I was paying attention.

"My point is that a young genius who was orphaned as a boy is in a special position to make this company his home, to invest in it emotionally, the way I have done."

"What about your son, Simon?"

"He's not my son."

"The red hair?"

"A coincidence. My dear Marcia cheated on me. Actually, I don't mind. Simon's father is an interesting guy. Used to host a talk show. A fun man to vacation with. Simon's a nice kid, just not super brainy. I'll find a place for him."

"Are you going to tell him?"

"Osgood? We'll see."

"I hear you're off to Davos."

"Ah, yes. The 'Woke Vatican,' as a friend of mine calls it. You should see those clever boys when they go off the deep end. They're terrified about enjoying themselves. Honestly, they make me feel like a pimp. They don't even know what cash looks like."

"Unlike yourself."

"If I recall, we're here today because I bumped into you at a taco stand."

"You were slumming."

"I suppose there's something wrong with slumming?"

I let it go.

"Well, enjoy Switzerland," I said, rising to my feet. I felt a touch dizzy drinking wine on an empty stomach. My destiny lay with the burger stand in downtown Clifden.

He raised his glass to bid me a friendly goodnight. It

wasn't in my nature to betray him. But there was something else, something we took with us from our college days, an interest in the machinery of fate and the lives of great men. Nick had the ability to be impartially interested in the story of his own life, and I joined him in that interest. We inhabited the same vocabulary, the same ancient names and dates, the same anecdotes about sex and suicide and the gods. He was as sensitive to my essential Christianity as I was to his essential paganism. We possessed the means of mutual understanding, and the experience was valuable to us both.

When I got back to my rooms, I found that Paris Allan had slipped a new Jupiter Jefferson story under my door. It was called "The Fable of B."

All was not peaceful in Alphabet Land. Things had gone fairly smoothly since the days of the Romans—despite a few minor hitches here and there, the letters had worked it out and stayed together. But suddenly there was trouble on the street. Everyone was quarreling over little things. Q and U were sick of each other. The vowels and consonants were at odds. Z wanted to change the order. X thought he was too cool for Y. K was tired of being silent. Soon the whole crew had had it with rules and obligations. They drew up lists and compared beefs.

At an emergency meeting, B became upset because he felt short-changed in the realm of numbers. "I'm an important letter," B said. "Why should I have to wait all the way to a billion just to get in the game?" "But a billion is really big," A pleaded. "Not as big as a zillion," B replied. The next day, B had had enough. B walked and the alphabet disbanded—like the Beatles.

Chapter 8

Getting Odd

Arbuthnot was first to arrive at office hours the following afternoon. She breezed through the door with her hands in her pockets, not pausing to shake hands as she toured the premises from the elegant vantage of her height. She varied her style of dress from day to day, oscillating between casual and formal, a pendulum of fashion. The day before it was pink exercise togs. Today her attire was formal—a pinstripe suit, an oxford shirt, a paisley necktie. She sprinkled her quirkiness with bohemian charm, often favoring sandals in winter, as was now the case. She complimented me on the room and asked how I liked it, though she scarcely seemed interested in my response. As if in afterthought, she asked if I'd been talking with Quinones.

"Not yet," I said. "That is, if you're referring to this week's agenda."

"A gender scenario," she said, facing the cold fireplace. "Do you think a suit can do justice to a woman's hips?"

"Did you say that to your college professor?"

She whirled around and, to my surprise, her eyes teared up. I returned presently with a box of tissues. "I actually feel pretty lousy about that," she said. "He really was flirtatious but I wasn't a child and I ruined his career. The problem is they treat you like children."

"You let them treat you like children."

"There's all this legal stuff to contend with. It's an impossible situation."

Someone knocked softly. Arbuthnot needed to blow her nose, so I waited before opening the door. It was Liu with Sinclair.

"Hi, Kay," Liu said warily.

"Hello, Miss Arbuthnot," Sinclair added in a humorous British accent meant to lighten the mood. "Did you eat my biscuits?"

"Miss Sinclair, I fed those stale biscuits to your dog. He was starving. You really need to feed the poor creature."

"Poor? That poor creature owns 51% of the biscuit business. Don't let him fool you. He's a miserly wretch."

I switched on the gas in the fireplace and we arranged ourselves for our work on Hydria Technologies.

"Girls versus boys," Arbuthnot reminded us. She had nabbed the club chair.

"Good versus evil," Sinclair said, clarifying the situation.

"They're toast," Liu added for good measure. She and Sinclair were now ensconced at opposite ends of the chesterfield. I kept my station by the fire.

For starters, I floated a brief passage from *Hydriotaphia*. "'In vain do individuals hope for immortality, or any patent from oblivion, in preservations below the moon; men have been deceived in their flatteries even above the sun, and studied conceits to perpetuate their names in heaven.'"

Arbuthnot responded with a smart question:

"Is the drive for immortality instinctive?"

"I would think so," Liu said. "A great artist might accept physical oblivion, but he would still want his work to survive."

Arbuthnot said, "Because for a great artist, her immortal soul *is* her art."

"Which raises another question," Liu rejoined. "Hydria wants to corner the academic market, but does academia have any great artists?"

"They certainly think so," Sinclair said.

I said, "Who?"

"The professors, *mon cher professeur*," said Sinclair.

"You run the risk," I said, feeling the strength of the flames on my calves, "of suggesting that academics consider themselves superior to the great artists of the past."

"They strike me as a very self-confident group," Liu said. "The problem is when they retire. That's when reality hits."

"All they need is a little encouragement," Arbuthnot said. "That old author talks about how flatteries deceive. We need to persuade our customers that we aren't deceiving them—that they're worthy of eternal monuments."

"It could be a touch tricky," Sinclair acknowledged. "Those urns aren't cheap."

"Colleges might include them in their benefits packages," Arbuthnot suggested.

"That's a good thought," I said. "But we'll still have to close the deal psychologically."

Again it was Arbuthnot who saw us through.

"Can we bring social justice into the picture?"

"I wouldn't try humor."

"I'm totally serious," she said, looking totally serious.

Sinclair picked up the thread. "Whatever doubt retired professors may have about the quality of their work will be offset by their devotion to social justice. We can strengthen their delusions of grandeur with the pretense that they're morally superior. They'll never know."

I said, "It feels like selling the pyramids to suckers."

"I like that," Arbuthnot replied. "The idea of building

your own pyramid is pretty good. I think a lot of people would be interested."

"I was referring to human vanity. Look up Dr. Johnson on pyramids."

Her thumbs went flying and she read aloud the words on her screen. "The pyramids seem to have been erected only in compliance with that hunger of imagination which preys incessantly upon life." She met my inquisitive gaze with a faint smile that conveyed her dawning recognition of her own consummate genius. "What about social justice pyramids?" she said.

I said, "That could be the dumbest idea I've ever heard." Liu giggled and Sinclair emitted a canary-throated laugh. But Arbuthnot knew she was onto something.

"Bet it'll work!" she said. "We can easily adjust the urn-concept to sell pyramids as well. The urn could simply be shaped like a pyramid. Honestly, why not?"

Liu's approval sealed the deal and the women left in high spirits, all past discord behind them. They felt they had a winner in social justice pyramids and were confident of being on the road to victory.

As their jocund voices receded, the hallway seemed lifeless. Then I was surprised by the apparition of a man with a grave, sympathetic face. I would have guessed thirty-five. He approached in what appeared to be a valet's get-up—dark vest and jacket, white shirt, black necktie, gray striped trousers and, it is important to note, a bowler hat. He held me in the grip of his fastidious gaze, turned to one side, and called in a somber British voice to someone in the parlor.

"The coast is clear, sir."

At that moment Quinones entered my field of vision like an ice skater who has just landed a triple-axel. His tight black jacket exposed a silk white shirt, which shimmered on his

Taurean chest. His shoes were polished to a blinding luster, and not a wrinkle could be found on his person.

"All right," he said to the man, who regarded him with benevolence.

"Who's that?" I said to Quinones as he sauntered through my door.

"Who's who?" he said, seating himself.

I said, "The man in the hall?"

"Who?" he said.

I walked right up and shouted in his face.

"Who's the man in the hall, Rico?"

"What do you mean? There's nobody in the hall."

I went back to see. Sure enough, there was nobody in the hall. I elected to drop the matter. Some things prefer not to be explained. A curious phenomenon no matter which way you look at it, the world's existence, but the sooner you learn to live with it, the less likely you are to become a social engineer.

"Boys versus girls, huh?" Quinones said.

"We had a good discussion."

He smiled rakishly. "Any brilliant ideas?"

I started with the famous lines by John Donne.

As well a well-wrought urn becomes
The greatest ashes, as half-acre tombs.

That got us nowhere, so I served up a couple passages from Sir Thomas Browne, but left Dr. Johnson out of it, considering Johnson to be Arbuthnot territory.

"I remember that from my Borges class," he commented. "It's kind of a womb-tomb thing, isn't it?"

"Yes. That's one of Browne's conceits. The urn is like the womb. Similar shape, similar oblivion." I elaborated on my concept of nicking Browne's language while omitting his worldview. Quinones attended politely as I read aloud a lengthy passage, but he vetoed my final sentence with a firm shake of his handsome quiff.

"It's good except the part about life being a pure flame. I wouldn't say that to a customer who plans on being cremated. Too many flames in the mix."

"Good point."

"But I have another worry. What if the urn begins to feel like a trap? An eternal prison. Do you see?"

This was Irish territory, I mused—shades of Samuel Beckett and Flann O'Brien rising up in some hellish tavern, whiskies on the bar. The old Ireland of sin and famine. Gone were the bad old days, but gone too was the hardscrabble island that could send forth its poets to rival the English in their own language and make the nations bow. Gone were the days of world-class heretics. The new gods of Dublin were a dull, dull lot.

"Prof?"

"I hadn't thought of it that way, but again I see your point. What if, instead of relieving people's anxieties about death, we're actually making them worse?"

"Exactly. The only solution is to make the good outweigh the bad. Like Christianity."

"Honestly, Rico, that may be how it seems to an outsider but Christians wouldn't think of it that way. For Christians, life is more of a test—a field of endeavor. We think of the soul as a given. The individual soul goes out into the world and then returns to God for judgment. In our eyes, a human being couldn't exist without a soul. You'd be some bizarre animal making noises. An arrangement of animated matter—nothing more."

"Funny, I was thinking of the soul right before you said that. Could owning this product be considered an improvement over having a soul?"

"An improvement? Well, there'd be a great gain in safety, that's for sure."

"What do you mean by *safety*?"

"Heaven and Hell aren't for the faint of heart. And you can't have one without the other. Now think of being judged for all eternity."

"What about Purgatory?"

"Protestants don't believe in it."

He rocked around in his seat and started to experiment. He said, "Your soul is safer in a Well-Wrought Urn. Something along those lines...like an insurance policy?"

"We'd have to develop it."

"It would work better if Hell actually existed but you could somehow get around it."

"Get around it?"

"Like hiring a smart lawyer."

"What do you mean?" I said.

"A fallback. An alternative to...what do you call it? Judgment."

"A Plan B?"

"Exactly—a Plan B. So you could take death to heart but not let it ruin your life." He spoke slowly and with considerable determination.

If the Church is not for thee
Try Plan B.

Then we worked on variations.

If you committed heresy
Try Plan B.

And

To be or not to be?
Try Plan B.

And

If you think God is history
Try Plan B.

And best of all

If safety's your priority
Try Plan B.

We ended up amusing ourselves, if not making much solid progress. I followed him out to the door where we discovered Osgood sprawled in the Windsor chair, black tie at half-mast. Quinones asked if he'd spoken to Allan.

"Not yet."

"The girls are way ahead of us."

"I'll text you later."

It turned out Osgood hadn't come to discuss advertising. He crossed the room, flopped on the sofa, and stared at the ceiling. He fidgeted, opened his flap to speak, shut it, and stared some more. It was a fine ceiling. It had a smoke alarm on it.

I decided it was time to open a bottle of the house wine. I made brisk work of the cork and set the bottle and glasses on the low glass table. Then I pulled up my club chair.

"Well, what is it, my beamish boy?"

"You think Nick ran into you at that taco stand by accident?"

"Could you say that again?"

"It wasn't an accident. Nick planned it out. He wanted you to mentor me."

It was one of those times when you think you're seeing the whole picture from your nose to the horizon and suddenly every inch of perspective collapses and you find yourself face to face with a pile of bricks.

I raised the glass to my lips and said a blessing. It might not have pleased Nick's exquisite palate, but it was nonetheless the best wine in the world for restoring the bloom of life. Recently, I'd picked up a case of the stuff through a wine seller in the city of Wormtown. The vintner was an immigrant from Calabria, but by a stroke of rare good fortune he knew about it—a small French winery called *Le Fou*. The mysterious owner of the vineyard shunned publicity. It seemed *Le Fou* made its way to America only via providence. I first discovered it in a wine shop in Chinatown, in San Francisco, among the reds in a discount barrel with a foolish sign that said *Kung Fou* and a neatly drawn gargoyle on the label, smiling like an old gossip. I never knew when I would stumble on it again but I usually remembered to ask. The Italian guy somehow had a connection. Just one case, he said. The price was very reasonable.

Already I felt the leaves nodding and the buds opening in the sun.

"Look here, Mal," I said. "Nick and I go back a long ways. It's hard to believe he'd set me up like that."

"I promise you, he did. And it was a smart move. You're a wiz at languages and we're both Catholic—creating the likelihood of a bond. Yet there's some other thing as well. Something you two shared in the past...I don't know."

"Nick wants you to rise through the ranks. He thinks you're executive material."

"You know what he told me?"

"What?"

"I could have all the power in the world."

I sipped from my glass and let my thoughts sort themselves out. It was certainly an elaborate scheme. I wondered when Nick thought of it and whether any of it had to do with Mia. It might have all unfolded unconsciously, whatever Nick thought he was aiming at. Two rivals battling unto death—not a new plot, only the manifestation of a drive in the male psyche that wouldn't go away until men went away. Or maybe I reminded Nick of his Roman Catholic father.

"Does he know you have relatives in town?"

"I don't know what he knows."

The patient remained horizontal. Frozen rain was ticking at the window, but the gargoyle on the bottle smiled encouragingly.

"I spoke with them today—my relatives. I used to call them aunt and uncle."

"So how are you related?"

"Not by blood."

He reached out an arm and touched the stem of his wine glass. He didn't drink from it. He nudged it, and squeezed it gently with his fingers as he spoke.

"This gets a little complicated," he said. "My mother's a widow in Arlington named Jean Osgood. But the woman who brought me into this world was named Beth Knott. She died twenty years ago. I never learned what from. Her mother Claire was my aunt's stepmother."

"Beth and your aunt were stepsisters."

"Correct. My aunt is Mary Phoenix, John Phoenix's wife. Beth came into the family when Mary's father, Tyrone Knott, married Claire after Mary's mother passed away. Beth was a high school girl when Claire married Tyrone. Mary was much older than her stepsister."

"Who's your biological father?"

"No idea. The summer after high school, Beth moved to Manhattan. She put me up for adoption when I was three."

He sat up and tasted his wine.

"That's all I know, prof. This is delicious, by the way."

"It's an interesting story, but why confide in me?"

"It's this dinner I've been invited to. I don't want to be alone among strangers. You think you could make it?"

"Is that girl going?"

"What girl?"

"Never mind. Of course, I'll go."

"Did you hear about this crazy lawsuit?"

"Your uncle versus your boss."

"I wonder who planned that."

Early the next morning, I emailed an ambiguous excuse to

the group, including Nick and Ann Fitz, and visited Manhattan.

Olwin Bright had requested a meeting. Her email, which arrived around the time I was saying goodbye to Osgood, was composed in a telegraphic style:

Open position. Book review editor. Urgent. Requesting interview noon tomorrow.

Before daybreak, I was driving through the Connecticut Valley to New Haven, where I parked the Mercury at the train station, grabbed a coffee and a doughnut, actually two doughnuts, and boarded the commuter rail to Grand Central.

I got into town around eleven and hopped the shuttle to Times Square. The subway riders were stone-faced and unavailable. At the end of the line we stepped onto a subterranean concourse that smelled like spoiled meat and swarmed with confident vermin and their heirs. Emerging on Seventh Avenue, I slogged past curbsides where the mad and the homeless lay fallen among needles and trash. On a sidewalk where a row of theaters shrank back in a tubercular fog, a wild-eyed young man wrapped in a bedsheet handed me a slip of paper.

EMERGENCY!
READ OUR REPORT!
PREPARE YOURSELF!
THE SEAL OF TIME IS BROKEN!

Somebody tried to grab him and he ran off naked, his bedsheet slipping to the sidewalk.

Bad magic was drifting over the continent and New York was among the troubled cities. The blight of graffiti defaced once healthy streets, sprayed like liquid cancer on masonry and padlocked roll-downs. A few brave restaurants peddled their trade to skittish foot traffic. On 42nd Street I heard gunshots. A hot dog vendor in a green army jacket stuck to his post. His colorful umbrella stood firm. On Eighth Avenue, outside the Times' Times Building, a police cruiser swerved to avoid a dancing bum. Someone hurled a bottle, which skipped off the cruiser's hood, sailed into the crosswalk, and hit an old lady on the leg. She limped resolutely on.

The iconic sign in the front of the Times' Times Building continued to greet New Yorkers with the paper's famous motto, "You are living in the *Times' Times*." I hadn't been inside the place for over a year. The moment I entered, a woman with a third eye tattooed on her forehead demanded the purpose of my visit. She was elaborately dressed for a security guard. Her gray uniform flashed and sparkled along the gig line with gold buttons of various sizes, which were incised with a zodiac of emblems—yonis, navels, caterpillars, mushrooms, worms, planets, comets, flowers. Before I could make sense of this arrangement, she directed me to a second guard, who sat behind a desk and demanded the deed to my house.

"But I have an appointment."

"You still need to make a statement."

This guard had a very youthful appearance. She seemed almost a child, but she presided over her desk with elaborate authority. Instead of fancy buttons, she wore golden epaulettes, displaying a plus sign (+) on one, and a minus sign (–) on the other. Recognizing the stunned expression of a dystopian tourist, she pointed to a poster on the wall: "Admittance of visitors will be based on their expressed commitment to Diversity, Equity, and Inclusion."

"I have nothing to say."

"Just say the first word that pops into your head."

She held up a set of flash cards.

"RACE."

"Olympics."

"WHITENESS."

"Paper."

"SPACE."
"Time."
"GENDER."
"Biology."
"INTERSECTIONAL."
"Crosswalk."
"SYSTEMIC."
"Circulatory."
"REPRESENTATION."
"Mimesis."
"UNITED STATES."
"Home."

"Please stand over there," she said, her ruby red fingernail directing me to a cubicle.

I traversed the floor to a desk that was bare except for two things: a ticket machine that dispensed strips of duct tape and a screen where an instructional video kept repeating. The video was directing me to place a piece of duct tape over my mouth while, from across the building, I heard a distant rumbling sound like the coming round the bend of a Big Boy steam engine. I was doing my best with the tape when the boa constrictions of a panic attack became imperative. Then, as I was wrestling with the snake on my rib cage, a third guard loomed up before me, an eclipse in jackboots, wide as a tank and tall as a missile.

It took time to process the full picture, but the snake on my rib cage seemed, in a frightening vision, to be transferred to her hair. The other two guards were gazing at me and I thought I saw snakes in their hair as well. More immediately concerning, though, was the complete absence of cloth or covering for the colossal crotch before me. I looked once and ducked, for fear my Lilliputian head would be chewed and devoured by unimaginable teeth.

"I'm here to escort you to the elevator," the third guard

explained in a surprisingly civil tone of voice. "Tenth floor. If you need to use a restroom, try the Hilton."

I comprehended by now that, up and down the sides of her sleeves and pantlegs, sharp gold spikes bristled in rows. She escorted me to the nearest elevator and more than once I swerved to avoid her driving forearm, which was cranking like a piston by my ear. In the elevator bay, she inched closer. Not a moment too soon, a bell rang and the door opened. Inside the elevator car stood an assembly of persons in bug-colored topcoats, motionless as photographs in a montage, except for an occasional twitch here and there like a crack in the dimension of space. A criminal hardness froze their faces and if you looked closely you could see their eyes clicking back and forth. I recognized some of them—I'd seen them lying carefully on Capitol Hill and lying brazenly on news shows—but others had their hats pulled low over their eyes. As they disembarked, I slipped in behind. A recorded voice chimed in dulcet tones, "You are living in the *Times' Times*."

I ascended to the tenth floor, where I stepped out of the elevator and ripped the duct tape from my mouth. It was a busy place, gophers scuttling along hallways and faces blinking at me from cubicles. A woman of my generation, topless and wearing a bone through her nose, looked up from her photocopies and glared with open hostility. Layoffs and firings were routine at the *Times' Times*, and a great deal had changed in a short amount of time. The only head I recognized was that of a recent editorial page editor. It was impaled on a stake amidst a grove of potted olive trees. I remembered him well. He was critical of rightwing Christian intellectuals, but he was willing to hear them out. He used to occupy a charming bourgeois office decorated with a framed quotation from John Stuart Mill: "He who knows only his own side of the case, knows little of that."

Olwin Bright's office door swung open as I started to

knock. The Editor-in-Chief continued her phone call without interruption. I entered and her foot shut the door behind me.

Over to my left, a chrome coffee table, cluttered with copies of the *Times' Times*, abutted the long glass wall that overlooks Eighth Avenue. The chairs were chrome frames with lime upholstery. Olwin Bright occupied the one nearest the door, and a zebra throw pillow rested in another. I removed my coat and hat and piled them with the rest of my gear atop the zebra pillow. On the far wall, a wooden bookcase organized some hardcover books that turned out to be outdated reference works. The bottom shelves were given over to a sprawling arrangement of loose-leaf notebooks, boxes, and cardboard mailing tubes. The wall-to-wall carpet was a hard-wearing brown. The only sign of cheer in the room was a small aquarium that housed a solitary clownfish, swimming peacefully among the bubbles.

Olwin Bright, cross-legged and barefoot, was evidently enjoying her phone call. "You told them Critical Rage Theory was patriotic?...You're kidding me!...How marvelous!" She wiggled her toes. "I blame the parents...I don't think children are really upset by that kind of thing...."

Ending her call, she turned her attention to me. It was a dangerous position to be in. Olwin Bright was a wizard of infinite craft. The ability to manufacture lies, disguises, and traps is a universal mark of executive talent, but her ability was layered, dense, and calculating to a level of sophistication that crossed like beautiful weaponry into the realm of the aesthetic. The game between us wasn't the ordinary ape clash. It was a subtler struggle for authority like a war between two novelists bent on reducing each other to a minor character in one's own superior fiction.

"All the time I knew you," she said, as I sat down in the chair beside her, "I was aware of two things. One, that we had serious differences. And two, that you were actually quite gifted. My worry was that you couldn't adapt to changing circumstances." A pageboy haircut framed her face, black hair on a pale cheek. Her blouse and jeans were black. Some subtler mirror-work lurked in her silver choker necklace and, descending over the breastbone, a stiletto of white flesh. "I don't want you to be misled. Book reviewing is a dangerous business. It comes with an interesting set of risks and rewards." Her lips were red and warm, her eyes gray and cold. "Our previous editor, poor Edie, didn't last six weeks. She couldn't stick to our point system. It's a simple thing and it's all we ask. Do you know about it?"

"I can't say I do."

"To make things easier we've put together a scoring guide. The basic principle is this: the greater the intersectionality, the more valuable the work. A novel about a quadriplegic black lesbian orphan adopted by an abusive white hetero couple and bartered into sexual slavery in exchange for logging rights in the Amazon rainforest would obviously be hard to beat, so long as it's written by an Afrodescendent author whose preferred gender is pan."

"So, if I understand correctly, I'd be given a scoring guide?"

"Yes. It's a key part of our editorial equipment."

"Do reviewers use the scoring guide?"

"Unfortunately, some of them refuse to do so. In particular, some of the older ones still show a tendency to 'go literary,' as we call it. It's odd, because all the major publishing houses encourage new authors to follow our system. We kind of leaked it to them."

Then she reached over to the coffee table, retrieved a 9x12 envelope from among the newspapers, and handed it to me. It was marked "Offer."

"Take your time," she said, retreating into her private office.

I unclasped the envelope and emptied its contents. The newly printed contract would put me in charge of the most influential book review in the country. It stipulated, however, that I would be subject to immediate dismissal if I did not abide by the intersectionality point system. I laid it on the coffee table along with the benefits sheet, which was more than satisfactory.

The scoring guide constituted the bulk of the envelope's contents. It was organized around the three major types of grievance—racism, sexism, and classism—but these painfully familiar *-isms* required multiple subheadings, which ran into dozens of pages. There were one hundred and forty-nine types of racism, depending on who was being racist, how "overtly" or "covertly" they were being racist, and who was the object of their racism. There were ninety-seven forms of sexism. There was only one form of classism, an *-ism* defined by cross-references to racism and sexism. A major factor was, of course, the author's own race, preferred gender, class, etc. Irregularities in the system occasioned a curious jargon that would require careful study. A lengthy appendix listed forbidden authors.

Olwin emerged, booted and bearing another 9x12 envelope.

"Well?"

"I can't do it."

"Why not?"

"Because I think you're the devil incarnate."

"I take it that's not a compliment from your point of view."

"This place makes me want to sprinkle holy water on the walls."

"Try saying something sensible for a change."

"If I had editorial discretion."

"Listen, you clown—and you are a clown, you're the biggest clown who ever went to Harvard, and the competition's thick—either you take this job on my terms, to the letter, mind you, or you're going to be facing some very unpleasant consequences."

She dropped the second envelope on the nasty carpeting at my feet.

"Open it." She smiled pleasantly. "You don't sign your contract, and that finds its way onto Twitter. It'll be a real tragedy. I won't be surprised if your boss fires you on the spot, to be quite honest with you. Public relations is everything these days. And the digital mob can be so vicious with their doxing."

It was a 5x7 glossy from a Halloween party on the Upper West Side, from my last year at the *Times' Times*, not long before Olwin's promotion. I was standing between Sam Fallo and Tom Baldock. We were drinking. Sam was costumed as a giant bottle of hydroxychloroquine, Baldock was Swan from *The Warriors*, and I was Ulysses S. Grant. I recalled renting the Civil War uniform—the brass buttons and gold stars, the field hat, the embroidered cuffs, and the stogie I picked up along the way in a Spanish cigar store on Amsterdam Avenue. I didn't seem to remember going in blackface.

"Blackmail, huh?"

"Funny."

"There were plenty of witnesses at that party."

"They'll be too scared to say anything, you dunce. You're on your own. Sign the contract, Moses. Welcome back to the *Times' Times*."

"I have a question for you, Olwin." She regarded me with bland indifference. "How did you get my email address?"

I sensed a slight pause, just a flicker of doubt, before she responded with steely self-control. "I am Editor-in-Chief of the *Times' Times*. No one questions my sources."

"Then you can do whatever you like," I said, tossing the photo onto the table next to everything else: the contract, the benefits package, the *Index Librorum Prohibitorum*. She seemed more puzzled than upset, like a child who feels drops of rain out of a blue sky. But as I gathered my things to go, something inside her snapped. A spasm of emotion seized her face and left it a wrack of blotches and wrinkles.

"You're a damn fool!" she yelled at my departing back.

Having escaped the Times' Times Building, I cabbed up to my apartment, poured a small whisky, and tried to settle my nerves—which were in no more mood to cooperate than a wise old basset hound is to visit the vet. I sensed that Nick was vulnerable to the political pressures that Olwin commanded. To maintain its grip on global markets, corporate America needed men like me to atone for certain sins. For that matter, men unlike me would do just as well, so long as they were some shade of white—pale, pink, albino, cream, tanned, olive, buff, ivory, fair, vanilla, whatnot. I wondered whether Leonard Fest would hire me back. Leonard was a decent man, but his trade rivals might exploit the situation. I was sitting there like a morose lump of lead when my father's ghostly voice broke through the gloom. "And can any of you by worrying add a single inch to your height?" As a teenager I was, you see, self-conscious about my height, being a "walking stump" according to my classmates, and Dad had responded by riffing on the Sermon on the Mount. I can't explain it but that was the cure to my adolescent brooding. It stole through my defenses and lifted me out of myself. Pouring another drink, I blew the dust off the family Bible and reread the entire Sermon, from the Beatitudes to the practical advice against building one's house on sand. I knew then and there that I would do nothing in the face of Olwin's tactics. It was out of my hands.

I was back on campus by noon on Friday. The new cleaning lady was already in action. Daniela was a pigeon-chested Albanian Christian who baked her own baklava. We hit it off right away. In a further development, Carthage had secured the services of a retired hotel chef willing to relocate from Providence. His name was Chef Duke and I'm sure he was well paid. Chef Duke was not pleased with Gladstone's kitchen arrangements, which forced him up on his tiptoes whenever he reached for an omelet pan. But if he lacked Gladstone's temperamental artistry, he was capable and easygoing, and Cowboy Joe enjoyed many days of peace and rest. In addition to the arrival of Daniela and Chef Duke, a dishwasher appeared in the recesses of the kitchen, a forlorn young man named Whitey, whose mother used to preside over the campus from the very building where he was now presiding over the Hobart. I gathered his story secondhand, but the gist of it is this. His childhood having been sacrificed for the greater good of Saint Malachy College and ultimately the world, he was having a hard time holding down a job. His twin brother, Blanco, was pumping gas at the local Zippo station.

Due to my absence on Thursday, both teams had been granted twenty-four-hour extensions. It meant I was in for a long afternoon. First, I met with the boys. When I mentioned my recent trip to New York, their response surprised me.

"No one reads the *Times' Times*," Quinones said dismissively.

"No one our age," Allan explained.

Quinones and Allan were working on the insurance idea and Osgood wasn't helping. After going back and forth on it, the two of them agreed that a Well-Wrought Urn could be an insurance policy only if it turned out that the inurned had written an overlooked masterpiece. "Don't take *Hamlet* to the grave," Allan said significantly. But I don't think he was really buying it.

Osgood wanted to know who would be discovering these lost *Hamlets*.

"I don't know," Allan said. "Researchers?"

"A type of person that will no doubt be conveniently plentiful in the future," Osgood snarked.

"Don't be such a cynic," Allan replied with dignity.

Allan was doing his best to make things work, but the boys were out of synch and the session wasn't working. Their catchiest idea, which seemed to originate with Quinones, was branding the Belizean chocolate as "Zuma," after Montezuma. By striking contrast, Sinclair, Liu, and Arbuthnot were in top form. As team leader, Arbuthnot had rallied the others to the cause of social justice pyramids. Sinclair's work on the Mayan gods was sensational. It turned out she had quite a gift for drawing. Liu improved the ideas issuing from her teammates, and she could draw pretty well herself. The girls sailed on to victory.

Chapter 9

Tied in Knotts

I was dressing for dinner when I heard Osgood's insistent knock. With a tie on each shoulder, I came to the door. "You're early," I said. He'd requested an Uber and we needed to hurry.

"What happened to your car?"

"It's in the shop."

"I could have driven."

"Go with the striped one," he said, racing off.

I gave myself a quick overhaul, grabbed my overcoat and striped tie, and rushed out after him. Under the porte-cochère, he stood hailing me from the rear door of a waiting sedan. I climbed in ahead and as he spoke to the driver my stubby fingers went to work looping and knotting—for some reason I can manage this feat without a mirror, an oddball talent that has come in handy over the years. I was only vaguely aware of the driver until, about ten minutes into our journey, we were slanting off the road and Osgood started screaming bloody murder. The driver was a slight young man whose numb manner never varied as he slammed on the brakes. He apologized for the inconvenience, saying he hoped to pay off his college loans before he totaled his car.

"Where did you go to college?" I asked him.

"Saint Malachy College," he said. "I majored in creative driving. Creative writing, I mean."

We soon arrived at our destination, a handsome ranch house on a fine suburban street in Clifden, Massachusetts. It had a flagpole in front, with Old Glory on it. The outside lights were on, illuminating the flag as well as the path to the front door, where Osgood gave the brass knocker a good solid whack.

The door inched open, revealing an elderly woman wearing a black-and-white dress and a crochet shawl.

"Hello, Aunt Mary," Osgood said. Her powdered face was bleached with age, sunken in the cheeks, sagging in the neck. Her eyes were blue and rheumy, and her gray wig matched her shawl. "Mal," she said tremulously. He stepped into the house and the two embraced.

"Close the door, Mary, and bring the boy inside," came a voice from within that I recognized.

We entered an atmosphere redolent of fish baking in the oven and fragrant smoke from a sumptuous fire. Trailing behind, I recognized Judge Phoenix sporting a cheerful red cardigan. He came forward on his long legs and wrapped Osgood in his arms. "Welcome," he said to us both. Behind him two others rose from their armchairs: the choleric fellow from the reading room and a Roman priest. Natalee Phoenix, outfitted in a charming silver-blue dress, remained demurely seated on an ottoman by the meshed fireplace. A sizable crucifix hung above the mantel, where many photos peered out from the past. As the judge introduced us to Professor Harold Farbarker and Father Charles Xatse, a young man flew out of the kitchen, took our coats, and withdrew without a word.

"He looks a bit like McGaffney," Professor Farbarker said, referring to me as if I were a zoo animal.

"He does look a bit like McGaffney," the judge agreed.

I said, "Must be a handsome fellow, this McGaffney."

"C. D. McGaffney," the bow-tied, tweed-wearing, scarlet-faced pedagogue informed me, "was an eminence in the Philosophy department. You know, Plato, Aristotle—that kind of thing."

I nodded.

"A couple years ago, the administration pressured his department into hiring a veteran of the Somali Navy. Nice enough fellow, but in fact he believed he was applying for a job in hotel management. It was the fault of the college's recruitment agency. I hesitate to use the popular term 'headhunters.' In the end, McGaffney wrote the Board of Trustees an angry letter defending the practice of philosophy. They summoned him to a meeting and fired him on the spot. The case is still in the courts."

Osgood and I remained standing while Professor Farbarker blasted away like a loose cannon on the deck at the Battle of Trafalgar. The judge and Natalee were eyeballing each other.

"I hear you folks have met."

"More than once," she remarked. The effect was of her slipping beyond the range of his questions. But the judge was not easily thwarted.

"When my granddaughter was five, they were putting up the house next door. One day, she went over there to retrieve her basketball and one of the exterior walls fell over, just where she was standing. The empty window frame saved her. She picked up her ball and went back to practicing free throws. I watched it happen with my own eyes."

"Just so you know," Natalee said, staring defiantly at

Osgood, who stood wondering at her. The judge seemed pleased with himself.

As Osgood and I sank into the plush couch, the olive-skinned young man who took our coats introduced himself in a Brazilian accent as Gianni. He directed our attention to a well-stocked bar in the adjoining room and said he was serving fish and pasta for dinner. As regards drinks, the judge preempted further deliberation by handing us each a large bumper of red.

"Just a nice table wine," he said, relaxing into his cushioned rocking chair.

Professor Farbarker explained they had been discussing the episcopate's response to the college's destruction. "They were too busy to address the matter. We heard little more than a noble squeak."

"Now, now, Harold," the judge said. "Things were happening fast."

The professor's lengthy snort was succeeded by Natalee's more mellifluous voice. "The only ones who figured things out were the older alums," she said. "They seem to have a harder nose for reality."

Professor Farbarker had more to say.

"Things didn't happen so fast in New York, Chicago, Atlanta, Philadelphia, Los Angeles, or Portland. Shall I go on? The destruction mounted, the poor suffered, and where was the USCCB?"

The question hung in the air like a pop up behind home plate. I make this comparison knowing full well that one will find no baseball metaphors in Shakespeare. And one will find no tilting fields in Beckett. It's a miracle anything coheres at all.

"They're just a bunch of political animals inside the Church. At the crisis's very height, the bishops of this state published a document called 'Faithful Citizenship.' Impeccable timing. Just when we needed actual Christian leadership, they pledged their support to politics. They should have been state assemblymen."

"I'm sure they mean well," Mrs. Phoenix said timidly.

"Render unto Caesar," Farbarker replied without sympathy. "In principle, I'm open to discussing what they call by the dreadful name of 'faithful citizenship.' But Caesar is not love. The current episcopal tendency is to deify Caesar. They put more faith in Facebook than in the rosary. They listen devoutly to NPR and pray novenas for President Jed Bartlet. They fail to recognize that their idea of faithful citizenship is demoralizing to the faithful, who do not worship charismatic leaders or beg God for a government handout. A properly formed conscience will be sensitive to the difference between God and Caesar." Finding a wide opening, the professor sipped his wine in preparation to launching a final salvo. "They ought to show the courage of their convictions. They ought to step the hell down and insist that four black auxiliary bishops replace them!"

"Ha!" said Natalee.

"The politician," Father Xatse said, "is a man enchanted by power, even when the situation calls for the utmost restraint. The priest is a man who must be wary of power, even when the situation calls for its exercise." Father Xatse was bald as a bowling ball, fiftyish, rather handsome, and he spoke in a Ghanaian accent. I realized it was he who called to thank me about a small check I gave to the annual fundraising drive at the local parish. I'd written on the memo line, "Not for political purposes," and he called to say he appreciated the sentiment and would honor my request. Now he continued, "I think it is a hard job being a bishop. Most of those men are good men. But they are under pressure from the reporters—and the reporters have it out for Mother Church. They want to take *Ecclesia* down. They are very optimistic about a future without Christ."

"I know a lot of crooked reporters," I said, pained by recent memories.

"He used to be one," Osgood put in.

"A crooked reporter?" Natalee inquired.

My grinning at Natalee's remark couldn't extinguish the heat I felt. "A prostitute earns her money honestly, at least in a market sense. Her heart may be open to conversion. A reporter is usually more like a shrewd and expensive pimp."

"So what are you saying?" Natalee laughed.

"It seems the prostitute and the reporter both lie for a living," Osgood said.

"One lies on her back," Natalee said. "The other has to back up her lies."

"With anonymous sources."

"Who work for the media."

"Or for the FBI. The Federal Bureau of Id."

"Thus increasing the demand for reporters and prostitutes!"

Father Xatse smiled benevolently at the witty young couple. "The real power," he said, "is with the saints." Then he took up the topic of mission work that he and Natalee were doing in Wormtown. He assured us the local bishop was a good man. They were joining forces with a Baptist congregation at an interfaith shelter. "There is a hunger for the Gospel," he declared. "It makes us thirsty for God." I noticed Father Xatse had a talent for mixed metaphors.

Gianni announcing that dinner was ready, Mrs. Phoenix ushered her guests into the dining room. She arranged us at a crowded table where Father Xatse said grace. We were treated to spinach salads with cranberries and goat cheese, followed by a main course of breaded halibut, mashed potatoes, and steamed broccoli. It was bourgeois Lenten fare with no apparent shortage of bread and wine. Natalee, who sat opposite Osgood, couldn't resist teasing him.

"I shall call you the Knight of Carthage," she said, batting her lashes. "Thank you for your good deeds, Knight of Carthage."

Before Osgood could muster a reply, my elbow sent the porcelain saltshaker flying. It surprised us by landing upright and undamaged, by the right foot of Professor Farbarker.

"What were the odds of that?" said Mrs. Phoenix.

I took it as a rhetorical question. But Farbarker, raising a pontifical forefinger, seized the occasion to display his wit. "It reminds me of my colleague Tony Chernenko, who specialized in the year 1841. It seems the year 1841 was fairly uneventful because Chernenko never did much work on it. Early in his career, though, he made a name for himself in a new online journal. He wrote one essay and it made him a star in our profession, though at the time many of us thought it a satire. His main point was that the word *brainwashing* ought not to carry negative connotations. He argued that student brains needed washing. Professors, in his view, should be brainwashing specialists. Technically, he preferred the term *brainscrubbing* as it is more surgical. But he never wrote a follow-up piece. As the year 1841 continued to lose its grip on his imagination, he went on to rewrite the faculty statutes. He was the first faculty member at Saint Malachy College to be promoted to the rank of full professor purely on the basis of committee work. It was widely viewed as an important breakthrough. The last time I saw Chernenko was at a meeting of the History department—our last ever, as things turned out. We were debating whether the political climate at the college warranted concern. As I recall, the fire alarms were sounding and Chernenko had the floor. He said I was overreacting." Professor Farbarker leaned over, picked up the saltshaker, and thumped it back on the table. "Carthage was about to salt our fields."

"What surprises me about these academics," Judge Phoenix said genially, "is that they seem to think that the country will be saved by Marxism 2.0—" "3.0," came a friendly amendment from across the table. "And not by intelligent individuals whose parents did their best to have them properly educated."

"You'd never know the Marxists killed a hundred million people," Farbarker said.

"They certainly don't mention it to their students," the judge replied. "But it seems there's always a new Utopia on the market. One much superior to past versions."

Farbarker drew attention to my interest in the Aldine Press. We proceeded from a general conversation about Aldus Manutius and Venice in the 1490s to a thinly disguised contest to see who could remember the greater number of humanist typefaces, from Bembo through its derivatives in the Italian and French Renaissance.

"Of course," he remarked, "you must distinguish between a true italic and a sloped roman."

He was a tough man to beat, Harold Farbarker.

"I knew a Farbarker once," I said. "The name was originally French—isn't that correct?"

"It was originally Scots, Mr. Shea. MacFarquhar. During the Reformation, a cadet branch of the family emigrated to Paris, where, in the interest of self-preservation, they renamed themselves *Farbarquer*. But then, around 1600 my direct ancestor Guy de Blague Farbarquer relocated to Shropshire to marry an English Catholic named Ellen Blount. They say history is full of strange turns, Mr. Shea. I say, strange turns are full of history."

Father Xatse was discussing the Pentecostal movement in Ghana when I asked what part of that country he was from.

"From Cape Coast."

"I used to know a Dominican nun from Cape Coast. Sister Mary Kanjia. She died about twenty years ago."

"I know the family. Fishermen."

"What a small world it is!" Mrs. Phoenix exclaimed, delighted at the thought.

"She was unusually" —I struggled for the right word— "loving."

Our dinner conversation was, all the while, describing an orbit around an unspoken crisis. While handling the broccoli dish, the judge mentioned that the case of Farbarker v. Board would be heard by the Massachusetts Appeals Court on Monday. "It's not a complicated case," he said. "I don't expect a delay."

"We're praying on it," Father Xatse said.

"If we do succeed," the judge said, "our alums are going to have to step up. Not like last time. It's their last chance."

"The power of prayer is strong," Father Xatse replied. Professor Farbarker glanced at his watch. "Ten minutes," he announced. The priest explained that he, the professor, and Natalee were due at eight o'clock at a parish council. "Farewell, my Knight of Carthage," she said, gliding off in her silver-blue dress while Osgood stared gravely at her going.

Soon he and I were alone.

"They're going to want to talk to you in private," I said.

"I'm sorry I was so useless this week."

"I fear that Allan and Quinones have met their match."

"I'll text them right now. Maybe we can do some work later. Those guys are night owls."

Osgood had sent his message when Gianni came in to clear the table and set it for dessert. Mrs. Phoenix followed with a spatula and a cookie sheet of freshly baked chocolate chip cookies, which saturated the room with their addictive aroma. "I know it's a Friday in Lent," she said, "but Gianni went ahead and baked them, anyway." She added with a wink, "He's

Protestant, you know." Then the judge arrived and offered to show me his jazz records, but Osgood outmaneuvered him.

"If you don't mind, I'd prefer for Moses to stay."

We could hear the clattering of plates from the kitchen. Then somebody dropped a large object that apparently shattered.

"Well," the judge said, taking his seat, "I hope the ossuary in the family closet doesn't alarm him."

Mrs. Phoenix had toddled off and now returned holding a photograph, which appeared to be an old Polaroid. "We were terribly sorry to hear about your father's passing," she said. "By all accounts he was a very fine man." Attending silently, Gianni poured coffee and then resumed his duties in the kitchen.

"How did you hear?" Osgood said.

"I called your mother a couple weeks ago," she replied. "I had a strange feeling."

"She didn't mention it to me."

Mrs. Phoenix seemed to have forgotten the point of the conversation.

"How did you know where to find her?"

Judge Phoenix fielded the question.

"When you were a little boy, son, your picture was in a Virginia newspaper. You were with your school class visiting Mount Vernon. A friend of ours happened to see the picture and brought it home with her. Thelma Kroiz. She's still going strong at ninety-three. That's how we knew where you were."

"What happened to my biological mother?"

"Beth," Mrs. Phoenix said, reviving. "It's not a happy story."

"I'd like to know."

"Your mother, Beth, I mean, was a real looker. She also had the sharpest tongue of any woman I ever met. I was never that pretty."

"Now, Mary...."

"John, I wasn't. Beth was too cute for her own good."

"Who impregnated her?" Osgood cut in.

"She never said. Years ago I discovered this. A photograph of a man wearing a tie. It was under the lining in a drawer in her old room. I tucked it away in an envelope but it keeps fading. You can hardly see it now."

She handed the photo to Mal. "There's nothing on the back," she remarked. He examined it and shrugged. When he put it down I had a clear view of the washed-out picture. I recognized what was left of the face at once.

"Whoever he was," Mrs. Phoenix was saying, "our family was Catholic. Abortion was out of the question."

"Beth wanted to abort me?"

"It was very common, Mal. She went to a clinic and someone there recommended it. You mustn't take it personally."

"I kept my first name."

"Because you knew what it was," the judge said.

"Why did the adoption take so long?"

"Because Beth had agreed that Mary and I would raise you. She left you in our hands but then she changed her mind."

"Where did she go?"

"Los Angeles."

Mrs. Phoenix started crying. I sensed the pain of wounds that had never fully healed. She dabbed her eyes with her linen napkin and forced herself to rejoin the conversation. "Mal, I'm so sorry but she and I never got along. Of course, I was old enough to be her mother. She was in California but she remained your legal guardian—we never pushed her on it. We tried to leave well enough alone. It was her legal right to put you up for adoption."

"My mother told me she passed away."

"Overdose," Judge Phoenix said grimly. "I read the autopsy report."

"And her mother?"

"She died soon after old Ty passed. Multiple causes."

"So here I am," he said, taking his cookie. "Working for the very people you're fighting against."

"I never liked computers," Mrs. Phoenix said. "Thelma says they're the golden calf."

"That might be a bit extreme," her husband suggested.

"I don't know," Mal said. "This morning I was thinking that, when the devil tempted Jesus with all the kingdoms of the world, he showed him all the kingdoms past and present. Computers, technology. I mean, why not?"

I returned on Sunday to Saint Anne's, where again I found myself frustrated by the pastor's evident need to go off message. The Gospel reading was the Transfiguration. In my mind it connects to the poet's line, "Human kind cannot bear very much reality." Peter and the two brothers, James and John, are high up on a mountain as reality buckles and bursts and shines like an acid trip. And yet Peter denied Christ and the pastor grew passionate about politics and pop culture. The choir, at least, was worthy of the Gospel. Insipid guitars might have sent me fleeing down the interstate to seek sanctuary in the Church of the Rad Trads. They were admirable, the Church of the Rad Trads. But I feared a Catholic exodus from America, that is, an exodus in spirit. The slow time of the Mass, the sculptedness of space in word and gesture, the body's gravity among its senses: these were great sources of dignity for any nation—and especially needful for one bent on degrading itself.

At the regular meeting on Monday morning, Ann Fitz congratulated the girls. "Win some, lose some," Allan said, defusing any residual tension. Liu made light of the situation and Quinones flirted absurdly with Sinclair, calling her a "dominatrix." Looking back, I suspect that Ann Fitz and Kay Arbuthnot had arranged things beforehand, because, before we reshuffled the teams, in fact, as soon as Ann Fitz reviewed the new week's agenda, Arbuthnot suggested a change. As it happens, our first item for the week was "AeroCab," a hugely expensive air taxi designed to fly the superrich and their pals around the skyline with the greatest of ease. The second item was a line of swimwear for the heavy-set crowd, tentatively labeled "Fat's In." Arbuthnot proposed we postpone "Fat's In" in order to balance "AeroCab" with a clean energy campaign. The Project Director was right behind her.

"I get it," Osgood said. "Since AeroCab will leave an enormous carbon footprint while catering to the rich, we need to compensate by helping the world convert to clean energy, which operates like a flat tax on the poor."

"For Chrissake," Arbuthnot said, "The planet's dying on our watch."

"No, it's not," he said.

"Yes, it is."

"How do you know?"

"How do you know?"

"How do *you* know?"

"How do *you* know?"

"I asked you first."

"Science!" Arbuthnot said, springing her trump card.

"Science? Unfortunately, the science is indistinguishable from the politics. Indistinguishable. So that's problem number one. Problem number two is we still don't have clean energy that can compete in the market against oil and gas without tanking the economy."

"We'll get there," Arbuthnot said. "One step at a time."

"If you never start the journey," Ann Fitz chimed in, "you never finish it?"

Osgood shook his head and let it go.

"But who's going to fund this clean energy campaign?" Liu asked.

The Project Director had come prepared.

"I know Nick's been working with the UN on some of their global initiatives? Let me confer with him and get back to you? In the meantime, our teams can get started on AeroCab? This week Tanit will be Mal, Kiki, and Ricardo?"

"It's Rico."

"For Baal, I've got Paris, Sophie, and Kay?"

Something seemed rotten in the state of Denmark when Ann Fitz smiled and asked how I was. "Fine," I said. On the way out, Allan mentioned he'd be stopping by. But Ann Fitz's smile knew better. I never worked with Paris Allan again. That afternoon, no one visited until Osgood arrived wearing the most canine expression of sadness that ever went on two legs.

"What the hell is it, for crying out loud?"

"Take a look," he said, handing me his phone.

We sat down and I looked. Olwin Bright had wasted no time posting the altered photo to her Twitter account. The instant outrage was like watching a bomb detonate through the remnants of my career. I was a "racist," a "racist fuck," a "total racist," a "racist stooge," a "racist swine," a "racist tool," a "hater," a "hate-monger," a "hateful creep," "hate incarnate," a "hate jockey," a "straight-up hater," a "white supremacist," a "white Christian," a "toxic moron," a "rightwing extremist," an "American Nazi," a "clueless asshole," an "embarrassment to the Jesuits" (this from A. B. Dopp, author of *How History Happens*), a "piece of shit," a "scumbag," a "grinning devil," a "thoughtless turd," a "horrible person," a "privileged buffoon," and whatnot. Smelling the feeding frenzy, Olwin's lieutenants went to work, retweeting older posts from the smear campaign that got me blacklisted in the first place. When a troll discovered I worked for Nick Carty, the call for my firing went out like an APB.

I returned his phone to Oswald. "I didn't know you were such a Twitter aficionado," I said. It was a cheap shot, but it made me feel better.

"Give me a break," he said, tapping the screen to open the curtain on some new variety of entertainment. Curiously enough, I sensed just what was coming.

Dear Carthage Community,

As you know, here at Carthage we stand by the values of our diverse and inclusive community. Therefore, I am deeply saddened to report that one of our employees, Moses Shea, has entirely betrayed everything we as a community stand for. With heartfelt sorrow but a strong sense of social responsibility, I refer you to the Twitter link in this email. It speaks for itself.

While the situation is uncertain and unfolding, we expect it will be resolved fairly and in short order.

If you are unaware of racism in recent world history or its use today by Christians and other White supremacists, take the time to learn. Let us strive together in our determination to end acts of hatred in the community we aspire to.

The experience of hate can be traumatic. If you would like one of our counselors to visit you, please reach out to Human Resources.

In the meantime, you are advised to think of Moses Shea as a radioactive pariah without a shred of human decency.

With hope for a better tomorrow,
Ann Fitz
Project Director

"She's no true poet. She's a pampered, preening, skulking, cowardly, backbiting, holier-than-thou, honor-raping, cant-mouthing, commodity-modeling, angle-wangling, Mack-the-Knife-smiling, stab-you-in-the-back, kick-you-when-you're-down, kale-eating, conscience-killing slanderer."

"I'm not sure about your order of adjectives," Osgood said. "Now, can you turn off your computer and your phone?" He produced a small device and, when he was finished sweeping the entire layout, ushered me into the bathroom. "It's an RF detector," he said, putting the gadget away. "All your rooms are bugged—except this one."

I put down the lid on the toilet and took a seat.

"Nice toilet."

"Isn't it?"

"Did you get those emails I forwarded you?"

This took a moment to process. "You're scaevola21?!" I said, wide-eyed.

"I hacked Fitz's account weeks ago. It was easy."

"Did you hack mine?"

"No. Will you look at this?"

A,

Take a peek at my Twitter account. It's checkmate for chubby boy. Nick is going to have to fire him.

Love,
O

"So where does this leave us?"

"Don't you see? You can go to Nick. If he doesn't believe you, I'll back you up."

"I appreciate it, Mal. I really do. But if Nick is willing to fire me over Olwin Bright, I don't want to work for him, anyway."

"It's just that he's susceptible to political pressure."

"Of course, he is."

We sat there, two bright boys in action, me on the toilet and him on the edge of the big tub.

"My dad was a theologian, you know."

Osgood listened attentively.

"When I was a boy, he was attacked by his fellow theologians. It surprised me at the time that these men of God could be so petty. He'd made a name for himself with his books, but they didn't like it and so they tried to ruin him. It was slander then and it's slander now. But I learned from him the healthy art of turning the other cheek. He had the power to fight back but he didn't want that kind of power because it makes you as bad as your enemies. Instead, he just kept writing his books, as if his enemies didn't exist. And that kind of made them go away."

"You're going to turn the other cheek?"

"Let's see what happens."

Things were moving quickly now. Later that evening we learned that the Massachusetts Appeals Court had upheld Judge Phoenix's decision in Farbarker v. Board. The wire service noted that the Carthage Corporation, acting on behalf of the Board, intended to bring an appeal to the Massachusetts Supreme Judicial Court. Carthage's lawyers would argue that Carthage CEO Nicholas Percival Carty was a devout Catholic —thus honoring the title deed. It remained unknown whether the Massachusetts Supreme Judicial Court would take the case. But the situation put acute financial pressure on Farbarker because, as the bench ruled, he had only ten days to indemnify the campus, including the O'Connell Library, without forfeiture of the suit.

I neglected to mention that Donna Ramella had invited

me to lunch. She very much wanted to introduce me to her son. After checking with our new chef, I suggested that she and Fabio join me for a meal in the refectory. She replied with several badly mangled sentences expressive of polite objection, yielding to a profuse and confused medley of compliments and, finally, after I had picked my way through several homonymic misspellings and various syntactical calamities, to what appeared to be a yes. I gave instructions for her and Fabio to meet me by the marble bench at eleven forty-five the next day.

I don't remember any relevant details from that morning, other than when I went outside to meet my lunch guests, Sergeant Nachman was positioned in the BV. She had backed it halfway into her cocoon-like tent, which seemed to be swelling of late. I made sure to keep my distance. The sergeant and I hadn't spoken since Mrs. Ramella's previous visit to the campus, and I feared relations would be strained. I was scuttling across her line of sight, when she once again availed herself of her vehicular PA system. "Mr. Shea," she called, exercising her ancient power over me.

I soon realized that something was terribly wrong.

Point A. Sergeant Nachman was regarding me at close range through binoculars.

Point B. A radical modification in the Nachman hairdo—though her service cap remained in place, I suspect that beneath it she was bald as Mr. Kurtz.

Point C. A high-end pump shotgun slumped against the passenger seat.

Point D. The BV sported a new hood ornament in the form of a human skull. The thought that I hadn't seen Deputy Nachman in days winged across my mental horizon with an eerie caw-caw-caw.

The window lowered. "Good morning, Sergeant Nachman," I said with false heartiness. "Always a pleasure!"

"I'm afraid it is not a time of pleasure, Mr. Shea. It is a time of duty and sacrifice."

Although she said nothing more, she wasn't prepared to release me. One gloved hand drummed lightly on the steering wheel, while the other clutched the binoculars on her lap. The shotgun barrel looked recently oiled. In the near distance, Mrs. Ramella's green Ford Taurus was turning into the O'Connell Library parking lot.

"You must excuse me, Sergeant. I have guests for lunch."

"How many?"

"Two."

"That's helpful information, Mr. Shea. I will subtract them from the number of illegal infiltrators."

"Well, good luck."

"That number is growing by leaps and bounds."

"I really have to go now, Sergeant Nachman."

"It's Farbarker's lawsuit. The people from the college think they own the place."

"In a sense, they do."

"Not on my watch."

I pulled myself away with a shudder. Sergeant Nachman required overnight shipping to a cuckoo's nest, and Nick needed to get a handle on the situation before he fired me. I had little doubt he was going to fire me.

It was starting to snow. As Mrs. Ramella and her son approached through the windless flakes, I was struck by the appearance of Fabio Ramella. He was about six feet four, with an easy stride, and he was bearing a pot of white flowers. His black hair was trim on the sides but topped with a dense mass of curls. As they drew near, I descried the heralds of brute strength in his blunt nose, thick chin, and heavy lips, but the gaze and forehead were noble. To my imagination, he resembled a Roman centurion. I could fancy him with a sword at his side instead of white flowers, but, then again, if first impressions count, maybe it was that I saw the flowers and the sword together—and that they combined in some fashion to express the depths of his being.

Chef Duke was welcoming to my guests and more tolerant of my chit-chat than his predecessor had been. We ordered hamburgers all around and, when we were seated with our lunches, Fabio commented on the changes to the interior decorating. He pointed to a spot on the wall where a crucifix had hung, and to another where a painting of the Sacred Heart had resided.

"You know," he said, "that picture of Jesus's heart on fire."

Liu materialized and said a friendly hello. I was grateful for this gesture—a testament to her independence of mind. I introduced my guests and she said, "We call him 'the prof,' you know."

When she left us to our lunches, Mrs. Ramella required clarification regarding my professional status.

I explained, "'Prof' is just a silly honorific. I'm not really a professor."

"Like an honorary degree?" she said.

"Kind of."

Mrs. Ramella then steered the conversation toward Fabio's time at the college. "Tell him about that paper," she said.

Her son torpedoed one last French fry into a sea of ketchup, inserted it down his gullet, and acquiesced to his mother's wishes. "My first paper was a time-traveling assignment," he said. "The idea was to go back in time and explain to your ancestors that the country was a lie because it was built on the backs of slaves. So I went back to my great-grandfather's starting a bakery. My grandmother—" "That's my husband's mother," Mrs. Ramella clarified. "She told me that everybody worked all the time. It was during the Great Depression and money was scarce. It was freezing in winter because there was no central heating. They heated the upstairs with the big ovens in the kitchen. My grandma's sister died of tuberculosis when she was five. Then my great-grandfather had to serve in World War II. He was killed in Italy, in his own hometown—which is pretty ironic—and the family lost the bakery. But I went back in time and told them they'd built it on the backs of slaves."

"What did they say?"

"They looked at me like I was Jesus Christ and thanked me for the information. I got an A on the paper."

I could see that Fabio perceived the humor in this account, but his poor mother had worked herself into a fine Italian lather.

"What kind of lesson is that?" she said angrily.

"It's okay, Mom," he said.

"I know the slaves in this country had it worse than us, but we had it pretty bad. My husband says it's not a competition. Do you think it's a competition, Mr. Shea?"

"I try to see things from a religious perspective."

"That's wise," she said, calming down.

"The truth is," Fabio said as he raked over his coleslaw with the back of his fork, "I'm grateful to my ancestors. They worked hard." He abandoned the fork and pushed the plate aside. "Then I came here and blew it."

"You mean you came to Saint Malachy College?"

"It was a nightmare. Now I understand better it was just Marxism with a fancy paint job. I took this poetry class and we read a poem called 'Spain.' I'll never forget this one line: 'The conscious acceptance of guilt in the necessary murder.' It still makes me sick. I wish I'd never read that poem."

I'd forgotten Auden could write so badly. It was his Marxist period. No wonder he went back to Christianity after that.

"They always think your sins are worse than theirs," Mrs. Ramella remarked.

I was worried about Donna Ramella and the Donna Ramellas of the world in general. They weren't stupid. They had worked their whole lives alongside their fellow citizens in a spirit of equality. And now they were being falsely called out for the sin of racism by a much wealthier elite. To be sure, those sins were out there festering, but not in the hearts of ordinary Americans. I saw the potential for a rightwing political disaster for the simple reason that decent working people can only take so much before they start seeing red. I said to her son, "What if the true Saint Malachy College could be resurrected? Reborn from the ashes? You could enroll again and have a second chance to learn."

"I heard something about that," he said. "It would be worth fighting for."

The snow kept falling and Sergeant Nachman was elsewhere when I saw off the Ramellas, promising to stay in touch. I went back for office hours (just in case) and put some ideas down on paper about air taxis. I was attracted to Leonardo's flying machine and his iconic drawings. If we could giftwrap the AeroCab with a tissue of science and a ribbon of art, people might think of it as a rite of passage for an advanced civilization and not as another stinking privilege for the superrich. "Humanity's Next Ride," I thought. But that evoked the Hindenburg disaster: "Oh, the humanity!"

Then my phone announced an incoming call from Buffalo. I knew only one man in Buffalo. He got right down to business. He said to expect a courier package at four o'clock. He said he was following a friend's instructions and couldn't stay on the line. We would have to catch up another time.

Sure enough, dead on the hour, as I sat waiting in the parlor, a Budget truck pulled up in front and the driver hopped out with a delivery. She must have recognized me at once, but she didn't show it. Only when she handed over the package I knew: she was the businesswoman from the hotel in

Las Vegas, the one who knocked on the door and took my picture. Sunglasses and a snowsuit had replaced the eyeglasses and pedestrian pantsuit.

She said nothing.

I retreated to my rooms, locked the door, and inspected the package's contents. I was looking at a stack of photographs taken in Beijing—the Summer Palace is hard to miss. Olwin Bright was there with other employees of the *Times' Times*. I didn't recognize any of the well-dressed Chinese men and women in their company, until, as I was riffling through the pile, I saw the Chinese president walking side-by-side with Olwin. They were grinning at close range like amorous chimpanzees. Towards the bottom I discovered a series of compromising shots taken through a window with a telescopic lens. The photographs were grainy, but there was no doubt about the content. Olwin and the president were drinking wine together. She was wearing a sheer negligee. He was wearing a wife-beater T-shirt and smoking a cigar. Just between us, he's paunchier than he looks in a black suit. In the climactic shot, he appeared to be staring straight at the camera like King Kong in an unusually thoughtful moment. Olwin was absent, unless she was represented by a small black arc, cut off by the bottom of the frame, at about the level of his navel.

This, I said to myself, is the kind of thing that can get a man killed. I don't think it was fear, though, that guided my decision not to scan a few select pictures and send them off to Olwin in a nice friendly email. I imagine she would have honored my request for a retraction and an apology. But I didn't like the terms. It was a blackmail match and my guardian angel warned against it. If I haven't mentioned the old seraph by now, it's because the Church prohibits the naming of guardian angels lest they turn into Harvey, the invisible rabbit. Another factor: I was curious to see how Nick would finesse things if left to his own devices. Would he play the game as ordered? How would he manage it? What excuse would he bring to the table?

I stashed the photos behind some French novels and was heading outside for a spell of fresh air when, at the front door, I ran into Osgood and Natalee Phoenix. They needed to talk. We sought the recesses of the parlor, where Osgood said it was safe.

"Shall I tell him?" Osgood said.

They were seated together on one of the antique-looking settees. They were both wearing blue sweaters. They looked kind of cute.

"Go ahead," she said, studying his face.

"The situation on campus is about to get more complicated."

"More aliens?"

"Natalee was working the front desk around ten this morning when this woman showed up."

"Who?"

It was Natalee's turn to talk:

"She goes by the name of Camille Zion. Her real name is Camille Jones. She was my roommate freshman year. She's super smart—and unhinged. She gave all the orders."

"You mean this young woman was behind the mayhem on campus?"

"Camille was a Saint Benedict Scholar and a star hockey player. Also, she knows how to build bombs."

"But what can she do now? I don't get it."

"She said that if Farbarker wins, she means to finish the job. She's bringing in her wrecking crew. She promises there won't be a building left standing."

"Did you tell your grandfather?"

"He'd like to have her arrested but it's not that easy. Things are too much in flux."

"What does she look like?"

"White girl. Tall and athletic. She's inked up pretty good. Lately she's a blonde."

"Anything else?"

"She's a committed anarchist. She started as a radical feminist but she reached the conclusion that it was just a midway point. She says the only real alternative to patriarchy is anarchy: otherwise patriarchy will keep creeping back in. It can never be reformed sufficiently. To Camille, western civilization must be destroyed in order to give birth to something new."

"You really think she might start bombing the place?"

"Yes. So does my grandfather."

"Do you happen to know someone named Fabio Ramella?"

"I know the guy. He had a torrid affair with Ren Watt. Last I heard they were burning down Portland, Oregon."

"Well, he's had a change of heart."

"A conversion?" She laughed it off. "I can't believe it. He was one of the biggest jerks on campus."

"That's how it goes. Now I would suggest—and it's just a suggestion—that you reach out to him. I'll send Mal the email address of Donna Ramella—she's Fabio's mother. She'll pass your message along. You might want to let him know what's happening."

I relaxed that evening by watching an old film, Humphrey Bogart's World War Two saga, *Sahara*. Around that time in world history, Laurence Olivier was doing his Henry V routine, and a jolly good patriotic crowd-pleaser it was—and not a bad script. But where the British underdogs joined the Welsh, the Scots, the Irish, and the English to form their "band of brothers," Bogart, as Master Sergeant Joe Gunn, forges a longshot fighting force out of a Frenchman, a Texan, four Brits, and Sudanese Sergeant Major Tambul. A Nazi airman calls Sergeant Tambul the N-word and Bogie tells the Nazi,

"Wipe that smile off your puss or I'll knock your teeth through the top of your head." Bogie: the active anti-racist.

Finding myself idle, I went out the next day for an afternoon constitutional. No one had arrived to shovel the walkways or plow the roads, but the snow wasn't deep. I was trekking along behind the gym when three strangers approached from the maze. They wore homemade black riot gear and were masked below the eyes. One of them had her blonde hair in a ponytail.

"Hello," she cooed. "Whose side are you on?" She was tall and her dark eyes shone above her mask. Her silent colleagues took their position on either side of me.

"I work for Carthage," I said. The men at my side relaxed a little. "But being a Roman Catholic with a devotion to my Church and the great tradition of learning it has fostered over the centuries, I find myself not unsympathetic to the recent ruling with which you are no doubt familiar." The men tensed up. "All I'm saying is you have to put things in perspective. For better or worse, it was Christianity, more than any other institutional force, that preserved classical literature when the ancient world passed away. It fostered conditions that eventually made a dramatic revival possible. Admittedly, our knowledge of the medieval transition-period is fragmented and at times bewildering, but it's hard to doubt the essential role of the Church. Latin, the cosmopolitan language of the Middle Ages, was a living language that nourished a rich theological and intellectual tradition. It produced a liturgical drama, as well as Bede, Hrotsvitha, the *Dies Irae*, and the *Carmina Burana*. Monastic discipline prepared the grounds...."

In the course of this illuminating exposition, worthy in my opinion of a Pulitzer, one of the men at my side surreptitiously extended a leg behind me. Camille Zion, for it was she, interrupted my lecture with a quick push. I fell hard, breaking my elbow. If not for the blanket of snow, I might have cracked my skull.

Just as suddenly—as the first sharp pain lacerated my nerves—Camille Zion and her companions fled the scene. A group of young men was giving chase. I felt strong arms helping me to my feet. Fabio Ramella was asking how I was. He got me to a car and drove me to the nearest hospital.

Nick pink-slipped me at the end of the week. He called early Friday morning as I was heading to the bathroom. I took the phone in with me. The old boy didn't sound ruffled in the least. He said not to worry—we'd work it out financially—but Carthage couldn't afford to employ me any longer. I was a public relations disaster.

"How did you ever get such powerful enemies?"

"*Proprium humani ingenii est odisse quem laeseris.*"

"It is human nature to hate those you have injured."

"Unless you prefer to turn the other cheek."

"You know I've always had a Christian heart."

"I didn't know you had a heart, Nick."

"Has Osgood said anything about me?"

"He said you two had a talk."

"Well, try not to turn him against me, all right?"

"I would never turn him against his loving father."

"Say that again?"

"Make of it what you will."

"Did he say something?"

"No."

I mentioned the Nachman situation.

"Why the hell did we hire her?"

"Why did you?"

"Ann."

"I'd get rid of her if I were you. I wouldn't wait a minute."

I put him on the speakerphone.

"The problem is we don't know yet if the state supreme

court will hear the case. God forbid those mad saints come up with their insurance check. Farbarker. What a farce. Honestly, part of me just doesn't care. Sometimes you have to cut your losses and live to fight another day. There are other campuses, you know."

"It's a bad year for the classics."

"You can't blame me for that, Moses. I always liked your work—sorry about your elbow, by the way."

"Who told you?"

"Ann. Which one is it?"

"My left—at least I can still wipe my ass," I said with a flush.

He said the movers would get my stuff back to Manhattan on Sunday. There were other things we might have discussed but we were comfortable with trafficking in silences, Nick and I.

Later that day I called Osgood to break the news of my departure. I proposed a meeting at the Griffin Café. I insisted on driving, sling and all. I needed the practice.

Situated at the bay window with coffee and fresh berry pie, we spoke without fear of hidden microphones. The latest on the Farbarker front seemed promising. A host of alums were contributing generously to the emergency fund. In particular, a wealthy alum by the name of American Brock had committed to donating a major sum.

"The watch manufacturer?"

"He studied with Farbarker."

"Small world."

Osgood grew suddenly passionate.

"Why the hell should you have to leave? Fitz is the one who should be fired. I say we go straight to Nick and fix the situation."

"If I were you...."

"What?"

"Never mind."

"You were going to say something."

"My dear boy. Power is corrupting. Information is dangerous. You've got to be on your guard. As for Nick...well, Nick is Nick and the world is the world. You're going to have to make your own choices where all that is concerned."

"Natalee doesn't like him."

"Why not?"

"She says Carthage and Rome are old enemies." It took me a moment to take this in and meanwhile he continued. "Will you come to Mass with us on Sunday? It's Father Xatse in the Civil War chapel. Eight a.m. A simple Latin Mass. A lot of people are going."

"Whose idea was this? Yours or Natalee's?"

"She likes you, you know. She says she feels like she knows you."

That got to me after a hard week. If Osgood sensed my emotion he was tactful enough to stare out at the empty parking lot while I blew my nose and caught my breath.

Chapter 10

Old Enemies

It was a morning of double starts and mysterious, neurotic repetitions—one of those mornings when every effort seems to take twice as long. Around five to eight I found myself crossing the footbridge, where the little boy was back, keeping his vigil. He ran off with his scarf trailing behind him, the fluttering harbinger of my arrival. I stumped uphill, past the bronze statue of Corporal Brian Patrick Walsh, to where the young couple waited by the door into which the boy disappeared.

The pews were crammed with worshippers, a startling influx of families and young people. The three of us knelt on the floor in the back. A pimply teen offered me his folding chair and I accepted—though it was hardly necessary. The boarded windows stood out like negative space, while light filtered through the stained glass that remained. As my eyes adjusted, the chapel seemed larger inside than out. The altar was lit by two tall candles, which flickered on the faces of the saints on the reredos. A stark wooden crucifix hung from the rafters, Christ's face gazing down to one side, as if not to disturb us in our prayers.

Father Xatse processed to the altar, attended by a server. The priest wore a fiddleback chasuble, gold and purple, with an ornate image of Christ emblazoned on the back. The server wore a black cassock, and both men wore lace surplices. Father Xatse bowed before the altar, made the sign of the cross, and began.

In nomine Patris, et Filii, et Spiritus Sancti. Amen.
Introibo ad altare Dei.

The Mass sprang to life with its own instinctive rhythm, the priest kneeling and rising, the server kneeling for long stretches. The priest caressed the Latin tongue so that we could hardly hear him, and the server chanted back even more softly. When the time came, Father Xatse's homily addressed the raising of Lazarus, a type of Christ, but also, as the priest commented, a man of flesh and blood whose death brought Jesus to tears. "He wept cats and dogs," Father Xatse said. But the Ghanaian priest did not go off message. He said that Lazarus joins us to Christ, not only in worship, but in the blind grief of bereavement. In the scene at Bethany, we are with friends and family, with our own brothers and sisters, knowing the good of this life and absorbing its awful brevity. This account of mourning and miracle is, Father Xatse said, paradoxically about the good of this world. Christ was no stranger to our human world. He was fully man and fully God. On no other terms can we begin to approach his love.

Because it was a Low Mass, the congregation remained silent throughout. Each communicant received the Host on the tongue, as the server extended a paten under the chin in case of slipups. I was shuffling back from communion when I noticed Sophie Liu at prayer. Our eyes met in a twinkle. It was and remains a mystery to me—that she was in the chapel. When Mass ended, we joined Father Xatse in the Saint Michael prayer and a few Marian prayers. After that, I knelt with my eyes closed, a pious swine bent on gratitude. I strongly suspect the Lord dislikes pious swine. In my learned opinion, the swine into whom Jesus sent the legion of demons were just about to go tell their fellow swine downhill that they, the uphill swine, were the superior breed.

Those times when I pray for an extra couple minutes after Mass, I do a kind of Examen. I orient myself to God and try to see myself in his eyes. The feeling of being at home in a strange church is an intimation of heaven. I concentrated to stay in God's presence, but soon my knees rebelled. The three of us rose together—Natalee Phoenix, Mal Osgood, and I—and withdrew until we were standing at the bronze feet of Corporal Walsh. Because Osgood wanted to see me off and Natalee thought that was best done without her, she and I said our goodbyes.

When he and I reached Dido Hall, the moving truck was parked out in front, its cargo doors open and loading ramps in place. I recognized the same four-man crew at work in their efficient and orderly manner, hand trucks banging up and down stairs, a quick pace, arms lifting and arms receiving. The bookshelves were clearing rapidly. I made sure the gas in the fireplace was switched off before gathering the small bag of personal items I'd collected the previous evening.

Another word for furniture is movables—something sobering about that.

My young friend was leaning against a wall with his hands in his pockets; so I asked him to carry my laptop. Arbuthnot, Sinclair, Allan, and Quinones had decided, evidently, against the awkwardness of parting. I thought we all kind of liked each other, but the situation had wrenched me away from them. As we left the building, I said to Osgood, "You'll have to come to New York and visit. Bring that girl."

"Didn't you ever fall for a girl?"

"Once."

"What happened?"

"She married Nick."
"That's not funny."
"Yes, it is."

We crossed the street to the parking lot and soon we were standing by the Mercury.

"Why do you drive such an old bomb?"
"I get tired of buying things."
"You're not telling me everything you know, are you?"
"No. That's true. But it's not really my business."

He stood there with his hands in his pea coat and his John Lennon cap on his head, watching me go. As I drove ahead, my eyesight, repelled by the Nachman structure—which now seemed bizarrely tumescent, like the massive abdomen of a queen termite—grazed the deserted marble cube that rested in the field beyond. I thought of Flannery O'Connor assuming the form of a living statue and crossing the field with her peacocks to retake her place on the plinth. A bit like Lazarus. A symbol of mourning and miracle. If Carthage were defeated, the statue would return.

Would that mean America going backwards? I don't think so. When you get totally lost, one of three scenarios must unfold: you recognize you're lost; dumb luck saves you; or you perish. Of course, you may recognize you're lost and remain lost nonetheless. But the dreamworld woven on our screens by those who spin the narratives and double down on their mendacity without a sense of shame—such sorcery is doomed in the natural order of things. Luck runs out. Time to climb a serious mountain and do a reality check.

It was a fine day for driving, overcast but not rainy. With one arm draped in a sling, I found an hour behind the wheel to be about my limit. I stopped at Hartford for some grilled yardbird mixed with rabbit food. The plus-size waitress was on the qui vive for a sugar daddy. "Hey, sugar daddy," she said. "Hey, sugarplum," I said. That was my romance of the day. I stopped on the Merritt Parkway for a big hazelnut coffee and needed to make an emergency pitstop in Scarsdale before my bladder burst. Finally, I reached 250 West 85th Street to find the moving van taking up half the block.

When the men finished, my apartment looked much as it had when I returned from my frenetic trip to Las Vegas. The leader of the crew directed my attention to an envelope on my newly replenished shelves. The envelope had my name on it, penned in Nick's jumpy scrawl.

"From Mr. Carty?"

"I wouldn't know, sir. It was on my desk this morning with instructions to leave it for you when we arrived in New York." He pocketed his tip, thanked me, and returned to his truck.

Inside Nick's envelope, I discovered some Latin words and some English words. The Latin said, *Novi ingenium mulierum: nolunt ubi velis, ubi nolis capiunt ultro.* It was a racy bit from Terence's *Eunuch*: "I know how women are. When you want it, they don't. When you don't want it, that's when they do." The meaning of this squib from a comedian whose audience dined on figs and beccaficos zigzagged like a laser beam through the different angles Nick was playing. He was touching my brotherly sympathies in the battle of the sexes. He was pleading there are two sides to every love affair. He was championing the classics. And, just to be on the safe side, he was buying me off. The English words said, "Check your account." This news of a windfall came with a sense of collusion: now that he was playing the Catholic card, the last thing Nick needed was for me to mail an amicus brief to the Massachusetts Supreme Judicial Court.

When the banks opened I learned I could almost afford to retire. Coincidentally, the national news turned its attention to the suicide of Nanolith CEO Holden Crawford. He came visiting like a wandering ghost—the washed-out face, eyes that might have been damned but that I wouldn't call soulless. In life, he had indulged a dangerous taste for guns, brandy, and teenage girls. But his love of Bill Evans also came back, as did a kind of spare honesty in his demeanor and the frank and flowing range of his conversation. The poor devil had done me a solid. He was as unique a blend of genius, candor, and vice as I'd run across in scores of professional interviews. Hard to say what makes a man like that tick.

The CEO of Nanolith had jumped to his death from the balcony of his high-rise apartment in San Francisco. Curiously enough, he landed on a migrant worker from Guatemala who lay passed out on the sidewalk in a puddle of urine. To help put things in perspective for the general public, the *Times' Times* covered the news of Crawford's decease by running parallel lives of the tech magnate and the undocumented migrant worker Juan Lopez. Crawford's bio meshed with the facts and probabilities formerly known as reality. He was born in 1963 in Mineola, New York. His father was a well-connected Manhattan attorney, who died in a freak accident when young Holden was twelve, at which point his mother embarked on a series of tumultuous marriages. Crawford bounced from prep school to prep school before discovering his talent for physics, earning a Stanford degree, and getting hired at Xerox PARC around the time Steve Jobs was haunting the place. He started Nanolith with angel investors he'd met through the *Whole Earth Software Catalog*. By his fortieth birthday, the company was worth a billion.

As it happens, the *Times' Times* was unable to discover any actual facts about the man they called Juan Lopez, so they made up the name Juan Lopez and reported that he came from Guatemala. Juan Lopez was born in 1990 in a traditional farming community in the biologically diverse highlands of Quetzaltenango. His father died on young Juan's first birthday during the Guatemalan Civil War, which was fought between a US backed force of genocidal mercenaries and leftist rebels fighting for their homeland. The story of Juan Lopez linked to the newspaper's coverage of Guatemala's drought and the catastrophic failure of the coffee crop. Hardworking men like Juan Lopez, caught in the pitiless grip of American-made climate change, hadn't had a chance to adjust their farming and to plant new crops in order to make their lives more sustainable. Small wonder, then, that they were sleeping on the sidewalks of San Francisco where thoughtless billionaires were jumping off rooftops.

In the post-America America, Holden Crawford was no Richard Cory. He didn't symbolize the bitter mysteries of the human heart. He left no suicide note and whatever it was that caused him to jump was not intriguing to the powers at the *Times' Times*. His color was against him, as was his objective, rational, linear thinking and his work ethic. Nanolith's recent breakthrough in NGL had tripled his net worth. He'd had no droughts to contend with, no failed harvests to crush and cow his spirit, but in some strange sense he'd failed Moore's Law and, more to the editors' point, he was burdening the world with a carbon footprint the size of the Chicxulub crater. Holden Crawford was responsible for Holden Crawford's suicide. On the other hand, the injustice of Juan Lopez's death was plain to see. It was death by suicide—only it was another man's suicide. As the *Times' Times* spokesperson tooted solemnly on cable news, "We Americans have grown selfish. There's nothing funny about it."

Osgood called that evening. He was pretending to be mad at me.

"You knew," he said. I had just downed a painkiller to calm the screaming ganglia in my elbow. I lay on the divan in my living room, with the phone to my ear.

"You should have said something," he continued.

"Like what?—'Hey! By the way, Mal....'"

"Were you in on it from the start?"

"Not at all. I'm embarrassed to say I was reading from Nick's script all along. You were right about that—our meeting in Las Vegas was no accident. But don't get the wrong idea about Nick. He doesn't just use people. He finds a use for them. He considers himself a beneficent deity. That's his view. If Nick thought he was evil, he'd be a lot easier to deal with."

"He clearly has the power to make people sin."

"Maybe."

"When did you learn the truth?"

"That he was your father? The Polaroid—the one Mary Phoenix showed us. It's Nick's picture from thirty years ago. He and I were living in New York back then. He was estranged from his wife. We used to get together on occasion and do some hard drinking. I never met your mother, though. Not that I know of."

"Does Ann Fitz know?"

"I doubt it."

"Does she know you and Nick went to college together?"

"Yes."

"But why didn't you tell me?"

"That we went to school together? So what?"

"He said when things quieted down, we could probably hire you back—he's staying in your old rooms, by the way. He says Carthage is an empire and the situation here's a sideshow."

"If it's a sideshow, why is he going to such lengths to prepare his case in Boston?"

On the street below a horn complained and suddenly the whole herd started up. Then the racket ceased as if they'd evaporated.

I said, "What does Natalee think?"

"Of his being my biological father? Natalee says it sounds

like a strained coincidence cooked up by a second-rate novelist. She says it's very inartistic of me."

"Well, that's a serious indictment. I want you to know, Mal—I did my best."

"It's not what anyone expected."

"There are dangers in meddling. In the end, we all have to make our own decisions."

"But would it be his script?"

"In his mind it would be."

"He says he's a Catholic."

"Time will tell."

"And until then, what am I supposed to do?"

"What is it Paris likes to say? *Nobody said it was going to be easy.*"

"I guess each of us is trying to write the script. Me, you, Nick."

"I feel more like a secretary these days."

"Whose?"

"That's a good question."

Next day, I gulped another painkiller and drifted up to 97th, where I went down the elegant stone staircase into Riverside Park. On the path lined with leafless cherry trees, cyclists passed joggers, who passed dog-walkers, who passed me in turn. I was in no rush. A few kids were shooting hoops in the cold weather. If you follow the path to the tunnel under the Henry Hudson Parkway you'll see waves of graffiti and a landslide of garbage, but, if no one happens by to relieve you of your wallet or your consciousness, you can sit on a boulder, rest your feet, and ponder the improvements that have come to the riverside since Henry Hudson sailed up the estuary in his ship the *Half Moon*. Behind you, a majestic skyline runs south to the docks where the luxury liners come to port. North, it mounts above the hills to the New York Presbyterian Hospital, where my mother gave birth once upon a time, and where not long afterward she died. West, the sky expands beyond the Jersey shore with its random buildings scribbled along the horizon like a stochastic oscillator. Before you, the Hudson. That morning the wide water was divoted and the color of tempered steel. High up, sea gulls soared in esurient rings.

I dined out (twice) and did some reading in the evening. Occasionally, I like to tackle a bit of non-fiction, to see how the other half lives. I opened a book I'd been meaning to get to called *Whither the Lion and the Unicorn?* It was a pro-and-con defense of the British Empire. Winston Churchill, who dominates the book, is of course one of those larger-than-life figures who parade across history like abstractions in human dress. Churchill says imperialism the way Edison says invention or Bach says music. He projects it like Governor Curzon and his wife sitting enthroned on the back of a large caparisoned elephant, while a turbaned servant shelters them under a parasol, and a mahout drives the elephant, and yet another servant, far below, stands at attention. Nonetheless, Churchill was the only man for the job. Without Churchill's indefatigable will, who knows what would have happened? Some say the Nazis would have raised their flag in Manhattan or draped it from the rim of Big Ben. And yet, as if history were but a game, the custom of hanging Churchill in effigy is honored at Churchill College, Cambridge. Gordon of Khartoum, whom Orwell idolized, died trying to abolish the slave trade in Sudan. His ideals were not native to the region. Yet he likewise is misrepresented and hated. It may seem an absurd exercise in ingratitude, this egregious revisionism, but it starts to make sense if you examine the assumptions of these ambitious professors, raging zealots for whom the gray areas of history are conquered territory. I feel no special affection for the British Empire—nor for the American Empire, for that matter. I've read *The Quiet American*, an excellent novel. But if you have a clear eye and a strong stomach for these things, you will find that the western empires were generally superior to the eastern tyrannies. Nonetheless we indulge them, the would-be tyrants who strut and fret in their tower of outrage, while their cutting-edge twaddle nudges us step by step like a collective death wish to the scaffold.

As I put down the book and reflected on my response to it, a gray mouse crawled out from a hole in the baseboard, applauded with its tiny pink hands, and crawled back. It was a city mouse and I'd seen its ilk before. Despite its being an ironic mouse, and most likely a devotee of Hamlet's *Mousetrap*, I'd have to call the professionals.

The week's mail included another letter from the good folks at Amor Christi Books. It opened with a new sales pitch from the publisher, John ("Jack") O. Jansen III. *"What do literature and Covid-19 have in common? Both require a deep cleaning!"* He went on to explain that this literary cleaning-process went by the name of *Immaculation*. Apparently, Amor Christi Books had developed a new line of Amor Christi software, which would immediately go to work immaculating every document on your computer—*and improve the text!* Jansen's letter included a long litany of personal testimonies. Loretta from Rock Springs had this to say, "I can finally read in peace, without worrying my children might accidentally see something they shouldn't." She was going to have her work cut out from her, Loretta from Rock Springs.

It was midweek when the situation at Saint Malachy's first caught the nation's attention. What happened was this. In the middle of the night an explosion ripped through one of the remaining dorms. No one was injured and the dorm happened to be in an isolated location. It burned to the ground when a fire hydrant failed due to lack of maintenance.

Now we need to consider that the fall of Saint Malachy

College barely grazed the national radar when it occurred. It is, of course, notoriously difficult to get hardworking Americans to notice even the clearest indicators of a spiritual crisis. If the Hebrew prophets ever had a single descendant among us, he probably tried folk music, and, when that didn't work, tried rock and roll, and, when that didn't work, toured the world without rest, and, when that didn't work, won the Nobel Prize and gave up. As for the school's violent demise, it didn't lend a sheen to those extremely urgent advances in higher education that have served the interests of a rising class of college administrators, a species of professional so successful at reproducing itself—being similar in that respect to the swampy infestations of *governmentus bureaucratus*—that it appears to be capable of parthenogenesis. And so the national character prevailed. But a faint recollection of some debacle at a liberal arts college lingered in the national memory and people were curious.

The first report on Wednesday was a straightforward account of the time and place of the explosion, the cause of which was unknown. Soon afterward, the names of the Carthage Corporation and Professor Harold Farbarker were linked to the story. Soon after that, though prior to any official statement, Farbarker was subtly and insidiously cast as the villain of the piece. He had prevented the Carthage Corporation from making the necessary repairs in the first place. And now, having won his controversial lawsuit, he was incapable of insuring the campus in order to keep it safe.

Nick responded with a masterful news conference. Nothing too showy, the crucifix on the wall above his head was tasteful and understated, while the Bible on the conference table wasn't larger than your average coffee table book. A quick call to Central Casting procured twelve bishops who joined Nick at the table, each immaculately dry-cleaned, cross-festooned, and topped with an amaranth zucchetto. Before them were prayer books, copies of the *Times' Times*, study missals, hymnals, Butler's *Lives of the Saints*, Covid-19 vaccination cards, and other props of virtue. The group was just beginning to pray the rosary when journalists arrived in the hall. They waited in a hushed silence for several minutes, video-recording the proceedings through the glass partition.

When the prayer session concluded with a reverent bowing of heads and a collective heaving of carbon dioxide, the bishops filed out and the media filed in. The religious mood in the conference room was not entirely abated. Someone had swapped out the sea snails around Tanit's neck for rosary beads, leading the press corps to mistake the Carthaginian goddess for the Virgin Mary. Attired in somber black, Nick welcomed the assembled journos and invited questions in a diffident and humble manner. For a man who was famously quick-witted, he spoke slowly and softly, pausing to the point of awkwardness and mumbling apologies. He seemed weighed down by cares. He said he didn't know what had gotten into people. It was never his intention to cause upset. In challenging times, the only solution was generosity of spirit. He modestly pointed out that he'd always been a good listener and he was prepared to listen now.

"Mr. Carty, is it true you are a pious Catholic?"

"Gosh. It's an embarrassing question, frankly. As a boy my Catholic parents drilled into me a core truth, that piety isn't supposed to be a show. It's in the heart. So I never feel comfortable flaunting my faith. But if you ask, has the Church been an immeasurably profound part of who I am? Have I placed my faith front and center of my mission in life? Only God can answer that. You might have to take it up with him."

This provoked a ripple of laughter.

"Let me just add," Nick continued earnestly, "I was as surprised as anyone that the appellate court didn't remand the case. I always intended to maintain the chapel. In fact, there are two chapels on our campus, a private chapel in this very building and another chapel nearby. They have never been deconsecrated and never will be. In my mind, they're very special places. All I'm saying is, if the gist of the case is respect for church property, I couldn't agree more. I have always considered this a private matter and I'm sorry to rattle on this way. That's all for now. Thank you so much for coming."

The CEO of the Carthage Corporation had just deposited the press corps in his pocket when the BV shot past the window behind him.

Fortunately for the press and its hallowed pledge not to let democracy die in darkness, there was one man who remained on the job, one man who wasn't rubbing shoulders with the cossetted gang in the conference room, one man who was following his nose to the action on the street. That man was Newsprick. Believe it or not, Baldock was back. What can I say? The man had more lives than Captain America. A week after they fired him, the higher-ups at *Eyewitness Void* got off their thrones and bowed to reality. And the reality was that Tom Baldock was a very, very popular individual. From what I understand, it was an exceptionally busy period for the aging stud. His days of unemployment would have broken a lesser man. He appears to have subsisted on amphetamines and whisky. He never slept. The glittering salons of New York, rewarding his newfound fame, measured his talent and ruled in his favor. I mean, they got out the ruler. Baldock served unfailingly in every democratic, non-judgmental, gender-fluid position that his erotic fate decreed. Having given upper-class Manhattanites a great gift, which was nothing less than the likeness and image of the godhead they worshipped, he became a kind of saint in their eyes. The singular stipulation in his eight-figure contract was that he henceforth be known professionally as Newsprick. That morning, from what I gather, he called his producer, a rising operator named Bonnie

Angel, and his cameraman, a glorified gopher named Harvey Gormengeister. He told Angel and Gormengeister to hop in the OB van with the Newsprick logo freshly painted on the sides and drive all the way to Clifden, Massachusetts. Then he made a couple other calls and leaped into action, his cherry red Porsche Panamera E-Hybrid tearing up the highway with two teenage girls on board, a case of scotch in the boot, and a vial of Viagra in the glovebox. He reached campus as the bishops were exiting in their limos. The moment Sergeant Nachman went flashing past, he climbed into the OB van and was hot in pursuit.

The action was taking place in the parking lot by the remains of Newman Hall. A group calling itself the Blatant Beast was staging a protest while, at the same time, videoing their demonstration with their phones. As a double-activity, it's not that easy to do, but they had perfected it with practice. Camille Zion was leading a herd of demonstrators who bellowed and bleated and barked and beat the air with their fists. I couldn't help but observe that a number of women had managed, through many years of surfeit, to load their frames with hundreds of pounds of sheer flab. They seemed highly indignant.

To my surprise, I noticed a familiar figure blending in with the protestors. He'd adopted their ritual attire and covered his white hair with a black balaclava, but I knew his pigeon-toed gait. He was sneaking about with a brick in his hand. I wondered if Ann Fitz knew what her boy was up to.

"Farbarker out!" chanted the Blatant Beast. "Farbarker out!"

This was evidently music to the ears of Sergeant Nachman, who cut her siren but left her lights flashing while she leaned back against the BV, arms folded across her chest and a look of grim satisfaction on her face.

Camille Zion took the lead.

"What do we want?"

"Social justice!"

"When do we want it?"

"Now!"

"What if the cost is high?"

"Social justice!"

"What if it sets fire to inner cities and leaves them in smoke and ruin?"

"Social justice!"

"What if it devastates the people it's meant to serve?"

I detected a hint of puzzlement. A few of the masked faces consulted their phones to see if they were still there but returned with their hearts strengthened.

"Social justice!!!"

"What if it ruins businesses and schools and leaves the poor helpless wards of a power-hungry state?"

"Social justice!!!"

"What if it lines the coffers of oblivious billionaires?"

"Social justice!!"

"What if it's the résumé-building, social-climbing toy of media sex maniacs?"

At that, the masked mob trained their phones on Baldock, who—as attested by a succession of uploads to popular video sharing sites—was watching from the shadow of his Newsprick van while Gormengeister pointed a broadcast camera back at the Beast, and Angel twiddled the knobs on her production console. For a moment, nothing happened. The Blatant Beast went silent and some of the larger females started passing around a bag of Ding Dongs. It seemed the protest had hit a wall. Staring in frustration at her screen, the ambitious producer told herself that a director was needed, a budding Tarantino to master the profitless sprawling seconds and discipline the chaos. But the delay didn't last long.

A prankster shouted out:

"What if we ourselves are nothing more than a violent gang of deluded nihilists, and our protest the purulent abscess of much wealth and peace, purchased by the sweat and blood of fallen warriors whom we dishonor with our very breaths?"

"Social justice!!"

Camille Zion took it from there:

"Will anything stop us?"

"No!!"

"Say it again!"

"No!!"

"Say it three times!"

"No!! No!! No!!"

The man known as Newsprick emerged from the shadows waving his microphone at Zion, who leapt to him like a gazelle bounding over the hills. He opened the interview with a couple of personal questions, and she presented herself as a former student who was hoping to complete her B.A. in order to pursue a career in secondary education. Then she explained that Farbarker was a clueless white male who was notorious on campus for his unwanted sexual advances.

"Is it okay to say 'scumbag' on the news?"

"Tell it like it is."

"Farbarker's a total scumbag. He tried to sleep with me. He freaked out a number of girls in my class. He's gross."

"So you don't want to see the college come back?"

"I wouldn't mind if they would just get rid of the old white guys. Honestly, I just want to shoot them. These people suck you dry. They're out of their minds and they have been for a long time. There's no talking to them. They should be exterminated."

As Gormengeister panned over to survey the Blatant Beast, his lens lingered on Sergeant Nachman, who appeared to be listening attentively.

"That's enough, Harvey," Angel droned into Gormengeister's earpiece. "Get back to Tom."

"So if you could simply eliminate a number of faculty, the college could potentially return and you would receive your degree?"

"Potentially. They would also have to change the name."

"Any suggestions?"

"Free College!" came a cry from the Beast. The many-voiced chant went up, "Free College! Free College! Free College!"

Bonnie Angel was not happy with the results. But when she edited and posted the Newsprick interview with Camille Zion on the *Eyewitness Void* website, the response was encouraging. They had clearly found an audience. The story took off and Baldock's instincts were vindicated. Already, it seemed, to be "farbarkered" was to suffer unwanted sexual advances. The celebrated historian A. B. Dopp made the rounds on cable news to trash Farbarker's book on the Civil War, *A Forgotten World of Tough Trade-Offs*, dismissing it with the flabbergasted grin that the cognoscenti reserve for special fringe cases.

Harold Farbarker had become those who hated him. As in all such moments of collective moral dementia, the scapegoating took on the excitement of a sporting event, a raucous smash-up conducted with demonic glee, a sadistic, grinning entertainment—and hence an escape from the exhausting demands of dialogue and compromise. It was a time of maledictions and hexes, of digital voodoo dolls and celebrity witch doctors for whom truth was a spell and the moral world a televised struggle between darkness and light.

Though in a sense well-scripted, the week's coup de grâce was surprising nonetheless. The fatal events were set in motion Thursday afternoon, when American Brock flew into Boston to be met at the airport by his former teacher. They dined at The Langham before driving to Clifden, where Mr. Brock took accommodations in a room upstairs at the Griffin Café. Friday morning, the watch manufacturer and the professor drove to the local bank, and a large bank check was deposited in the joint account held by Harold Farbarker and Tommaso Carlucci under the name "Friends of the Griffin." In short order, arrangements were made for a clerk of the appellate court to receive an electronic copy of a receipt from Magnus Indemnity, verifying that Saint Malachy College was fully insured against whatever cards the Fates might send wheeling across the table—from everyday accidents to bombs, bricks, and earthquakes. At Mr. Brock's suggestion, a copy of all communications was emailed directly to Carthage's top lawyer, Gideon Litchfield, Esq.

Litchfield wrote back asking for the courtesy of a week's time. He was confident that the Massachusetts Supreme Judicial Court would hear the case, and he thought it wise to spare everyone involved unnecessary costs. For now, he was requesting a weeklong extension so that Carthage could alert its employees and vacate the premises in due order. Farbarker acceded to this request, on the condition that he and his party be granted permission to tour the campus that afternoon, beginning with the newly reclaimed Virgil Hall.

Apparently, no record exists of Nick Carty's meeting with Harold Farbarker and his party. We know it took place in the conference room, with Ann Fitz present, as well as American Brock, Judge Phoenix, and his friend Carlucci. I would be interested to discover whether they visited the private chapel and inspected the octopus tank. In any case, we can be sure that Nick was civil. He always maintained a cold grip on his passions—which is to say he indulged them with pinpoint accuracy. He wanted the Massachusetts Supreme Judicial Court to hear the case, but no mere legal decision would rattle him to the core. He was too strong for that. He remained confident that Carthage would prevail in the end.

When Farbarker and his party exited the building, they were met by a seething mob. The Blatant Beast had grown considerably overnight. It was now a masked, dancing millipede with five hundred phones. To start the day's festivities, it smashed the old sign for Virgil Hall into pieces. Now it positioned itself on the lawn to greet the four ambassadors from Saint Malachy College. A helicopter swooped down from above as Baldock and Gormengeister sprang from their van like paratroopers. Camille Zion approached Farbarker and aimed a vicious stream of obscenities at him. Rocks were thrown and one knocked off Carlucci's fedora. Farbarker and his party were caught in the jaws of the Beast, unable to escape and guarding their faces with their hands, when Fabio Ramella arrived on the scene, leading a squad of powerful young men who charged the ring and pushed back hard on the rioters. Fabio seized one of the short, squat protestors by the ankles, swung the black, bomb-shaped object around several times with the perfect footwork of an Olympian hammer thrower, and hurled it at the rioters, scattering them like duckpins. The technique proving effective, Fabio's brothers-in-arms followed suit.

Gormengeister was aiming his camera at Baldock, who was reporting from the field in a smart new bomber jacket with the collar popped. Bonnie Angel was operating the studio equipment in the back of the van. They were broadcasting live. Angel suggested in his earpiece that Baldock give a friendly wave to Camille Zion, who rushed to the microphone to speak out against the sexist tactics of her former classmate Fabio Ramella, a well-known rapist whose toxic masculinity was all too obvious to behold. As she was shouting above the percussive throb of the helicopter, the BV executed a brilliant 360 drift entry onto the lawn. Here Bonnie Angel saw the opportunity of a lifetime. She beckoned from the van and took Sergeant Nachman into her confidence. "The world is watching," she said excitedly. She showed Nachman the studio on wheels and equipped her with a spare earpiece. It was a dangerous collaboration.

Due to Fabio's efforts, Farbarker and his three companions were making progress in the direction of the porte-cochère, where Manny Murphy sat waiting in the Benz. Sergeant Nachman in her purple uniform cut a wide swath through the rabid mob. She unholstered ol' Sam, called Farbarker by name, and shot him in the head at point blank range.

"That's okay," Bonnie Angel said, as the action unfolded on her screen.

Nachman shot Carlucci in the head as well.

"No worries," Angel said.

Ol' Sam pointed at Judge Phoenix.

"Not him! Not him!" cried Bonnie Angel into her microphone.

Duly corrected, Nachman turned and fired at the heart of American Brock, but the bullet was deflected by a Marian Medal he'd been awarded the previous week. Then, while Angel was contemplating the impact of a couple dead white guys on her career and if and when she should erase the record of her afternoon's work, the former head of Public Safety marched over to Baldock and shot him twice before he could interview her. Another bang pierced the air, and instantly blood oozed down like oil from under Nachman's service cap. Her limbs twitched as her body buckled and fell. Manny's gun had spoken.

Epilogue

Harold Farbarker died instantly. Sergeant Nachman had forever stemmed the majestic flow of his incomparable oratory. But the slain professor was victorious in death. Having ascended to the mystical faculty in the sphere of the sun, he must have smiled down on us like the sun when the Massachusetts Supreme Court refused to grant a review of Farbarker v. Board. Soon afterward, Virgil Hall was rechristened Farbarker Hall. A great bronze statue of Farbarker holding forth in full academic regalia marks the spot where he was felled by a single bullet. Tomasso Carlucci also departed this earthly plane. Always the athlete, a loyal friend, but never much of a bookworm, he suffered the indignity of having the library renamed in his honor. The Carlucci Library, home to a small but priceless collection of genuine Aldines, was named after a man with very remarkable rebounding skills. As for the third casualty of that bloody day, I will pass over in silence the gruesome discoveries made by police at the Nachman residence in Clifden. You can read about them in a book called *Justified Madness: Irene Nachman and the Quest to End the Patriarchy*, written by a former faculty member of

Saint Malachy College. For my part, though, I will always associate Sergeant Nachman with Schumacher, the gamekeeper in Jean Renoir's 1939 film, *The Rules of the Game*.

The Blatant Beast fed lavishly off the destruction. It clashed with the state police crowd control unit and broke acres of glass before withdrawing to its parents' basements. It disintegrated overnight into hundreds of unathletic, socially useless, semi-literate monads. But the Beast was only sleeping. Soon it was revived by fresh loads of newsfeed beamed at light-speed across the limitless inane.

The big surprise was the survival of Tom Baldock. Baldock was evidently unkillable. When Nachman went berserk, she plugged him twice—in the shoulder and above the ear. Breathing raggedly, he was rushed via helicopter to a hospital in Boston, where a brain surgeon removed a slug that would have slaughtered a Brahman bull. It caused massive hemorrhaging and ripped up the part of the brain that distinguishes fact from fiction. But as Baldock noted in his first interview after the shooting, the damage was unlikely to affect a man in his line of work. From what I understand, the lasting effects were limited to the shoulder wound, which impacted his tennis stroke. The indomitable Newsprick made a hero's return to New York, where the Mayor awarded him the Bronze Medallion for "exceptional citizenship and outstanding achievement." A parade in his honor is postponed indefinitely until the end of Covid.

Nick Carty moved on, as I knew he would. And yet, I suspect the defeat affected him more than he ever acknowledged. He recovered the money he'd spent on Saint Malachy College and relocated Hannibal to the north shore of Long Island, where another Catholic college had been cannibalized by its faculty and administrators. Did any of the Massachusetts crew go with him? I don't know. When a new biographer inquired into his fleeting return to Catholicism, he remarked cryptically, "It was election season." Eventually, he would leave the daily operations of the Carthage Corporation to others. He would semi-retire to Capri and become a heretical nun. Yes, Nick's sex change surprised a lot of people, but the price of Carthage stock skyrocketed.

As for Mal Osgood, he placed himself in the hands of a strong woman. "If you want to join the patriarchy," she said, "you have to go through the matriarchy." Since Natalee put an end to his plans as an imperial scion, he bid Nick a final farewell and tied the knot. He is now Vice President for Information Technology Services at the resurrected Saint Malachy College, where his children are a regular nuisance.

What of Ann Fitz? I never heard her questioning voice again. Nor did I ever hear news of Kay Arbuthnot, Sophie Liu, Ricardo Quinones, or Kiki Sinclair. Other than Osgood, the only one of the young titans who stayed in touch was Paris Allan. No one could have foreseen the changes that lay in store for the former track star, who proved himself a dashing trickster with more than one trick up his long sleeve. He shed his dream of a tech utopia. His devotion to Moore's Law wavered and went. But he bet on his alter ego and achieved real standing in this world. Jupiter Jefferson has his share of enemies, as will anyone who inspires envy in the venomous and the dull. But he is widely admired for his deadpan takedowns of the charlatans and mediocrities who preside over our major institutions.

One day he visited my rooms in Farbarker Hall. He stood in the doorway and his white suit made me think of a tall Mark Twain. Or a black Oscar Wilde. Usurping my Saint Malachy College rocking chair, he rocked back and forth and slapped his big hands on his trouser legs.

"Hey, prof," he said. "Did you teach me anything about writing?"

"All I said was, 'Art, not graft.'"

"So that's why I'm getting clobbered."

I looked at him with surprise.

"The critics," he said with a grin.

"As far as they go—which isn't very far—my advice is to limit your attention to critics who've done the reading. The ones who know literature."

"As opposed to having wonderful political opinions."

"That's right."

"But satire's an unusual case, don't you think?"

"Yes, I do. A satirist like you is critical of society, but at the same time you're not writing editorials. You have to hammer out a form."

"You mean the way the whole exceeds the sum of its parts."

"And that is not a political problem. It's an artistic problem—with a subtle touch of the theological, by the way. It's a challenge to transform one's righteous indignation into a work of art. But submission to form is what makes the process happen. The artist serves the form."

He sends me his excellent books as they appear.

Manny Murphy went to work for the US National Park Service. He relocated his family to Wyoming. One day a picture postcard of golden eagles arrived, informing me of his whereabouts. I was gratified to hear that things worked out for him.

Mia Mazur died right before Nick's court case fizzled. I must have gone to bed thinking about her, but I'm unable to determine the exact sequence of events. What I recall most clearly is a dream where we were holding hands, a pair of kids walking through the Cambridge Common in summer. Bright sunlight edged the pregnant clouds and drenched the distant scene. We seemed to read each other's minds. She had suffered but it was all behind her. She was at peace. She laughed and pointed out the old sights. The Puritan. Christ Church. The

Civil War Memorial. She had filed an amicus brief and I thanked her, thinking she was praying for my soul. She needed to call someone and I waited nearby as she smiled in her young beauty and the wind ruffled her auburn hair, until I realized I was the one she was calling.

On the Easter Monday following that busy Lent, American Brock dropped by 250 West 85th Street to ask if I would return to Saint Malachy College to help him put together a Literature Department. After exhaustive research with his team, that is, Natalee Phoenix, he spoke of a shortage of literature professors who actually knew something about literature. He wasn't sure what it was they did know, but he was sure literature wasn't it. I asked for a week to mull things over. I was living the life of a metic in the great town, pottering about my apartment, rereading Shakespeare, sallying out for a fine meal, but my conscience—that "prick," as the writer Devin Adams calls it—got the upper hand.

I was back on campus in time to watch the garden outside my western windows bloom. In April, a throbbing lilac bush unfurled its blossoms, flooding the air with thick purple scent. I had lilacs and daffodils, hyacinth and lilies, and a compost pile of literary associations to go with them. Landscapers performed a long overdue clean-up and the grounds began to put on their former beauty. I enjoyed my daily walks. Summers and winters, I returned like a migrant bird to the shores of Manhattan, but I spent much of the next five years teaching literature and grading papers. Those undergraduate papers were often a challenge. "Sir," as the old joke goes, "your style reminds me of the remark in Hobbes. It is 'nasty, brutish, and short.'" But they learn—the hopeful, the awkward, and the heartbreaking young. They learn so long as you steer them in the right direction and know when to get out of their way.

Judge Phoenix served as president that first year of the restoration, but it was really American Brock who did the heavy lifting. I would often see him striding over the campus with his notebook, surveying the condition of things. Under his kingly command, the statues returned to their plinths, new dorms arose from the ashes of the old, and the chapels were fully restored. That first fall, a handful of students returned, including Fabio Ramella, who pursued a degree in History—which was just as well, because, as regards his continuing in Sociology (his former major), we were stymied. We had no Sociology offerings at all until a young scholar arrived from Purdue and put that dangerous department back in business. I recall being impressed by her dissertation, *Bureaucracy and Irrationalism*. The next year, the incoming class numbered a mere twenty. But the student body grew over time, and so did the number of new hires. A lawsuit led by Tony Chernenko, who specialized in the year 1841, failed badly, and the *ancien régime* was done.

I will end this peculiar novelistic chronicle with a brief account of the day that President Brock and the college honored my years of service. In their kindness, they erected a Roman pillar and (I am embarrassed to say) named it after me. A gorgeous specimen of Carrara marble with a bluish tint, it rose to a noble height adjacent to the amphitheater. It put me in mind of another fluted pillar—that belonging to Carthage's guardian angel, the goddess Tanit. But this was Roman marble.

A small, friendly group was gathered on the stage, including me, President Brock, and a few of our fellow academic blowfish. The amphitheater's semi-circle was populated with overworked young faculty, pallid and sluggish in the seasonable May weather. As President Brock delivered his speech and gestured to the monument a short distance behind us, I thought for a moment I was shaking with nervous excitement. It turned out, though, to be one of those minor earthquakes that tickle central Massachusetts from time to time. A few frogs probably jumped for their lives, but it did no significant damage. With one exception. You see, when the tremors first started I noticed that the sluggish young faculty had grown suddenly animated. A look of tremendous satisfaction spread from face to face, as if they were watching the climax of a great play, or President Brock had announced they would all be receiving generous bonuses. The five or six of us on the stage turned around and the reality of the situation struck home: the new pillar was sinking straight down into the blessed earth—a process that continued without interruption until the thing was half its former height. Brock and I approached the marble stump like a pair of Athenian olive-pickers who'd witnessed the miraculous death of Oedipus. When we got there, we stood awhile in awe. Neither of us said a word. Then, as I turned my back on the depressing scene, a keen flash of insight struck my colleague's countenance. He said it was remarkable: not a tenth of an inch could distinguish the difference in height between me and the sunken pillar. I think it important to note that we were not on terra firma. It seemed to me that a marsh was hardly the ideal location for a dignified monument.

I turned back around to confirm this observation when a bolt of laughter pierced my side. I could barely suppress my chagrin. American Brock—for he was the one laughing—met my stoical gaze with a jovial pat on the back. It was the first time I'd heard the sound of laughter from his lips.

"Don't worry," he said. "We're insured for acts of God."

I said, "That isn't that funny."

"Yes, it is," he assured me, his strong beard glinting in the sun. "It's funny whether we like it or not."

Lightning Source UK Ltd.
Milton Keynes UK
UKHW012216030323
418027UK00006B/51